PHANTOM
CONSTELLATIONS

praise for daniel braum's fiction

The stories in this collection do not fit conveniently into a neat box. The Night Marchers is full of sadness, beauty, and unprecedented wonder. Two cups of literary dark fiction, a heaping scoop of magical realism and urban fantasy, a tablespoon of horror. If you're looking for something thought-provoking and elegant, yet still dark and somewhat mad, you'd be a fool to pass this book up.

— CHAD STROUP / SUBVERTIA

These tales are unlike anything thing else I'm reading today. Bold, adventurous, strange, and totally enjoyable. I can pretty much guarantee the stories in The Night Marchers and Other Strange Tales will be unlike any you've read before and will leave you wanting more. 5 out of 5 Stars

— FRANK ERRINGTON MICHAELS / HORRIBLE
BOOK REVIEWS

"The dark unreality and ambiguity of these stories make this collection an easy pick for fans of weird fiction."

— PUBLISHERS WEEKLY

"In these deeply melancholic stories, Braum writes of relationships with all the skill of our best realists, but always punctuates and torques his observations with a suspicion of the strange and the unreal. Underworld Dreams is an original high-wire act that deftly walks the thin line between genres without ever slipping."

— BRIAN EVENSON

"In Underworld Dreams, Braum takes the reader through a series of mystical vignettes packed with strange occurrences, intense emotion, and, yes, flat-out horror. Unsettling, violent and heartbreaking, this is a collection that weaves the supernatural into real characters and emotions so effortlessly it'll linger in your head and your heart, like a nightmare you don't recall having survived."

— PHILIP FRACASSI

"There's an urge to race through this skilled collection from one smart story to the other wondering what's next? But don't do it. Pause and savor instead."

— JACK KETCHUM

"One of the brightest young stars in the firmament of dark speculative fiction, Daniel Braum is among the best short story writers we've encountered."

— THIS IS HORROR

PHANTOM CONSTELLATIONS

strange tales and ghost stories by
DANIEL BRAUM

Cemetery Dance Publications
Baltimore
❧ **2025** ❧

contents

Introduction by the Author

Are you seeing what you think you are seeing?

Are your perceptions "taking in" what is real?

Are all the connections that we make, objectively "true"… or are they products of our minds assigning meaning and sense, where there is… none.

In this world nothing is certain. Both religion and science readily admit that there are places where the rules of what (we think) we know break down.

The stars in the sky care not of what we think. They exist unknowing and unaffected by how we see them and how we choose to categorize them. The constellations in the great darkness are phantoms; shapes we assign them- only as real as our shared agreements and proclamations of connectivity.

Phantom constellations are all around us. Our lives. Our loves. Our relationship with the natural world *and* the supernatural world. Our thoughts on things unnamed and things yet to be named, and things barely known and not yet known, and even the things we will never ever name, or know, or ever even be able to imagine… all are phantoms. All only as real… as we make them.

There are those who might say that our lives are governed by fate or by the stars and great external forces outside ourselves and others who might say that the course of our time on this earth comes down to human choices.

Whatever the answer may be, if there even is one, good fiction is indeed made of human choices. Especially when the scares and wonders are not named or familiar but things of the unknown.

The stories in this book are stories of people walking in worlds of Phantom Constellations, traversing situations and challenges full of uncertainty.

Phantom Constellations are everywhere. From the ends of the earth to the places next door.

Let's venture into these borderlands and twilight zones, and even into places that seem familiar. What will you see? Together we can decide what, if anything, is real and what are phantoms in the night.

-Daniel Braum
August 2025.
Long Island, New York.

scarecrow and the imposter

I know you're out there. Where are you? Where are you? Where are you?

The demon doesn't answer. It never does. It never speaks.

The glowing ball of a late evening sun dips behind the hay bales stacked next to the old red barn; its shadow reaching into the corn field where I've placed the straw man I constructed. Not to scare birds. Today this ragged body is meant to lure.

I bet it looks real to you. I know you need it. You know you want it. Come on now, come out. Come check and see.

Scarecrow is the slipperiest I've ever faced.

It comes. It harms. And it just… disappears. Then starts all over again. Somewhere else in another body. I've done my best to make it so it cannot resist this one.

———

The old barn is in real disrepair but still standing; the wooden boards themselves unsure how much longer they will hold together. I wonder how much longer the American Dream or a dream of any kind will be able to find shelter in quiet, over-looked places like this. Places discarded and left for time to ravage.

It's something Miri would have said. She once told me she wanted a barn, much like this one to turn into a hotel or gallery or something. They're everywhere on the endless road winding through the Catskills we were driving on one aimless summer afternoon, going nowhere *slowly* and joyously, flanked by lush green and quaint farmstands, seemingly transporting us back to when things were simpler and kinder as we rolled. As she spoke of the barn, I spotted a box turtle on the road ahead. I managed to swerve in time and pulled over to help it across. From behind, a car came around the bend too fast and hit it sending it airborne like a punted football into the trees on the side of the road. I looked for it fruitlessly even though there was no way it could have survived—

Something moves at the edge of the field. A thistle-brown jackrabbit dashes into the cover of the stalks. There's a black shape in the growing darkness.

Scarecrow.

I train my eyes on the shadow. On the corn stalks. Tall and still, no swaying at all.

It's just my eyes and ears and the trap I've set in the field. Scarecrow is too wary. Too tricky for electronics.

The shadow fluctuates. I see him and I'm able to hold my gaze. He's wearing the body of a tall man; he likes tall men. Denim pants. Work boots and a flannel shirt despite the June weather. Just like scores of others in the rest stops along the Thruway. It's hard to make him out and not because of the cap obscuring his face or the way he stays in the shadow. His skin reads as black, un-natural black, and I'm not sure if every inch of him is burnt or if the flesh has expired and is further in revolt with every second he rides it.

He crosses into the field cautiously but without turning back and I'm so close to having him. He's in my snare. Crossing *out* won't be so easy. The entire field is my garotte.

Fifty yards away, in a little clearing, the scarecrow of straw and rag that I created is suspended upright by a pole as its spine —a visage of human frailty, a manifestation of the vulnerability we all face, of the nightmare of knowing that our so-called control of the elements and the natural world is but an illusion.

Scarecrow emerges from the stalks; moves to the stuffed effigy of a man and stops before it. I can feel his contemplation in the quiet absence of bird sounds.

Has he realized what the animals know? Does he feel my hand in this?

He reaches to the straw man's face and tilts it up, in an almost gentle way if I didn't know better. Then he lifts it, trying to free it from the pole. He's taken the bait. He's in my trap. He's going to take it as his next body.

I dash into the field.

I've got you. I've finally got you.

Scarecrow doesn't see me coming. He doesn't hear me. He doesn't sense me. He's totally engrossed in transferring himself into *my* scarecrow.

Without *him* inside the weary black flesh can no longer hold together. The denim and flannel collapse into a pile.

I tackle the scarecrow he's now trapped in.

"I've got you. I've got you. I've got you."

There's no resistance. No fight. The straw thing is limp. Absent of any spark. He's not in it.

I shout my fail-safe word, sending the perimeter of the field up in flame, but it's too late. He's already gone. Ahead of me, again. Escaped and on to the next one.

How?

A smoldering piece of corn husk spirals to the ground. I grind it into the soil with my boot heel to extinguish it.

And I'm alone again, standing next to a rotted, decaying corpse, surrounded by smoke and burning corn, holding a lifeless mess of worthless rags.

My old "friend" Ava is waiting for me under the teak wood, canvas-roofed sun-shelter near the edge of her little man-made lake. Three quarters of it is ringed by trees—oak, birch, maple, a beautiful wall alive with the motion and sounds of red wing blackbirds and wrens and thrushes.

Reeds and willows and water lilies line the part of the lake adjoining the treeless clearing where the packed earth path from the main road ends. A floating dock tethered to shore, reaches fifty yards or so into clear, still water.

Padded folding chairs are still set up lakeside in need of being put away from a function, probably a wedding, wilted sunflower bouquets in vases adorned with ribbon at the end of each row.

The roofs of Ava's new guest cabins can be seen over the trees and wild blueberry bushes and scrub to the left of the clearing. Behind them, obscured by summer foliage is the "ghost house," the ruin of an old hotel pre-dating the Borsch Belt era, now just an old stone wall foundation and cast-iron boiler sometimes visible depending on the time of year and if there is no snow.

"Nate Arcane," Ava says as I step into the shade. "To what do I owe the pleasure?"

There is no question why I'm here. She likes to rub it in. That I need her.

And there's no doubt she's smarter. Stronger. And a superior practitioner. So, is it insecurity or just cruelty?

How quickly people forget, *how they like to forget* the things we've done for them. Back when Miri was still alive, Ava's then husband literally made a deal with a devil, or at least that's what she called the thing that wrote the document that he signed. She came to me. I researched for days. Skipped plans with Miri. Discretely asked everyone I could for a way to get him out of his own self-made crisis of greed. I never understood why gratitude was something she just could not show. Why my efforts never counted. An expectation of return is not why we help. It is not why we do things. Still, it stings; worsens the dull ache of being alone. No partner. No kids. No heirs. No shop. No assistant. No employees. Just me. Hat in hand, as always.

"A pleasure to see you, Ava. You're looking good. Did you lose weight?"

"Oh, I see what you're doing, you sly dog, but go on. Flattery will get you everywhere."

I hate the dance of small talk and niceties but I have no idea where Scarecrow will be next. No idea how he got away. Nothing at all. So, I put out word I was looking for help. Which I hate.

When people say they want to help often the translation is they want to help themselves. The old adage be careful what you wish for, is solid advice and not just in dealing with djinns in fairy tales.

Ava answered my call.

Obviously not a djinn and despite her blonde hair and penchant for bright clothing she bears no resemblance to genie-chic Barbara Eden, though from the scent of Oud and Silk Road spices wafting off her I can see them sharing a love of fine Omani perfume.

She runs in circles way above my pay grade and rightfully so. Finding her set up here, in the Catskills, among the forests and towns I roamed as a child is not a turn I would have ever imagined. The platitude, "change is the only constant" is so true though. Everything around here's changed so much from the Catskills I once knew. Even the Catskills I tried to show Miri, long gone. The mom-and-pop maple syrup set ups that I used to love to come upon are nowhere to be found. Development is everywhere. Roads are paved and new. It's more than fresh paint and construction. New faces, new families and new ways of thinking. Farm to table restaurants are the name of the game. Hotels and ubiquitous AirBNBs with price tags only the rich can afford abound. A resort casino that went up without even a nod to the Borsch Belt hey days the centerpiece.

Ava is strong enough and skilled enough to do anything she wants, anywhere she wants. Yet here she is catering to elite New York City escapees and people like me. Perhaps rolling in dough is the most potent magic of all. Being too rich to care about anything at all.

"You like it?" Ava says.

She motions with her hand to a scarecrow tied to a lawn chair set up on the square platform that is the end of the dock. A man with a rod and reel in hand who I recognize and remember to be her new husband, Vincenzo, paces from one side to the other causing it to bob. It's odd that he doesn't notice Ava's set up, then I realize not only does he *not* see it, he *cannot* see it. Ava's doing. He's not a practitioner. Not an equal. Just her man. Just a toy.

A black cat with a long-haired tail turns the last bend of the path and comes trotting along as if she owns the place, unconcerned by the plethora of threats inherent to the surroundings. She abruptly halts and crouches; her tail twitching as she focuses on something Ava and I do not see.

"Oh, Pepper, darling," Ava says then turns to me. "She must be stalking one of our resident ghosts."

"Easy on the bullshit, Ava. I'm not one of your guests don't treat me like one."

The whir of tree frogs and summer insect sounds fills the space of her non-response. I've think I've finally gone and done it. Finally pissed her off. I expect her next words to be to tell me to fuck off and take a hike. Instead, she reaches into the pocket of her wide-legged capris and produces a letter sized envelope of pulpy hand made paper and hands it to me.

"For you," she says, flatly. "He won't escape you. This time."

I take the envelope.

"Magic words?"

"Oh no, no magic words, darling. I mean there might be. The envelopes just a prop but hold on to it, props like that are helpful to people like you. I mean, what's needed is already done and in you now."

I put the envelope in my messenger bag, in between two of the bundles of hundred-dollar bills.

"Come, darling," she says, deliberately in that same singsong tone reserved for guests. "Come take a look."

She leads me on to the dock and we clomp our way to the scarecrow in the chair and her oddly non-reactive husband and his repetitive pacing with the rod and reel.

"Why the drama," she asks as we walk. "Why so obsessed with this Scarecrow?"

Telling anything true to Ava is a risky proposition.

"I've been chasing him for so long I can't remember why. It really doesn't matter anymore."

She looks at me like she doesn't believe me.

"Fair enough then," she says.

"I need to know. Tell me. How's he doing it?"

"Doing what?"

"You know. How's he getting away? Getting out of every thing I've ever tried."

"Oh, darling, he's just jumping away."

Jumping? What the hell is that?

"Hmmm, yes jumping away," I say. "How?"

"Does *how* matter? You said you didn't want him to get away."

"So, your spell stops him from jumping—"

"I said he won't escape you."

We reach the end of the dock. Her husband doesn't acknowledge us. He's not fishing. He's doing a dance and show of fishing with a blankness in his eyes. His face is sun burnt—a patch on his nose so bad its blistering.

The scarecrow in the chair is a hefty thing of stuffed burlap dressed in clothing. Its proportions are all off. A fly, all obscene and fat and black takes flight from one of its wrapped hands and it dawns on me there's a real corpse under all that wrapping, or at least something mixed and matched and stitched together. Ava's watching me look at it.

"He won't be able to resist," she says sounding disturbingly like a used car salesman. "You'll have him this time. Now either that's good enough or it's not. I'm gathering Pepper and going back inside and out of this heat."

I guess it has to be.

She tromps towards shore without a glance at her husband, her wood-bottomed clogs clomping on the planks causing the dock to rock more forcefully. Her husband's balance falters from the motion.

I follow Ava to solid ground and take out one of the bundles of cash from my bag.

"Oh, money? Your money isn't good with me."

"Then what, Ava? You have to allow me to pay—"

"Darling, I never said this is free. Let's just say… you owe me one when I come asking."

Exactly what I did *not* want to hear but I agree.

I see what Pepper has been stalking. A bullfrog mostly submerged in a wheel mark in the ground that is filled with water. I bend down and coax it into my hand with Pepper watching intently.

I put the frog safely into the lake.

"Ah, a man of mercy," Ava says. "Do know, you deserve mercy, too, Nate. No matter what you've done or what you think you've done."

It's the first non-selfish thing she's ever said to me. Pepper is watching me. Watching my hand, making sure I don't have another frog.

"I'll leave you to it, then. Call him. He will come. And you'll have him, I promise. I'll make sure you are not disturbed."

Ava snaps her finger. Out on the dock her husband comes to a halt with a jerk. He returns to shore, greets me perfunctorily as if he had not lost time and was not with a face full of sun burn. He and Ava entwine arms and walk into the path of wild blueberries, Pepper padding behind them.

Leaving me with the corpse in the lawn chair and the empty lake.

A blue heron emerges from the cat tails and tall steps through the reeds mercilessly hunting for frogs with its long beak. I wish them luck.

I return to the dock with Ava's envelope in hand. A black water strider glides across the still water, its legs making small circular wakes. A trout surfaces and swallows it; a brief iridescent glint of sunlight on its scales before it returns to the depths. I open the envelope. I can barely make out Ava's flowing scrawl on the thick, fibrous sheet of paper inside. The purple-black ink is there one instant gone the next.

I read the few words I can discern—

Motion on the other side of the lake startles me. There's a kayak moving towards me that was not there a second before. A man in hunter's camouflage and mosquito netting is paddling methodically.

Scarecrow.

I step back as he approaches and realize he doesn't see me. Ava's "bait" or whatever spell she has done must have him mesmerized. He reaches the dock, grabs hold, and climbs out of the kayak onto the platform effortlessly.

It's Scarecrow alright. Tall and lanky as me. Face obscured by netting and thick sunglasses. I hate that I find myself admiring his hunter's jumpsuit, and the way he's stowed his knives on his belt.

He goes right to the body in the chair. I know this flavor of wrong. His gait, the way he moves feels like every gut punch that ever bruised my life.

He takes the body underneath it's armpits, lifts it up, and holds it before him as if sizing up a new suit.

I throw myself at him. Wrap my arms around his.

He's dead weight. He's not struggling but something's happening. The electricity in me feels it—a kinetic certainty sure as the instant before a cloudburst. He's trying to jump away.

Not this time.

I can't see his face but I can feel *him*. Feel panic beneath his mask.

Ava's scarecrow remains slack. Scarecrow is still in the body he arrived in. He's trapped.

It's working.

His fight comes alive and he tries to shake me off. He's strong. But not strong enough. He can't break my hold. We push against each other stepping back and forth. The platform's rocking. We're going to fall off—

Something changes. A painless jolt hits me. A joy-buzzer-pulse radiating from my groin to my toes to my teeth. Every nerve in my body flares and I become aware of all the currents running through me. Every synapse. Every iota of electricity that powers my cells, my organs, my ears, my eyes. My sight becomes a jumble of grainy colored dots. The lake and dock and all the trees smear into a blur. Scarecrow and I lose our footing. We're going to smash onto the planks—

Everything freezes.

Everything a motionless still life of the instant before we smack down on the hardwood.

The crash doesn't come. The impact doesn't come.

I'm motionless, too, yet I'm also falling. Every signal every sensation in my body telling me I, too, am a smear, sliding along an invisible wall. Scarecrow still pressed against me.

I will myself to hold tighter. No way I'm letting him go.

I feel him. Willing himself away. Doing whatever it is that Ava calls jumping—but its not working. I've got him. Whatever Ava's done is preventing his escape. Wherever he thinks he's going I'm with him.

The snow-grain-dots turn gray then black and the only sensation left is that sense of wrong that is Scarecrow close to me.

I scream "I've got you."

I hear the words in a smooth female timber.

Miri.

Miri's voice.

I remember when she spoke the words. It was the first night she stayed in my loft. Her first time in and around all the physical minutia littering my world.

She decided it was a fine time to teach me how to stitch the rips in the beat up leather jacket I refused to retire.

"Here, I've got you," she says as she guides me with the needle.

That first night wasn't just the first time I let her stay. It was the pinpoint instant I let her in. For real. For good. The exact moment that I committed to her. No wedding ring. No words. Only me crossing a threshold. Me realizing I was on the other side of a dividing line. I knew that I would do anything for her. That she was forever.

Miri's words repeat and slur.

My sight returns.

Grainy shapes coalesce into her face.

Her open, eager face full of possibility. Her face as it was in my car, on that lonely road that day I was showing her the Catskills. The instant before the car behind us slammed into that beautiful, helpless box turtle—

The crash comes.

I hit the planks. Hard.

There's scuffling. I see someone racing down the dock to shore. Scarecrow is running away. He disappears into the path through the blueberries.

I try to move. A wave of lightheadedness stops me. A stray fishing hook has pierced my lip. I spit blood.

Ava's spell worked. But he's getting away. On foot though. I can catch him.

As I force myself to my feet I see the lawn chair's empty. Ava's scarecrow isn't there.

I run to shore, gasping for wind.

The wedding chairs are gone.

I don't see any of the familiar trees and scrub. There's a neat row of well-manicured apple trees behind the blueberries. Ava's guest houses are nowhere to be seen.

I realize I'm standing on sand, not soggy lakeside sod laden with frogs. An artificial beach.

I take the path through the blueberries to the road. Scarecrow is no where in sight. Which way did he go? Did he cross the road? Did he go into the forest?

Where the stone foundation and iron remains of the Ghost House should be is a quaint, three-story hotel that I have never seen before.

A summer wind blows through the apple trees carrying the smell of maple sap cooking somewhere.

Everything is… wrong.

I stand in the parking lot in front of the hotel taking in the sweet aroma of caramelizing sugar.

How is it that everything is… almost the same but is… different.

Next to the hotel is a well-tended vegetable garden, fenced in with tall chicken wire for deer-proofing. Abutting the garden is an area enclosed by a low rock wall. I walk over. There's a plastic round animal shelter in the center. Stainless steel dishes of water. A family of box turtles munch away on a plate of fresh greens, oblivious to me, as late afternoon sun shines down.

Someone has cleared the acre of scrub between here and the lake. All the reeds and growth on the shore are gone. There's a beaver dam causing a gentle overflow. A three-foot waterfall drops onto a slope of exposed boulders at the edge of the trees feeding a small secondary lake.

Lush lavender in bloom and thriving green herbs fill two wooden barrels repurposed as planters flanking the hotel's wooden front door. A black metal wagon wheel is on display at the start of the driveway.

I want to hunt Scarecrow. I want to tear apart every inch of forest looking for him. But I'm so spent.

I take a deep breath and steel myself to go inside.

The door opens into a restaurant, an old-fashioned wooden bar to the right of the small waiting area where I'm standing. The dry air-conditioned air tinged with a hint of smoke and grilled meat is a relief from the humidity.

A young woman is handing menus to a couple at one of the tables.

On the far side, across the long room is the front desk. Big windows with the shades open give a view of the road and the forest. Windows on the other side offer a view of the vegetable garden and the lake beyond it.

I plant myself on one of the bar stools.

The bar tender ceases drying a high ball glass and turns around to me. Its Ava's husband, Vincenzo, all done up dapper in slacks, a white button-down shirt and pin-striped dark vest. He's bright-eyed and alert and sun burn free.

"It *is* you, Nate," he says. "Didn't expect to see you here… um, all good?"

"Hey, Vincenzo, nice to see you man. Yeah, all's good, what's up?"

"Well… you know, I guess everything's… all worked out then?"

Everything's wrong. Everything's different.

"Yeah, you know, yeah it's all worked out."

"Amazing. Wow, good to hear it," he says. "A drink then, this calls for a toast. I'm having one with you, boss be damned."

"Must pay being in good with the boss, Vin. So, where's Ava at?"

"Ava? What the fuck, Nate. Why the hell would you ask me that—"

I glance at his hand. There's no wedding ring.

"Just making talk, uh I… haven't had my coffee today."

"Neither have I. You don't see me asking dick questions though. Jesus."

He turns away from me, collecting himself.

"Give me one second, man."

He retreats to the far side of the bar and picks up the phone on the wall. He sees me watching so he covers his mouth.

A small push from the arcane fixes that. I touch my finger to my ear and I can hear him.

"Yeah, it's definitely him he's here," Vincenzo says. "Okay, I'll ask him."

He hangs up and returns to me with our drinks.

"You okay, man? You're looking rough. And your bike's not in the lot."

"Yeah, I was… out for a run in the woods, fucked up my ankle and took a spill."

He slides a high ball glass full of something over to me and lifts his.

"Well, cheers man and welcome back. Down the hatch then."

From behind someone presses themself against me and covers my eyes. Strong hands. Soft skin. A hint of mint and basil and pine wood.

"So, I guess this means you're *not* leaving town," the voice I can never forget says into my ear. "And that you're sorry after all."

Miri.

"Mirabelle Leah," I say. "I could never stay angry at you."

"Asshole," she says. "*You* angry at *me*?

She sits on the bar stool next to me. Miri. Long lost. Long *dead,* Miri. How can it be? Here she is real as rain taking me in, suspiciously with her cloudy green eyes.

"Such an asshole. Since when do you use my full name, you know how much I hate it. But here you are after you said I'd never see you again."

She's dressed up. Her hair blown out and make up on. I touch her hand. Its real. Its flesh and blood. I gently pull her to me and bring my lips to hers.

It's been so long. I come alive with the thrill. But nothing's the same. We knock teeth. She pulls away.

"No. No, Nate, you don't get to do that."

We stare at each other for a heartbeat, eye to eye knowing what comes next, then kiss again. I put my hand on the small of her back.

Our teeth knock, again. We hold our lips against each other, motionless. Then slowly search for a lost rhythm I thought we both knew.

"Nate, no. I have to go."

"Please. Stay. Or come with me. Somewhere, anywhere. What could be more important—"

"The big wedding. The Fourth is two days away and I have to set this caterer straight. I'll tell Chantal up front you're back. Rest or clean yourself up or whatever. I'll be back in a couple of hours."

I reach for her. She stands and walks to the exit. I watch.

This is *her* place, not Ava's. *This* is the hotel she always wanted. The place I always wanted for her.

She stops. Turns and looks back at me like I want her to. I want her to stay and show me every last inch of the place, every little detail of her dream made real.

She pushes the door, passes through, and disappears into the end of the day.

I remember the last time I saw her…

She's barely a step inside and she's peeling off her scrubs as if that will free her of the weight of yet another long emergency room shift.

The sun is coming up. Later, when it sets, the night time city will be alive with Fourth of July revelries. If past is prologue, all the pyrotechnics will wake up the ghosts of New York and I will be out there with them.

"I'm ho-me," she says in an upbeat cadence, trying to hide her fatigue.

Her success has become a cage. Long hours. Human trauma. Human tragedies. The minutia that come with responsibility fill her quickly and are slow to exit. I know her so well. Her bright, beautiful, mind yearns to be free. Yearns to explore. Every day is a vast ocean of potential and possibility. Every shift, every bit of red tape, every single thing she juggles is a stone threatening to sink her.

No matter what, she always shows up, shows up for us, and with a brave face. It's something I've not yet learned to do.

"Welcome home, hon-ey," I say, doing my best to match her tone. "How was your day, um, night?"

"Second year of residency, does it get worse or does it get better?"

I don't know what to say.

More important than her medical talent is that she still truly believes she is here on this earth to help people. Ahead are more long hours. Running a business. Running a practice. Navigating all the steps the world will require when all she wants to do is to be the healer.

"Better," I say.

It's not quite a lie. I know that my life is better having her in it. The cornucopia of lamps, and vases, and chairs and end tables she has brought here not only have transformed my loft from a crash-pad-hideout-work-shop into a semblance of a home; the mementos are physical evidence that I exist, and that I matter to someone. Healing is not just medicine and the medical arts. Healing takes time. Healing takes space. We wear our wounds in our bodies and manifest them in our surroundings. These are things Miri knows instinctively and it shows in everything she does and every place she inhabits.

I return to my books, charting Miri's location in the apartment by sound as she goes about her unwinding routine. After a few moments all is quiet and I am immersed in the star charts I am trying to correlate with the accounts of the sphinx that walked through Brooklyn, and my crude drawings of rooms in my grandmother's house that do not exist.

Her strong hands cover my eyes.

"Hello, lover," she whispers in my ear. "I have a surprise for you."

She's excited she was able to sneak up on me. I've been distant. I've been sullen. She's been trying. More than trying. She's adopted the Sisyphean task to snap me out of the dark cloud that is my life. None of it her responsibility. Her life, our life, shouldn't be like this, this dance of light and shadow and ups and downs, yet I do not know how to stop the patterns and ebbs and flows, I do not know how to fix "us."

"Get up, get dressed," she says. "I'm taking you antiquing. Upstate. It's gonna be fun—"

"Now? Today?"

She is a treasure. She is a gift. I should just say yes. My

books can wait. There will always be time for ghosts. But I do not. It is *almost* that I cannot.

"Maybe you can go with Stacey instead?"

She thinks about this for a moment.

"Maybe. I will, if you promise you'll go out with your friends too…"

"I have no friends."

"Yes you do and they miss you. Carlos reached out to me just last week. When was the last time—it doesn't matter, it's never too late."

"Is it?"

She removes her hands and retreats back into her routine. I retreat back into my books.

I hear the shower run. I hear her in the kitchen. I sense the sun has risen, though there are no windows. Above my desk I notice a small wooden dragon hanging from the cavernous ceiling. I remember Miri buying me the dark blue and gold painted Tibetan-style ornament but I have no idea how or when she managed to get it up there.

I hear her approach again. From behind she gently lays her hands on my shoulders.

"Hello, lover," she says. "I know you need tonight to go out and go be you. I'd like the opportunity to try and persuade you otherwise."

I lean back and reach for her. My left hand brushes the smooth, soft, skin of the side of her toned leg.

Tomorrow I will start anew, I tell myself. Tomorrow I will be up and start the day at breakfast with her, like she tells me she wants. Tomorrow I will not spend the day with my face in these books. Tomorrow I will plan that trip upstate for her, not the tour of the Catskills of my long gone past but all the places and sights and things that I know that will delight her silly. Tomorrow I'm going to be a better me, a better me for her.

She kisses my neck.

I will take the day with her then tonight I'm with the streets and the ghosts. Tonight, a Fourth of July with her friends will just have to do.

Miri leaves at three in the afternoon; passing through the door into the New York summer humidity and bangs of M-80s and Cherry Bombs going off unseen in nearby streets.

"I'm picking up Stacey and taking the Thruway up," she says after she notices me standing there watching her go.

"Not the Taconic?" I say.

"They just re-did the rest stop. No way we're not stopping for fries. See you after the long weekend, lover."

The clear, night sky is alive with whistles and crackles and deep, resonant pops and vibrant tendrils of fire made of colors unseen in nature. Everyone in the city is crammed into the Sea Port on South Street watching the launches racing up from the barges and Brooklyn Bridge from expensive vantages many of them outdoor tables laden with fancy cocktails and fresh, trendy foods.

I'm watching the bridge too; my eyes trained down, not up.

It is a prime night for apparitions. Jumpers. Men and women lost at sea. Lost souls crossing from the outer boroughs into Manhattan, doing in death as they did in life.

A tremendous firework explodes, igniting the sky with a

blossom of sizzling white sparks expanding beyond the entire span of the bridge. A lone human form appears and tumbles over the railing, disappearing into nothing before reaching water.

My phone rings.

There's a pang in my chest. I'm sure it is Miri. She only calls if she's having a shitty time and is bailing out of plans. I see it's not her number.

"Nate, it's Stacey. I'm so sorry—"

Stacey bursts into tears. There are people with her. Voices and truck engines running and a commotion of bustle and noises.

"We were leaving the winery," Stacey says through sobs. "I was in the rest room—when I got outside, I saw a man get in the car with Miri and they drove away."

"Stacey? What? What's going on—"

"He was tall. I couldn't really see him well but he sort of looked like you, Nate. I knew it couldn't be but he reminded me enough of you that I actually wondered if it was you. And they just drove away, leaving me there."

Explosions bloom in the sky. A quartet of red bursts ignite, transforming the world into a perverse semblance of daylight in reverse. I don't know how long I stand there. I'm aware of people filing past me. Happy couples arm in arm. Raucous drunken groups. Families with young ones in tow. Foreign business men in suits. Permutations of clusters of people of every age and every kind. I notice a young couple so lost in a kiss they are oblivious to it all. I close my eyes and walk.

The humid air, heavy with the smell of the river and gunpowder, gives way to the ubiquitous reek of trash and diesel exhaust as I wind into the heart of the city. I pass restaurants going strong into the summer night. The thump of bass, and miasma of hundreds of voices enrapt in their own personal worlds are living things accompanying the artificial light reaching into the shadows and darkness. I walk until the sun is almost ready to come up then I force myself to head home.

I learned that Miri's car went off the road. And down a rocky embankment. End over end it crashed from one boulder to another and exploded. A crumpled metal death trap of fire. They recovered what was left of Miri's body. No evidence of the man Stacey says she saw, or any other, was ever found.

───────────

I close the door and will myself to let the memories stay outside so I can focus. I try to discern clues and shreds of meaning from this place Miri kept for me, *no, the other me*. My room, no, *his* room.

The bed is not made; the sheets are as he and Miri left them. I look for a story in their folds and shapes. There are ash trays on both night tables. Apparently this other me still smokes. Has he convinced Miri to take up the habit?

The cigarettes in the ash tray are not very old. They were here a day or two ago, no more.

What did they talk about? They fought. Broke up. I, no *he*, left.

There is a solid wooden desk beneath the window. I sit and try to imagine him. I see the lake through the window. The floating dock is serene and empty.

I should have never trusted Ava. No, I should have never trusted myself. Ava didn't lie. She practically told me what she was doing. She made a point in saying her spell wouldn't stop Scarecrow. I saw what I wanted to see.

Ava said Scarecrow'd been doing something she called jumping. Transporting to different here and nows. To adjacent, slightly different realities existing simultaneously and then back again. All reflections, and iterations of each other.

Ava's spell didn't stop him; it hitched me to him. Hitched me along on his ride. For her own sick, amusement, I bet. Why else does Ava do anything?

I check my phone. Its dead. The charger by the bed fits but doesn't charge it.

I run the faucet and splash cold water on my face. I clean the blood from my lip. There is a plastic jar of dried shrimp pellets on the toilet tank.

I smooth my hair down, brush off my shirt, put Ava's envelope in my pocket, and take the turtle treats outside to the garden. The turtles have finished with their greens and are in various places in their enclosure. I toss pellets, one at a time, to each of them.

Why am I trying to figure out how to go back? Shouldn't I be figuring out how to stay? I can just… do nothing and stay here. Miri is here. Everything is here. The only problem I can think of… is the other me. Of course he'll be back. He's me. He and Miri are broken up but how can he stay away from her?

I take out Ava's envelope. No words appear. Not a scintilla of anything arcane. Just thick pulpy paper.

Vincenzo said this place's Ava was the competition. So, it won't be too hard to find her. And I know just what to look for.

A few minutes walk down the road from Miri's hotel the brush and scrub give way to blueberry bushes. I see the sloped-roofs of Ava's guest cabins among the tops of intentionally planted young trees. The cluster of two-story structures appear the same as the ones I know, right down to the one closest to the road, the double-sized one Ava uses as a lobby.

I circle it and peer through its many windows. Inside, everything is made of luxurious wood. Hardwood floors. Log walls. Long exposed wooden beams near the high ceiling. I enter and find myself before Ava herself standing behind a hardwood counter that is the front desk.

"Nate?" she says.

She's dressed in retro-sixties chic, a paisley patterned blouse and solid dark capris, looking much like "my" Ava. Her perfume is familiar; strong florals that evoke white blooms, but is nothing I've ever smelled before.

"You're you but you're not you," she says before I speak.

She moves from behind the desk and for a second, I think she is going to greet me warmly with an embrace. Instead, she takes my hand and spreads my fingers inspecting the spaces between them as if I'm livestock.

"I had a feeling this was possible but I didn't expect to see it," she says.

"It? You mean, me."

"So prickly," she says. "You're so much like... you."

"Well, you're practically a super villain where I'm from."

"Flattery will get you everywhere, darling."

"You even sound like her," I say.

"Come, let's talk somewhere more private," she says.

She takes me by my elbow and leads me outside to a picnic table made of teak. A black cat jumps up.

"Hello, Pepper," I say.

Pepper ignores her name and tries to see if I am holding any frogs. It is only when I take out the envelope and show it to Ava that she loses interest.

Ava turns the envelope over and over inspecting it as intently as she checked my hands.

"The other Ava made it," I say. "It has something to do with how I got here."

"Well, it does look like something I would make," she says. "Though I'm afraid it's just an envelope."

"The other Ava said what she had done was already in me."

"I hate to play for the other team, darling, but I think this other me's full of it. I don't think she did anything, except maybe giving you this old thing to convince you that you had the proper lure for your demon."

A bullfrog rips a deep resonant croak from somewhere in the darkness. Pepper's ears stand up.

"I'll never be as good as her, I mean…you," I say softly.

"Darling, so much of using the arcane is just giving things a lit-tle *kick*. It works best when pushing things to do what they naturally want to do."

"The other you said something like that too. Only more self-serving."

She returns the envelope to me.

"At least I'm consistent," she says. "It's probably just a prop. Maybe it's meant to distract you. That's something I would do. I feel like you know that though, or it's something you should know."

"I had no choice. I needed her help," I say. "I couldn't even find him myself."

"And here you are. Asking for my help, again. Do you think have no choice, again? What will it be today? How to send you home?"

"Home...? No. I want to stay."

"Oh, Pepper dear, this just became more interesting than I thought. If you want to stay then, why not just... stay?

"The other me."

"Oh, yes," she says. "Yes, I see the dilemma. You can merely stay if you wish, nothing to it. No fuss. But to do it right you have to kill... yourself. You have to kill *our* you."

Pepper is staring at me again. She's not watching my hands for frogs. I swear she's listening. Waiting to hear what I'm going to say.

"You're right. I have to kill him. If I'm going to do this, I have to do it right. I have play it safe. I have to be sure, right?"

"You've thought about it already. I like that. I always liked you, Nate. Such an interesting wounded bird you are. Don't forget, everything, everyone, including you is deserving of happiness."

Killing him. *Becoming him* is the only way to be happy. He has it all and he's just thrown it away. He's thrown everything away, everything. Everything I've ever wished I could have just one more chance for.

"Where can I find him?"

"Here, of course. He lives in one of my cabins, correction lived. He's been a good solider, I'm sorry to see him go. You'll have to hurry; he's done with our little taco-stand of a one-horse town and is hitting the highway any minute now. I'll show you which one is his, but first I have something for you."

"For me? I'll pass. If you're anything like the other you there's a price for everything. A steep price."

"This other me sounds like a swell gal. I can only imagine the fun we'd have if we got together."

"She's a monster," I say. "She likes to watch things burn."

Ava places a pistol on the table. It's a heavy thing of black matte steel; obscene and out of place on the smooth glossed table top. I don't know where she produced it from. Out of thin air? She isn't carrying a bag. No way her clothing could have concealed it.

"You told me everyone is deserving of life," I say. "And happiness."

I say it like a question. Like an accusation.

"I did, didn't I? And I meant it," she says. "Though I readily confess, I think it will be oh so much fun to find out and see which of you is *more* deserving."

His cabin is exactly what I would choose, a place that does not stand out. Non-descript. One story. No different than the rest of them. A motorcycle with two stuffed side bags waits outside the door. The bike is sturdy and black. The kind I'd dreamed of riding through the wooded back roads a hundred times but was too afraid to ever buy. No brand name. No markings. Only a small blue sticker of a dragon silhouette barely visible on the fuel tank.

I remember Miri on one mild, sunny endless summer day, long ago, once upon a time. Were at an estate sale. She notices me pick up a blue wooden ornament the from the piles of detritus from someone's soon to be forgotten life.

"That's Sangpo," she says. "The myth goes something like, Sangpo was the dragon that loved people and only wanted to help human kind. In Sangpo's time, dragons lived among humans and sometimes shared mystical secrets and knowledge. Every time Sangpo tried to help someone or even talk to a human it wound up burning them because all it knew how to do was breathe fire. It had so much guilt from this it decided to never speak again. And it went to live as far away from humanity as it could. Far, far away in the forest. The world went on and grew up around it, a world that forgot about dragons. A world that no longer needed them. A world maybe never needed them in the first place.

"That's depressing," I said.

"It's also not true. We need dragons."

I put it down. She must have returned and bought it for me. I envision her going through all the trouble to surreptitiously hang it to try and inspire me as I undo the safety of Ava's pistol and slide it into my back pocket.

Easy now, don't blow your ass off, I tell myself. This is just like running pick-ups back in Brooklyn.

The cabin door opens before I knock.

I am standing there. It's me. The man standing there is me.

He's tall and lanky. Like me. Only trim and fit, at least twenty pounds lighter from the way his black t-shirt and black jeans fit the way I wish mine did. His face is a visage of my face back when it was chiseled and not so worn from wear. Lean and mean and healthy. Unshaved. Smooth skin. He's wearing a polished, silver chain around his neck.

"You. It's you," he says. "I was hoping you would come. Come in."

I walk past him, slowly as he holds the door open.

I should shoot him now. Right now, when I have the chance. Is it going to be in the head? Or in the chest?

"Will you sit?" he asks.

He seems... curious, not-threatened; genuinely curious about me.

The place feels wrong. The same radio-station-tuned-to-sickness wrong that radiates from Scarecrow.

The one room space is the tell-tale empty of someone about to move out. There's a bare futon frame. A small kitchen table with an old book, a box of matches, and six square pieces of cheap wood on it. A closet door in the corner is open revealing empty space inside. I cautiously sit in one of the two chairs at the table. He sits across from me. He doesn't notice me adjusting the gun, or he doesn't care.

"There's so many things I want to ask you," he says.

"Speak."

"Perfect. Just like me. Right to it. I hate the bullshit too. So. Where you are from, is there a Tomas?"

"Yeah. He was my boss and yes, he's a bastard."

"Right. That figures," he says. "And did the thing with the sphinx happen? Was there the tunnel to the moon—"

I push out of my chair and to my feet.

"Really? What the fuck. This is what you're asking me? Cut the crap, if we're...you know, the same how could you just walk away from Miri?"

"Oh, you sentimental, soft-hearted fucker," he says. "Miri's a good girl but—you should know she asked me to give it all up. Magic. Demon hunting. The arcane. All of it. Everything. You of all... people... should get it. That's asking me not to be me. I don't know what happened to you—"

"That's right you don't know! You have absolutely no idea what my life is like. I'm nothing. Just drifting... Do you know how many times I said I would kill to have what you have? I'd give up everything I have for her."

"Would you? You'd give up everything that makes you, you for *her*? What would you be then?"

"I don't have to be me. I can be you..."

"You poor, miserable thing. Being me isn't going to make anything right. You're still going to be you. She's still going to be her. Think about it."

"I have thought about it."

"Obviously not very hard."

"I know I'm not a self-righteous bastard like you. Even on the days where it takes maximum torque and a giant pipe wrench just to exist, at least I know I'm doing good work. Do you? What about you? Do you have a Scarecrow here? I bet you do. I can't even begin to tell you all the things I've done to try and stop him—"

"Oh, I *had* a Scarecrow. Let me see your neck."

"What?"

He pulls the silver chain out from his shirt revealing a six-pointed Star of David. Seconds ago, it was hanging over his heart.

"Come on," he says. "Show it to me. Show me yours."

His star is silver. Simple. Just like mine. My grandmother gave it to me, here in the Catskills one summer when I was visiting her in her little shack. It was the summer I turned thirteen.

I do as he asks.

"I thought so," he says. "Does it even mean anything to you?"

"You bastard. How dare you—"

"You stupid fuck. I'm trying to help you. Don't you see I'm trying to help you? I'm not going to sugar coat it and coddle you like a fucking baby. Scarecrow, how was a pathetic thing like that even a challenge for you? You truly must be... the stupid me from the other world where I'm not me... where I'm soft and weak and a chump. Have you read this?"

He thumps the book before him on the table.

Worn-down, gold-embossed Hebrew writing is on its burgundy leather cover.

"It's so... basic. So easy," he says. "Have you done any work at all? Have you even ever tried? Scarecrow... is nothing. Easy meat."

"So easy, huh? I've faced him. I knew the people he's killed. I've met their families. I've even fought him with my bare hands. I bet he'd steamroll over you like a—"

"He's dead. He's dead... here. I killed him, but thanks."

I should shoot him in the chest. Now. Less of a chance to miss.

"You're lying," I say. "You'd never find him. No one can. You can't find him if he doesn't want to be found—"

"Really, thanks for bringing him. It was so long ago I'm gonna enjoy ending him again."

"Now I know you're lying. You can't fool me, you're me. All bluster."

"Listen to the shit you tell yourself," he says. "Finding him is easy. Things like him are born from us, from inside us. When they get out, they sulk around and hide. They love cramped hiding places; their favorite spots are the corners of rooms in the dead space between a wall and a badly placed door that doesn't open all the way."

I don't speak. He's quiet; watching me as I look around the room. When he sees that I see the open closet door he smiles.

"He's here," he says. "He's right here."

"What the hell sort of nonsense are you even saying?"

He stands, darts to the closet and closes the door, revealing a man facing the wall in the space behind it. Scarecrow. His face hidden under the mask and netting but I can feel his sense of alarm, his animal panic as he realizes that he is seen.

He turns and takes one lurching step towards us then halts with a jerk. He brings his arm up to cover his face and stands there, shaking.

"Why do you look surprised?" the other me says.

"That's not Scarecrow. That's something you did. A trick."

"I assure you this is not a trick. In fact, it's something *you* did. He was born from you. From the parts of you that are wounded. Unloved. Unhealed. He's made of every blow that ever caught you. Every slight that made you feel... small. Everything that ever made you feel invisible. Not appreciated. Kicked around. It took the shape of all these parts of you and came into the world kicking and screaming, petty and malicious and ready to make the world hurt the way it hurts."

"You're lying!"

"You know I'm not. Well, if you were even competent enough to do the most basic part of your job, you would know."

The other me grabs Scarecrow by the neck and pulls the netting and hunter's mask off its face.

It's me. My face. Another me.

Scarecrow tries to speak but it cannot. Garbled, guttural sounds escape its twisted mouth.

"Don't worry, relax. I know what you're thinking. He's not *really* you just a thing *you* made. Or I made or some other us made. I stopped thinking about it long ago. I *will* tell you it hates you, hates you for making it, for making it exist, the ultimate unfairness of all. It's obsessed with you. Obsessed with doing you harm. There are some texts that say he loves you. For creating him. I'm telling you, and from experience, he hates you more. That's why he's always hunting the things you love."

I take out the gun. Point it at Scarecrow, then at the other me, then move my aim back to Scarecrow.

"Don't bother," the other me says showing no sign of concern over the pistol. "It will find a new body. Here's how we do it. Listen, I'm only going to tell you once. Consider this a lesson a gift."

I keep the gun steady as he speaks.

"First you rob it of what it feeds on," he says. "This takes some focus. A little time. Discipline. And clarity. All things you apparently lack. You're still in the thick of all your shit."

"You don't know me. You don't know anything about me."

"I told you to listen," he says, sternly. "What did Scarecrow do to you? Can't answer, right?"

I've been chasing him for so long I can't remember why. It doesn't really matter anymore.

"Answer. Why don't you answer?"

"I don't owe you anything," I say.

"You don't. You're right. I'm trying to help you, you stupid fuck. Let's see, did it kill someone? Your parents? Your sister? It probably would try to kill *your* Miri if given a chance now that I think about it. Come on, answer. Why the obsession? The answer is you don't know why. You never did, you just tell yourself it is a thing that always was and just… is."

"I don't have to listen to you. You're wrong—"

"Look at it. It's such a simple thing. Such a stupid thing. Still, it's too dangerous to be allowed to exist. I'm doing what you were supposed to do."

He grabs a knife from Scarecrow's belt and stabs it in the gut. Scarecrow's face is all surprise, then disappointment and pain. I see its love, too. I see how much he wants me, or maybe the other me to love it. His broken face pleads for help.

"I want you—to hurt—like I do," Scarecrow manages to say. To him. To me. To both of us. His voice, so close to my voice, is an affront. Scratchy and hoarse. Twisted and barely audible. It is the opposite of love. It's the worst thing I've ever heard.

The other me stabs it again. Again, and again. In the gut. Fast, rapid thrusts. Then he slashes its face. Slashes it again. Scarecrow's sadness turns to rage. It wants to move, it wants to hurt us but it can't, because of something the other me has done. The other me brutalizes it; mauls it's face into a bloody mess of hanging flaps of skin.

"Toss me those matches, will you," he says to me. "Burning isn't necessary. It's just something I like to do."

Scarecrow. The thing that brought me so much, pain. The thing that killed so many. Yet all I want to do is help it. Show it mercy.

I do not comply. The other me stomps to the table and snatches the matches and the six wooden panels.

"Oh, I see in your eyes you remember fire," he says to me, or maybe he's saying it to Scarecrow. "Do you remember what comes next?"

He strikes a match and throws it. Scarecrow's face goes up in flame, an unnatural conflagration as if he were truly made of straw and not flesh and blood. I watch his skin bubble and turn black.

His body, a blaze with fire, becomes a burning ember in the shape of a man. It shrivels and shrinks. Smaller and smaller until it's just a doll-sized man-shaped thing floating in the air.

The other me places one of the square slabs of wood beneath it. It hovers there. Then he places one above Scarecrow. And one on each side of it. The six pieces float inches from flame yet they do not burn. The other me snaps his finger and the pieces respond by coming together to form a box. Whether the fire inside is extinguished or just contained along with Scarecrow I cannot tell. The wooden box floats, motionless and still. Before I can speak, the other me throws a match at it. Instead of bursting into flame the box disintegrates into black ash. Falling flecks of it disappear before reaching the floor.

"What have you done?" I say.

"Hope you were paying attention. That's how you do it. Almost finished. This one's almost gone. Just a little bit left."

He returns to the table and sits in his chair, still unfazed by the gun I have trained on him. He takes off his left boot. And then his black sock. His foot is cris-crossed with thin, white scars. A healed constellation telling a story of cuts I cannot even begin to decipher. He takes Scarecrow's knife and makes an inch long incision on the meaty tip of his big toe.

Blood wells from the gash and drips to the floor. He contemplates it with a satisfied expression then hands the knife to me.

"Okay, your turn now. The only part left of it is what lingers in you. Let it out. Bleed. So the last of it can dry up and die."

I keep the gun steady on him.

"Do it," he says.

"No."

"Of course you won't."

He puts his sock back on. Then his boot. He stands and his face becomes a portrait of disdain.

"You're just an echo," he says, more to himself than to me. "You're the part of me that fails. The part of me that won't move on. The part of me that won't take the medicine."

I tell myself to pull the trigger. To do it.

"I'm going to kill you. I'm going to become you. Then Miri and I will—"

"You can't. And you won't."

I will myself to shoot. To squeeze the trigger. To blow a hole in him. To blow his head off. My hand will not obey.

"Let me go!"

"I'm done with you," he shouts. "You're worthless. I can't teach you. I can't fix you. Be gone. Trouble me no more. I cast you out. Go back to where you came."

He makes a pushing gesture in my direction and I wince. Nothing happens though.

He sits and brushes the cover of his book with the back of his hand and lets out a big sigh.

"I'm still here," I say. "You're the failure. You can't even do… whatever it is you think you've done. You can't even do that right."

"Oh, you poor thing. How wrong you are. It's done. You're gone. You have one hour left here, tops. Say your goodbyes, or not. Go anywhere you want but get the fuck out of here before I regret the stupid, pointless mercy I showed you by letting you live."

He ignores the gun still pointed at him and comes to me and puts his hand around my neck. He pulls me, then pushes me out the door and I cannot resist.

Outside he gives me one last push that sends me stumbling and shakes his hand at me like he's shooing a pest, then climbs onto his motorcycle.

He starts the motor on one try; its revolutions break the

mountain quiet. He revs it and pulls away without any further regard to me. I watch him disappear down the tree lined road.

He said I have less than an hour so I dash to the road and break into a run. Back to Miri's place.

I push open the door, startling the young hostess manning the waiting area. I look around, frantically, for any sign of Miri. The young woman signals to Vincenzo behind the bar who proceeds to the phone on the wall behind him.

I'm deciding whether to stay or to try and find which cabin is hers when the door behind the front desk opens.

Miri.

"Oh, thank god," I say. "Am I ever glad to see you."

"Hello," she says, flatly.

"I'm here. I'm back. You're back. How was your meeting, oh it doesn't matter, let's get out of here. Let's go."

"We're not going anywhere," she says.

"We need to go somewhere private. Your room. Or… my room. It's very important, we have to go now."

"Calm down, whoever you are."

"It's me, baby. It's me, Nate."

"You're not him."

"I can stay. I can be him. I can be your Nate. I'll give up magic. I'll give it all up."

"You're not him."

"Okay, I can explain. Please just listen. I've figured it out. We don't have a lot of time. I know I'm not *actually* him. He's gone. He left. He left you. But me, I'll do anything for you. I've been down this road before. I know what I did wrong so I know how to fix it. Fix us. Well, not us. How to fix me. This is a chance. This is our chance, please—"

"Just calm down, turn around and walk away. Walk out that door and never come back here."

"Miri, please. Please let's take this chance together. Do you know how lucky we are to have this chance? We're so close, we can be happy. You. Me. I know how to be happy now. Together we can be happy."

"He warned me about you. He warned me, you're an imposter, you're the thing he called the Scarecrow."

"No, I'm not. I'm me."

I run and throw my arms around her.

"He did something that's gonna send me back. But you can come with me. Just hold on to me."

She breaks free of my embrace.

"Back off," she screams. "Back the fuck off."

She's swiped Ava's gun from my pocket and has it pointed at my head.

Everyone erupts into a panic.

"No, Miri. Please don't do this. I want to stay here, with you. But I can't. You can come with me. You can come back with me—"

I take out Ava's envelope. Maybe I can find some clue. Some answer. Maybe it will give me the strength to fight. To fight whatever he's done so I can hold on and stay—

"Oh no, it's happening. I can feel it. Please. We can go back together—"

I reach for her again.

She fires. The crowd gasps.

Miri's yelling. Her voice has become a garbled sonic blur, sliding together with whatever I'm screaming as I feel myself disappear.

I pop into being lakeside at Ava's place right smack in the middle of Saturday night dinner service set up on the shore. A three-piece jazz band is on the dock playing for a dozen tables of Ava's patrons.

Ava is standing right next to me. A waiter all in black balancing a tray of cocktails next to her.

"Oh, Nate, you're back," Ava says, unfazed by my entrance. "That was fast. Did you have a nice trip?"

She takes a martini glass off the tray and extends it to me. I don't take it.

"You… god damn you, you knew all along."

She grimaces at my refusal of the drink, then sips it herself.

"I wasn't certain of anything," she says.

"You used me as your guinea pig. Tell me I'm wrong," I say. It comes out like a growl.

"Nate, I think you need a drink, darling," she says.

"Fuck this and fuck you, I'm leaving. Goodbye and good riddance, Ava."

"Not so fast," she says.

Pepper appears from the darkness.

"I did my part," Ava says. "You're rid of Scarecrow, aren't you?"

"Miri. She was there. But now she's gone," I say. "Do you understand what I'm telling you. I couldn't stay. I couldn't bring her back."

Ava sends the waiter away to a table.

"She was never yours," she says. "There is nowhere where you have a happy ending. Nothing you do, nothing you try is going to change it. Take comfort in that, poor thing."

"You don't know that. How could you know that? You don't fucking know that."

"There are other worlds than this one, darling. Some of us can tune in simple as you tune into a radio station. Some of us, or some *things* like your Scarecrow, can skip around to and fro and come and go like a radio signal bouncing off the atmosphere. So yes, I do know this."

"You're disgusting. I'm through with you. I'm leaving. You're never going to see me again."

"Not so fast," she says.

Pepper circles me, brushing against my legs as she orbits.

"My price is due."

"Fuck you," I say. "I'm not giving you anything."

Pepper halts, bares her teeth, and releases a growl. The guttural sound is unearthly.

"We entered into a bargain, fair and square. If you re-neg, there are consequences."

Pepper resumes her circling. She is not a cat at all. And I can tell she wants me to refuse.

"What do you want? What more could you possibly want from me?"

"Sit, Nate. Tell me, tell me everything."

She leads me to a table. Her waiter rushes over, pulls back a chair for her, and we sit. I find myself across the table from this witch that I hate and her little black demon surrounded by what in a better world, in a just world should have been a perfect night.

"This is what you want? Do you want to know about your first husband? Should I tell you about Vinnie?"

Just a few minutes ago, everything was in reach. Just a few minutes ago, I was this close to having it all.

"Darling, I suppose," she says. "But only if you must. Why not start with something more interesting. Did you run into me? What am I like there…"

July first. The last of the day's light is fading.

It's humid the way only New York in summer can be. Fireflies are rising from my freshly watered lawn. I hear the young couple next door pull into their driveway. I went out an hour ago and brought in Chinese food. It's on my counter, cold now. A family I recognize from around the neighborhood were there bringing in food too. There is nothing I want to see on the TV. Even what's new feels old. I know the world is beautiful yet everything is full of emptiness. I cannot escape this certainty.

I go into the garage and take the cover off my motorcycle. The young guy who comes to me to learn about the arcane keeps it in ship shape.

I decide I'll go into Brooklyn and pick up a stack of books from my loft and check on the old place.

The westbound traffic on the Belt Parkway is a clogged artery. I'm grateful for the few breaths of salt air that reach me through all the fumes and exhaust.

I arrive on my street to a gathering of people lighting off wads of jumping jacks and roman candles from bottles in front of my building. Bigger rockets launched from unseen places nearby light the skies. They've been going off all month pretty much like they always do. I decide to keep driving.

The monuments of the city's skyline loom over their reflections in the East River. Are the same ones, or ones just like them, watching over Miri? That other Miri. All the other Miri's. Even if

Ava said there are none, I like to believe that in all the iterations along the string of infinity that is existence there has to be just one where we got it together.

Without thinking, I find I've driven to a new parlor of the arcane that recently opened downtown. Against my better judgement I go inside.

There are walls full of books. Clouds of aromatic smoke. Dim lighting. The sizzle of fresh food. An uplifting buzz comprised of a dozen stimulating conversations happening at once. An old friend recognizes me. Another person's handshake becomes an embrace. Someone I cannot quite place offers me a thank you for something I've forgotten that I'd done. Someone interrupts us to be sure they send regards from a friend who had recently visited New York from far away and asked for me. I accumulate professional and personal invitations before I can cross the room to the bar.

These are my colleagues. These people identify as my friends; I suppose that makes it true. These are the strangers who recognize me.

I know I'm saying the right words. I know I'm smiling in the right places.

This is not the life I ever wanted.

I'm an imposter.

All these things should give me joy. I don't feel a thing.

I do not feel anything.

The other me. He was wrong. I'm not the Scarecrow. And I'm not him. Correction, *I'm* wrong. I'm not an imposter. I *was* me. And now I'm just an echo. An echo trapped in this here and now that shouldn't be. Here I am, I'm the ghost here. I feel like I've always been just a ghost.

Above The Buried City

I'm disappointed at how peaceful Gonzales looks just lying there, eyes closed, his coffee skin tinged yellow in the morgue's fluorescent lights. I took some small comfort in the fact that he'd spend the rest of his days rotting behind bars, with nothing else to do but think about what he did to Naomi. But from the almost serene expression, it doesn't look like he has it too bad now.

Warden Jeffries slams the clipboard with Gonzalez's death certificate and medical records onto the metal counter. "One day healthy as an ox, and the next, poof, he just drops dead, just like that."

"Yeah, I don't like it," I say.

He flicks his lighter, again and again. The constant sparking without a flame makes me nervous.

"Hell, it's way too late to be here. You should be home with that pretty little wife of yours."

"Girlfriend," I say.

Flick-flick-flick. The harsh fluorescent light finds its way into the deep lines in his face.

"Just sorry you had to come," he says.

"Only doing my job, Marty."

He's one of the few that knows a good DA is more than just a lawyer; he knows that I was there every step of the way. For the investigation. Meeting the family. Not just for the pretty stuff, like half the suits in our office who view the job as only a stepping stone. So yeah, late or not, I'm here.

"Gonzalez's attorney and her freaky-hoodoo-mama sidekick are outside, waiting for the body," he says.

"She's a real piece of work."

She came to the trial. Every day. Wearing the same set of clothes. A stranger from another world. Her Mayan face, with its sloping nose, and deep-set brown eyes remained emotionless as I recounted Naomi Westin's last moments. Gonzalez wept like a girl.

Jeffries flick-flicks the lighter. "Your call."

"They couldn't have had all the paperwork just waiting and ready to go. It's like they expected it."

"Certainly are in a hurry."

"So, hold him," I say. "Can you do that for me, Marty? Ten million law-abiding citizens of the Tri-State-Area want us to err on the side of caution."

And Naomi deserved it. Close as we had to a royal princess, she was the shining spirit of New York. Of my New York. Despite the upper crust and their restaurants full of wealth, celebrity, and privilege, *my* New York is still the greatest city of the world, full of people with good old-fashioned virtue, like Naomi was.

She shunned the vapid socialite scene for charity affairs, and her politics classes at NYU; only appearing in public to aid her pet causes— mostly having to do with combating Central American poverty and aiding New York's immigrant underclass. Still, her make-up free, scar-lipped face was all over the magazine covers and Page Six. A photograph of us from one Thanksgiving, serving turkey dinners at the shelter downtown, hangs on my office wall. In the picture her smile looks the same as it did in school, when we were both wide-eyed rebels with a cause. I remember the feeling of my arm around her, our smiles beaming as the picture was snapped, and my chest feels full of rocks. Gonzalez took her from us. So he belonged in prison. Dead was second best.

Jeffries abruptly stops his lighter flicking. "Good fucking god," he says.

Gonzalez is sitting up on the gurney, coughing. He throws the white sheet off his lower half, then stops because he's coughing so hard. Jeffries radios for back up. And I'm frozen; staring right into Gonzalez's open eyes thinking this can't be happening, the rocks in my chest tumbling over and over.

Gonzalez looks confused, then disappointment dawns on him. Something akin to the forlorn expression of a suspect waking up in a holding cell I've seen countless times before. He looks past me to the double metal doors. On the other side is a long hallway, then the waiting room where his attorney and freaky groupie are, and then the parking lot and freedom beyond. I think he's gonna go for it and I'm gonna have to tackle him.

Two corrections officers burst into the room. They slam Gonzalez back down onto the gurney and tie the restraints. I'm suddenly aware I'm breathing heavy. Sweating as if it was I who restrained him.

"Naomi," Gonzalez cries, as they bump through the swinging doors and wheel him away.

A sweet smell rises above the disinfectant reek. The familiar mix of vanilla beans and flowers that Naomi wore. Whether it came from an expensive bottle or drug store shampoo I never knew, it was just her. From the corner of my eye I think I see a woman standing there next to the examining table, and I turn, but nothing's there. A trick of the light on the stainless steel. I'm so tired I'm getting loopy. But if I hadn't been here, who knows what Jeffries might have done. It could have been a disaster.

Jeffries finally lights his cigarette, takes a noisy drag, and exhales. "Now I've really seen it all," he says.

I expect to find Marissa winding down from her gallery shift on the couch with a coffee, but all the lights except for her changing room are out.

Outside our windows, the city lights blur into the skyline. Each light a life, overlapping, impossible tell where one begins and another ends.

My phone rings. It's Abrams. I'd been wondering if he'd call tonight or take me into his office tomorrow. Dean and Gweneth Westin are hosting an event tomorrow, he tells me, and with what happened with Gonzalez, it's essential that I be there.

"I'd rather not go," I say.

I can't face Naomi's parents and there's no good way to tell him.

Marissa flits in from her changing room, a slender shape in the dark apartment. She's mastered the art of discerning when I'm on for work. She fills a watering can in the sink, apparently paying me no mind, but I know she's listening. Suddenly at 11pm, our neglected plants need watering.

"I'm sure someone else would be honored to come," I say. "Jan Manetti has been working hard on the Astor Place cases."

But Abrams wants me. The Westins want me.

Marissa stands on the table to reach the cyclamen dangling in front of the living room windows. The outline of her long blond hair glows faintly with city light. An edge of purple lace slides above her low riders as she extends to pour the water.

"Alright, tomorrow at seven it is," I say, giving in to Abrams, then hang up.

"These need repotting," Marissa says.

"Going out?" I ask.

She is. Third time this week. And I'm too spent to get into what's at the heart of it. But she'll be back for the Westin's party. People from her New York, the New York she wants for us, will be there and she won't miss the opportunity.

A minute later she's out the door and I'm alone with the plants. I can almost feel their thirsty roots absorbing the water as I give in to exhaustion and let myself drift. In the blur of pink and white lights I see the shape of the silver mask that's been sitting in our evidence room since the trial. Naomi's face is beneath it. Her mouth moving. I can't hear the words as I fade.

The skyscrapers framing the Great Lawn fill the view from Dean and Gweneth Westin's floor to ceiling windows; a modern backdrop juxtaposed against their collection of Aztec masks and Mayan stelae. Jade statuettes and stone carvings are displayed on simple white pedestals throughout the penthouse. I can't wait for the fad to pass.

Marissa is chatting up Juan Farber, managing partner of

Rivera, Larca, Weintrob and Associates. Her high-necked, black dress comes just below her knees and nicely hugs her curves. She stands straight, the stem of her glass balanced between her slender forefinger and thumb. I picture her holding one of her paintbrushes with the same grace and effortlessly manipulating her chopsticks on our first date. At Nobu. I'd made the reservations weeks in advance for Naomi and I, but she told me we would never be more than dear, dear friends.

I don't look away in time and Marissa calls me over.

"Richard, you remember Juan Farber, from the golf outing," she says.

He knows me from the trial. They all do.

"A pleasure, Richard," he says. "Even after you put the bastard away, the motions never end. Is every judge in this town mad or what?"

I smile politely and when I don't speak, he does.

"She's quite the woman," he says, tipping his martini toward Marissa. "Suze is thrilled with the paintings you chose for our new extension."

"And we'd all love to see you at the gallery again soon," Marissa says.

"The way Suze spends I'll have to reel in a few more clients before doing that. Gimme a couple of days."

I force a laugh to match theirs. When Marissa laughs she is again the magical girl I met at "W" bar commiserating Naomi's rejection. The girl who had half my clothes off on the cab ride to my apartment. The girl from Nebraska who worked her way through F.I.T. tending bar. The woman who wants a life and all the world with me.

"How you two make it on Richard's government salary is beyond me."

Juan won't say anymore. Not here. Not in front of Abrams.

Abrams is across the room with Dean Westin and bunch of his Wall Street chaps in a huddle of cigar smoke, caviar, and laughter. I excuse myself and join them, claiming "duty calls."

Marissa frowns. I'll hear about it tonight.

Dean's vodka-reddened face becomes serious as I join their circle. But after a second, the visage of the broken father passes and he claps me on the back.

"Cigar, Richie?" he asks.

I'm about to say no when Abrams' phone rings. He turns and steps back a pace to answer it.

"Yes. I understand. Right away," he says. His party face goes blank and he is once again my boss, the District Attorney of New York.

He folds his phone and finishes his martini in one obscene swig.

"Mercurio Gonzalez flat lined, *again*," he says.

Gonzalez's attorney is in the waiting area, holding paperwork up to the one-way window while arguing with the two corrections officers barring the door. She's just a dime-a-dozen suit from Legal Aid. It's the woman behind her who concerns me. Rosita Velez. The one Jeffries calls freaky-hoodoo-mama. File says she's Gonzalez's next of kin. Forty-five. Born in British Honduras. Belizean papers now. Declared address is a Yucatan resort village on the Mayan Riviera. Her long dark hair frames a face like one of the Westin's stelae come alive.

"Do something. Don't let this happen," I say to Jeffries.

He unzips the body bag. I'm not sure if to show me or to convince himself.

Gonzalez had been the cagiest cat burglar in department history. A string of thefts, all Central-American artifacts like the Westins' collection, had perplexed us for years. Until Naomi Westin picked the wrong night to bring her weekend Romeo to the family's Greenwich Village brownstone. Gonzalez stumbled upon them necking amidst Daddy's priceless collections and pulled a gun, so the police report goes. And Romeo picked the wrong night to play hero. The gun went off in a struggle and that's where Naomi's story ended. They never found Romeo. I played it over hundreds of times in my mind. I figured him as one of the sons of the elite with a daddy who didn't want to get involved. Probably whisked him away to Europe faster than you can say big fat Police Benevolent Association donation.

Gonzalez, the cops said, was found weeping at her side. And the freak had placed one of the artifacts, a silver skull mask, on her face. I would have liked to have spoken to that Romeo. Just for that final look into Naomi's private world. With Gonzalez behind bars, the thefts stopped. But no amount of wishing brings Naomi back. Leaving through the morgue doors is not how this is going to end for him. Not with the stunt from the other day. No way.

"He's dead. For sure this time," Jeffries says.

I pull off the white sheet. Angry red lines of the autopsy incision divide his chest into a "Y.".

"Come on, Marty. Do anything. I don't care. Lose the body. Burn him."

"Nothing I can do, Richard," he says.

"I'm telling you, something's wrong."

He tries to put his arm around me. I push it off.

"I know this is the pits," he says. "But everything's in order."

The guards open the door and step aside.

My phone buzzes. It's a text from Marissa.

"Going to Montauk. Staying with friends. Not sure when I'll be back."

And just like that, Gonzalez is wheeled out the prison door.

Marissa being gone doesn't translate into big change, not with my hours at the office and her at the gallery nights and weekends. She hates Montauk. Means she's staying with her sister and is thinking of leaving me, for real. I know I should call, that it's time we hashed it out. Worked it out, one way or another. But I don't.

I'm ready to leave for the office when the precinct calls on my cell. The Robinson-Dutt Gallery, in Soho, reported a break in and theft, sometime in the early morning. The only object missing is a jade-lapis mask. Mayan. I go straight there.

Two police officers are pacing the top floor gallery, looking for prints and evidence among a few dozen pedestals displaying figurines and pottery. The room is as minimal and boring as the Westins'.

A man with salt and pepper hair, in a black shirt and dapper black suit, stands at the front texting on his cell, his silver thumb rings clicking on his phone.

"You look familiar," he says. "This doesn't have to do with—"

"No. Just asking a few questions."

He goes back to his phone.

"Such as, where does this stuff come from."

"Mexico's Yucatan Peninsula. Some Guatemala and Belize," he answers, full of attitude.

"I meant from whom."

"Why?"

His why implies, "Am I in trouble?" I know their sources are shady; the whole damn industry is questionable. But today I don't care. I know Gonzalez is responsible and I want him.

"Just trying to get an idea why only that one item was taken," I reply.

"Easiest answer is because it's the real deal."

"And the rest?"

"Honest answer?"

"Please."

"Maybe, probably, real. Depends on who's buying. Come look at this."

He leads me to a hardwood pedestal displaying an oversized coffee table book.

"The lore is fascinating. Full of lost civilizations and human sacrifice," he says while flipping through the large, glossy pages. He's talking like I'm a customer now. Good.

"The Mayans believed the cenotes, these deep natural wells next to their pyramids, were portals to other worlds and that they were sending their sacrifices through them. They suited them up with masks like this one."

He stops at a page with a stylized image of a shirtless Mayan priest pushing a sacrifice off a pyramid top. A silver mask is over the victim's forehead and nose giving his face the visage of a skull; a raw red hole is where his heart should be.

"Thing is, most of what we know comes from the art, like this, which is a restoration from a stela from Chi-Chen-Itza. The practice went on for centuries but very few skeletons were found.

That's why artifacts, like our stolen mask, are so rare, and valuable."

"So where are all the skeletons?"

"The cenotes, although all dried up now, were too deep for anyone in antiquity to retrieve them. So it's a big mystery. Plays nicely with the lost Mayan civilization mystique."

"What do you think?"

"That it's a great story that sells a lot of pieces. Question for you. Do I get the form for the insurance claim from you guys or somewhere else?"

Back in the office, there's a message waiting from Coop, my contact at Homeland Security.

"Shitty day," I tell him when I get him on the phone. "This better be good."

"You're not going to believe this," he says. "Go to your computer."

I open Coop's e-mail and an image of Gonzalez passing through airport security comes up on my screen, clear as day.

"This is great. Where are they holding him?"

"They're not."

I slam my fist on the desk and push all the files off.

"I had you flag his passport for a reason!"

"Easy. Easy. Shit like this happens all the time. I mean not like this. Records came up as deceased but he clearly wasn't."

"Don't tell me to take it easy. He's dead, for fuck's sake. I saw him."

"Guy looked fine to me."

"He's a convicted felon. He belongs in jail, not on the afternoon plane to Cancun."

Coop's silent. If he tells me the guy already paid his time or it's all in my imagination, I'm going to kill him.

"I'll notify the field office in Mexico City," he says after a few seconds. "Uh, so, how's everything else. Marissa?"

"Everything's fine, Coop," I say, fighting to maintain calm. "I'm hanging up now."

I look at the photo of Naomi and me, then I ring Marissa. She doesn't answer.

One of Marissa's bras and a workout tee hang from the weight bench in our second bedroom. An empty canvas on her easel next to my desk is plastered full of invitations to gallery openings. I try her again and when she doesn't answer I read the trial transcripts again and dig through my old files but it's useless. I go online. At first just looking at maps and searching Mayan mythology, but then I book a flight to Mexico.

Sometime in the night, I hear the door slam and erratic foot clomps across the living room. I open my eyes to see Marissa standing in the bedroom doorway. She's holding the flight confirmation from my printer, alcohol emanating from her pores.

"You're not going to Mexico without me."

"Sorry, work," I say.

"He's fucking dead, Richie. And yeah, you were the one who put him away. But you can't spend your life as Abrams' dog."

Her fingers nervously grasp each other and I want to still them in mine.

"At least talk to Juan, please. For me," she says.

"I will," I say, sitting up in bed.

She didn't expect that. And neither did I.

"Really?" she asks.

"Really."

"Don't fuck with me just to shut me up, Richie."

"I said I will and I will. *After* I capture Gonzales."

She thinks about this in silence for a moment, a sour look on her face. Then she walks over and sits on my lap. I can feel her heart beating, hear the shallow breaths in sync with the rise and fall of her chest. It's been so long since we were this close. I really smell the alcohol in her sweat now, along with a mix of cigarette smoke and her best perfume. Her seduction perfume, not intended for me. She runs her fingers along the back of my head and presses me to her and I don't care.

Marissa is asleep, naked among the tangle of sheets. Unable to sleep I crawl out of bed. I go to the closet and take out the locked metal case with my pistol in it. Abrams had us get certified and wasted a few Saturday afternoons at the shooting range before he lost interest. My paperwork is in order, but I can't take it with me to Mexico. I put the case back, gently cover Marissa, and wait for morning.

I'm in the morgue watching them wheel Gonzalez away. This time I turn and the woman standing there does not disappear. Naomi. Wearing the silver skull face mask. The world blurs and we're standing somewhere high. A sprawl of Mayan buildings beneath us. A giant green snake with white feathered wings flies overhead. Its spiral coils disappear behind a bright painted pyramid.

"No. Just go. Stop," she says. Her lips below the mask, tortured.

I wake up in the cramped plane seat with her words echoing in my head. Marissa is next to me flipping through my print outs and the photo of Gonzalez.

"You don't really believe it was him?" she asks.

"I know what I saw."

"You saw him dead. *And* this is a photo of a guy that looks like him."

"The burglaries started again."

"You're going to find him in his grave and we're going to spend the rest of the week on the beach."

"And then we'll have nothing else to do but drink margaritas and go sight-seeing."

"And para-sailing. Don't forget shopping."

"They don't take credit cards in Mexico."

She smacks me playfully.

When we step off the plane the humid air hits like a puff of dragon's breath. Noisy birds chase lizards across the runway; lush tropical greens grow right to its edges.

The terminal walkway is adorned with stylized posters of

idyllic beaches, romanticized bullfighters, and Mayan priests high atop pyramids.

An hour later, we check into a fancy spa on the Mayan Riviera that Marissa selected. It is one in a row of hotels and shops on a steep cliff overlooking the long white beach and the turquoise sea. Remnants of Mayan ruins litter the grounds; gray iguanas of all sizes sun themselves on the ancient stones. The wall outside our room is covered in lush blood-violet bougainvillea and bright red hibiscus the same shade as Marissa's sundress.

A fist-sized humming bird whirs past with a click-click-click. The bright emerald greens of its feathers and ruby red throat catch the sun as it flits from bloom to bloom. For some reason I find this poignant, and I feel an epiphany struggling to surface into thought, something about Marissa and I, but instead the image of the "Y" cut in Gonzalez's chest fills my mind.

A breeze laced with clean sea air and pleasant soap meets us as we open the door. I drag our bags into the bedroom. A gecko on the wall lazily eyes me.

"It's wonderful," Marissa says from the bathroom.

I hear the rustle of her shedding her clothes. She runs the shower.

The spacious sun-lit bathroom is covered in sand-beige tile, a few turquoise and whites thrown in here and there. Marissa's shape is softened by the frosted glass and running water.

"Join me," she says.

The past day with her has been wonderful. But I fear it is only a temporary shift brought on by telling her I'll to talk to Farber. It's easy to see how a carefree life like this, or even just a job that I leave at the office, could be so, so nice. But I don't want to feed her empty promises.

"Maybe later," I say. "No time to waste."

I feel the disappointment in her silence. I stand listening to the water run, the steaming glass obscuring her. Every inch of me wants to throw open the door and press her against the shower wall. But I walk away, stopping just a second for one last look before I go.

―――――――

By the second afternoon I've questioned a host of locals, tourists, and the one policeman I found in the area, with no sign of Gonzalez. I'm ready to widen the net, so I hire a cab to the little tourist trap towns at the edge of the jungle.

The first one is a just row of flimsy constructed shacks, open on one side, facing the dirt road. They all sell the same things, Guatemalan crafts, Mexican blankets, and souvenir trinkets—the most common being little soapstone pyramids and replica masks. A few sun-burned tourists browse and haggle with disinterest as they wait for their tour bus.

At the jungle's edge, a dozen yards back behind the stalls, are rag-tag shelters. The real town. A teenage girl weaving bracelets looks up at me suspiciously as I walk over and start looking around.

"Do you know Senorita Velez?" I ask.

"No ingles," she says, and glances at one shack apart from the rest before looking down and avoiding my eyes.

The shack is the last of the row, offset from the rest by a garden of herbs and plants ringed by conch shells and stone. Looking at it, that feeling of rocks in my chest returns.

As I approach I hear scuffling and moving around inside so I run over and open the flimsy door. The window is open and the table full of jars and herbs beneath it are in disarray.

I dash outside and around the shack. Someone is ahead, running through the jungle. I follow, swatting branches and vines as I run. Birds chatter angrily. Something the size of a cat darts across my path and disappears into the brush.

I emerge into a clearing in front of a huge mound covered in earth and trees, an unexcavated pyramid. Stone bricks protrude at the base, tree roots clutching them in place. Halfway up is a man. Long black hair, like Gonzalez. I scramble to catch up with him, grasping onto saplings for footing. He circles around out of my view. I follow his trail of broken trees and crumbling earth to the far side of the mound where it stops for no apparent reason, like he jumped or just flew away. The cenote below holds only stagnant water teeming with insects, its surface undisturbed. For a half hour I circle the pyramid, peering up trees, and kicking rocks; checking for signs of a hideaway but find none.

He has to be here. But he's gone.

I buy a green coconut from one of the stalls and the lady chops off the top with a machete and puts a straw in it for me. I take out the picture of Gonzalez to try a little old-fashioned canvassing.

As I go from stall to stall a young boy follows me swiping a stick in the air like a sword. I'm met with a litany of nos.

"How about you?" I ask the boy in frustration.

He smiles and slashes the stick-sword.

"That's the boss. He's a great warrior. He told me someday a great army will come to take back Texas and California!"

"You saw him? Where?"

The boy's mother scrambles from her coconut stall.

"It's ok, tell me," I say to the boy.

The woman pulls the boy away by the ear.

"I'm sorry. I did not see anything, mister," he says.

"But I did," someone says from the stall across from us.

A Mexican teenager in cut-off jeans and a weathered black t-shirt with big red Rolling Stones lips leans against a pile of bright Mexican blankets. In his Nike sneakers and sleek black sunglasses, he looks as much a tourist as I do.

"Got any Marlboro reds?" he asks.

"Sorry," I say.

"I'm dying for a 'boro red. Come on."

"Don't smoke." I show him Gonzales' picture. "But I might, if you've seen this guy."

"Is it worth case of reds to you?"

"You're full of shit," I say, and turn to walk away.

"I can take you to his grave," he whispers.

That gets my attention. The women in the stalls glance at him with disapproving eyes.

"Walk with me," he says.

Everything else has turned up dry so I follow. He leads me five minutes into the jungle to a tiny clearing. A few dozen rectangles of earth framed with conch shells and whitewashed stones form three uneven rows in the moist rich brown earth. The dates on the wooden crosses show most of them died much too young. An old shovel, some two by fours, and beer cans litter the far corner.

The boy points to the freshest patch of earth. It has no cross.

"There's a body there," he says. "But it's not him."

"And how do you know?"

"How do you think?"

"You dug it up? Now why would you do that?"

"Ask my grandfather. I'd rather be in Mexico City but I'm back in this shithole till school starts again. And when I'm home, I work. He'll tell you himself, he's going to want to meet you with you asking all these questions."

"And your grandfather is?"

"I'd lose the attitude, mister. With all the questions you're asking he's someone you want to meet. His bar is the Serpent's Nest. Best one we have around here. Plays dominos most nights around eight. And don't ask me why, cause I couldn't tell you."

I don't trust the kid. It's the boredom and arrogance in his eyes.

"You want a case of reds? Then let's start digging."

"Shit, not again."

"I'll tell your grandfather you're a good kid."

"Whatever, just don't tell him about the cigarettes."

The staff at my hotel said the Serpent's Nest is the place all the locals go but from first glance at the place, I know they've lied. Marissa's happy to be here. The roof is thatched and cleverly designed walls slide open to the night. The dance floor sports expensive video screens and the bar looks ready for hordes of spring breakers.

"Come on, let's go burn off dinner," she says.

I pick at the last of the dirt under my nails. I wonder who that poor soul we dug up is. Gonzalez is out there, somewhere. I hope this old man helps me find him.

"I have to take care of something," I say.

"Then I'm starting without you."

The kid's grandfather is sitting at the bar across the dance floor playing dominos with the bartender. He's wearing a long-sleeved linen shirt and god-awful plaid dress pants, despite the heat. The two goons flanking him are doing a better job than the bartender at masking their boredom.

"Your grandson sent me," I say, and the two men look at me like I'm nuts.

But the old man takes my hand, eagerly. "Oh, yes. I'm Don Luis."

Beneath his sleeve are green and blue blurs, tattoos so faded I can't tell what they once were. They're an odd backdrop for the smiley yellow character of his cheap Pokémon wristwatch.

"Makes my granddaughter laugh," he says.

"I'm sure your grandson's a bit too old to be impressed."

"Aye, my grandson. Every time he comes home from school, I know him less. I should be thankful he comes home at all."

One of the thugs nods with fake empathy.

I reach for the picture of Gonzalez. "Have you seen this—"

Don Luis stops me, then laughs and knocks on the bar top.

"Esteban. Miguel. We will be in my office."

I stand and look for Marissa. She's engrossed in the music and has attracted a circle of young men. The pang of jealousy is unexpected.

"She's safe," he says. "They know you are with me. They all do."

I follow him through a door behind the bar. As we walk, the thumping bass of the dancehall reggae is enveloped by night sounds.

"Best not to talk in front of the men," he says. "They're superstitious fools."

The hulking shape of the buried pyramid looms over the trees. I picture it as part of the skyline of some lost city.

He takes me to the clearing where Gonzalez disappeared. He lets me take it in for a second.

"Treasures. Treasures. Beneath us, everywhere," he says. "One artifact can keep a family going for months. A much better alternative than working in the resorts."

"An honest day's work for an honest day's pay," I say.

"It's pitiful. One step up from servitude."

He produces a tiny figurine from his pocket.

"The people who made this are dead. They have no use for it. If they could know the world of good they were doing, do you think they'd object?"

"Do you?"

"I send things north. It's my business. It pays for the bar. Sends my grandkids to real schools in Mexico City. Our mutual *friend,* Señor Gonzalez, well, he's in the business of bringing them back. Bad for business. Having him locked in your jail was a blessing."

"This is where I chased him and he disappeared. You have people. We can stake out every giant mound of dirt from here to Belize."

"They say these are places where the dead cross between worlds. And I've told you my men are superstitious fools."

"But not you?"

"I know he's clever and he's hiding somewhere I can't find him. You're a clever man, shall we hunt together?"

He reaches into the crook of a tree overhanging the cenote and pulls out something wrapped in paper. He hands it to me. It's something solid.

"My grandson says you know where Velez lives. We've been

watching, but she's a crafty bruja. Gonzelez escapes every time. He will return there soon, a couple of days at most. The police will not question you if you leave right away."

"I'm not going to shoot anyone."

"Take it anyway."

"I didn't come here to shoot him."

"Then take him away. Then, back to your jails, if you can."

"I just came here for justice. The man's a criminal."

"Sí. Sí. You're the long arm of the law. I get it. Do what you have to do, Sheriff, just don't give my grandson any cigarettes."

I take out my roll of bills. "I owe him—"

"Keep it. Go to your girl. Dance with her. Enjoy the time you have. He'll be back."

———

In the morning there is a covered bowl of fresh fruit waiting outside our door. We take it to the beach. Marissa sketches me eating. She fills pages of her pad with the long line of the coast.

We pass the days in the sun. In the shade of the pool bar. I try not to think of the gun all wrapped in paper in the hotel drawer.

The afternoon of the third day, Abrams calls. Marissa listens as I check the message.

"Gonna call him back?"

"No. Not now."

It is so hot we take dinner back from the restaurant and eat it on our balcony. After, she runs the shower and turns out the lights. We spend the rest of the night in the comfort of the quiet, dark room.

Toucans chatter outside our window. Marissa straddles me, my hand in the concave hollow of her lower back, her fingers spread across my shoulders. Beyond the noisy birds is the powerful lull of the breaking waves.

I become aware someone is in the corner. Naomi, the death's head mask above her razor thin white scar; her lips forming silent words.

"What is it?" Marissa says.

"Nothing."

Gonzalez has returned. I can't hear but I know it is what Naomi is saying.

The sun comes up, filling the room with light. Marissa goes back to sleep. The bed is a twist of limbs and sheets, the clean smell of sweat—the smell of us—not yet washed away by the morning air.

A hummingbird flits among the hibiscus. And in this still moment my mind is quiet. I see the bird loves every flower. Fully and completely. Drinking it dry before moving to the next. It has to— to keep aloft. I wonder why haven't I moved on from the office? Why Marissa and I aren't married? And it dawns on me. Just like that. We have these beautiful moments. Always have. But they are moments. Islands in time, like chains of flowers. I know I will end up like Jeffries, a lifetime public servant, with her always second. And it's just not fair.

I take the gun out of its paper wrapping and leave, careful not to wake her.

The buried pyramid looms above the trees, a silent sentinel, guarding the closed stalls.

The row of shacks is alive with morning bustle as I walk to Velez's and stop at her open door. She is grinding herbs and seeds. A big fruit bat hangs upside down in the corner. Masks, knives, statuettes, and pottery are crowded among her table packed full of jarred herbs. These are not the trinkets of the village outside, these are real. Gonzalez's illicit fruits. A treasure trove of evidence.

"What a fool you are for coming," she says, without looking up, as if she was expecting me.

The bat opens its eyes and licks its brownish-red fur. Then it opens and re-folds its fleshy wings.

"I know you've been talking with Don Luis. Why would you listen to such a thief?"

"I'm not here to judge anyone," I say.

"Then I hope that you will not. Mercurio has paid his debts. Two life sentences."

"I'm just going to bring him back. The rest isn't up to me."

She looks at a stone knife on the table.

I take the gun out of my pocket.

"Now look at you," she says.

With her disdain, I feel far, far away from New York, from the sterile halls of the airport, from the plush soft edges of the hotel room and Marissa's embrace. I could leave now. Take as much as I could with me to the authorities.

"Where is he?"

The bat tilts its head inquisitively.

"Such a fool," she says. "Even now, you have no idea what they have done for you."

"You're under arrest," I say. A fear reflex. The words are feeble. The reek of herbs and humidity swallows them.

"And you think you are right, but you're just another outlaw."

I try to picture myself talking with Farber or running away with Marissa. But I can't. I can't summon the feeling of Naomi's arm around me. The gun feels heavy in my hand. I flip the safety off with a click.

"Don't hurt her," says a voice from outside.

My eyes are drawn to his white un-buttoned shirt, first, the "Y" scars on his chest, angry and inflamed. Everywhere else, his olive skin looks sun-touched. But something's wrong, like that healthy glow is just a mask, a disguise that's fading. I wished the gun made me feel stronger. If I shot, I'm not sure what it would even do.

"You're alive?" is all I can think to say.

"No." Gonzalez says.

"Then what the hell is going on?!" I yell.

He traces the line of the Y from his shoulder and stops at his heart. "It does not beat. It stopped that night."

"Let's just make this easy, okay?"

"I loved her. I want you to know that now."

"You fucking killed her!"

"It was an accident," he yells. "You don't know. How could you? There was no one else that night but me. No break in. No missing boyfriend."

I keep the gun trained on him, but he doesn't care and puts the items from the table in a bag as he's talking.

"Naomi wanted me to stop all this. And we argued. Someone

called the police. Her parents, I think. They never approved. The rest is as you know."

"And you said nothing? All this time."

"Who would believe me? Not you. But ask her. She says you can see her. She's trying to tell you to just go. So please, go."

"And let you go free?"

"No, for you to go and live your life and stop holding onto her. It's not too late. The future is bright for you. This body doesn't have much longer. And after today, you'll never see me again."

He stuffs the last of the artifacts into the bag.

"I'm bringing you back."

"These don't belong in New York. Or as chits for criminals. I'm taking them where they belong."

"The cenote?"

He doesn't answer.

"Show me."

"I cannot."

Something hits the side of my face and I realize I've forgotten about Velez.

Gonzalez bolts out the door and into the jungle. The bat drops from its perch and flaps out the window. I grapple with Velez and push her off me. She stumbles into the table, jars and bottles crashing around her.

I run after Gonzalez, cursing his head start.

The jungle seems alive with obstacles, mounds of rubble and half excavated buildings. But I know where he is going.

When I reach the pyramid, he is already at the top and is throwing artifacts into the cenote. I raise the gun and take aim.

"Just go," he calls. "I forgive you."

I squeeze the trigger. Not sure if I meant to the first time, but with the second and third bang the sting of his words disappears. He shudders, stumbles left, then right and drops the bag. I take aim again but just watch as he closes his eyes and jumps. There is no splash.

I climb as fast as I can. But he is not in the cenote. I kick at the artifacts that have fallen from his bag. A stone knife. A bowl. A statute of a serpent. I pick up the serpent and throw it. The stagnant water swallows it with a deep glug.

This is not how its ends. I know Marissa and the hotel are waiting for me. Farber and New York are waiting for me. But I won't be a stranger in a world built atop my city.

I drop the gun and take the knife in both hands.

"I'm sorry, Marissa," I whisper.

She'll wonder. She'll hurt. And I wish that the gates of glowing, glittering New York will open up and receive her because there's nothing left of our dream but a spent flower.

I hold the knife high, plunge it into my chest, and jump.

Twenty-Nine palms
in reverse

Twenty-Nine Palms, California. 2009

Yuli isn't here for the reason Noam thinks.

He pulls the key from the ignition and exhales, his other hand still gripping the wheel. The line of sandy brown earth and grey exposed rock snaking its way through the Joshua trees and cactus and brush all the way to the mountain ridge in the distance barely qualifies as a dirt road. Yuli opens the rental jeep's door and dry desert heat hits, the hot, fragrant air overcoming artificially cool and sterile. She secures her camera strap around her neck. The jeep's engine is still rumbling, unhappy about the steep, jagged incline Noam just gunned his way up. She didn't think he had it in him.

He's spotted something.

"Don't tell me," Yuli says. "I want to try—"

"Why bring your personal spotter then?"

She shushes him by blowing him a kiss the way she always does, then flips her hair and searches the ridge for bighorn sheep through her long lens. There are none. Movement in the corner of her vision catches her attention. Too tall for a bighorn. A person? Someone walking? She can't zero in. She searches the stillness between the jeep and the ridge. It's a prehistoric landscape of surreal rock formations, and ancient twenty to thirty foot Joshua Trees, their crooked limbs towering over patches of barrel cacti and silvery bush-like cholla undisturbed by tourists and climbers from LA. There are no other vehicles. We're probably outside the park, she thinks. She lowers the camera.

Canine prints, and tracks of a bird, probably a road runner or quail, are in the earth before her, a story of passage in the dried-up evidence of a flash flood. Then she sees what Noam stopped for. A tortoise. Crossing the "road" only a few yards away. Its domed shell scarred with healed over cracks. From its size, she guesses it might be even older than the Joshua Trees. She picks it up, turns it around, and places it in the safety of the rock formation from where it began its crossing. She glances at Noam leaning on the jeep in his jeans and white tee as he's scanning the ridge in the distance, looking cool as a cucumber with his week-old scruff and mop of unruly brown hair and his expression unaware of her and focused on the landscape before them. She finds him—and the whole moment beautiful—a frame of a 1950's movie come to life.

"The first time I came out here I was still in school," Yuli says.

"We were all such dopes. I don't remember having any water and was probably wearing sneakers. This guy who was with us, he wasn't bright at all, we all thought he was stripping to pay his way through school, he yells from up ahead, 'Hey look, there's a big boa sleeping up here. I found a boa!' I knew enough about snakes to know there are no boas out here but the first thing my mind thinks is wow, he's found a boa and it's probably someone's lost pet and we have to save it. So we catch up with him and I stick my face in the rocks where he's pointing and yeah, there *is* a big ass snake coiled up sleeping in there. Only it's not a boa, it's a six foot plus thick, thick diamond back rattlesnake—"

"Yuliana. You're doing it again," Noam says.

"Am I?"

Noam nods.

"I am. Sorry. You know, it's just… California is where I started. Where I started being me. I want to show you everything. I want you to know all of me."

"I wish we could be somewhere that's new ground for both of us," Noam says. "That's what couples do."

"I'm taking California back from my past, so it's ours now, too. That's *also* something couples do."

She notices movement again. She was right. Someone *is* way out there at the foot of the ridge. A woman. Dwarfed by the Joshua trees. Slowly walking towards them. Yuli brings her camera to her eye, pushes the lens to the max, trying to zero in, unable to keep the woman in the frame. She zooms out, spotting her briefly before losing her among the ancient trunks.

"And there you go," Noam says.

He's holding the tortoise, its legs moving in the air. He places it on the other side of the dirt path.

"You're not supposed to put them *back*," he says. "You're supposed to help them *cross*."

"Cross? This isn't even a road. This isn't even anywhere," Yuli says. She walks to him and kisses his check. "Is my spotter getting grumpy? Need some water and AC?"

"No, I'm… not sure we're in the right place. I don't think this is the right ridge. There's supposed to be a pool of run off. A watering hole. Maybe we shouldn't have gone up that incline."

Noam scans the plain with his binoculars.

"See anything?" Yuli asks.

She's hoping he finds a mountain lion. Steve and Steve from the guest house said they're out here but nearly impossible to spot during the day unless moving. And they won't be moving unless going for water or prey.

"Um, nothing," Noam says after a pause that feels too long.

Before she can ask him what's wrong or tell him to get over himself, she's not sure which, he lowers the binoculars and points.

"Kestrel, fifty feet ahead," he says. "See that Joshua Tree? The one that looks sorta like a wind mill?"

"Check. See it."

"Third branch up, halfway to the spiky leaf-tufts at the end. There's a kestrel trying to stuff a dead baby snake in its hollow."

"Oooh, I see it."

The tiny snake, not dead after all, doubles back on itself, lunging with fangs bared.

"Oooh, look at that. You're so good to me."

"Now that's what I like to hear. Don't ever say I don't do anything for you…"

Yuli photographs the snake as it frees itself and falls. She wonders about the pause in Noam's reply. Did he see the woman out there too?

The sun is ready to go down. The big blue open desert sky behind the ridge will soon be filled with color. The kestrel takes flight, its gliding arc the only motion in the windless, natural garden.

There is something kinetic in the stillness. It dawns on her it's been too long since she's felt this connected and alive.

Steve and his husband of the same name designed the guest house themselves, and had it constructed entirely from materials found on their sprawling acreage just inside the border of the National Park. The low building's stone and timber contour is made to resemble the ridge on the horizon behind it and fit in with the natural landscape. Yuli chose it because she hoped Noam would love it.

The four of them finish dinner and sit at the long, reclaimed-wood table by the big window granting a perfect view of outside. The Joshua trees are not nearly as tall as the ones from this afternoon.

"Steve's grandfather bought the land decades ago, before the Park was a Park," the Steve who is a former chef says. "So we're literally grandfathered-in around the no building and living inside the park rules, as Steve likes to say."

"Well, the hippies and climbers always knew Twenty-Nine Palms was the place to be," the other Steve says. He's the one Yuli spoke to when booking and is also a guide. "They knew the LA people and hipsters would one day creep in."

"Which one was your grandfather?" Steve asks as he gathers the plates.

Yuli gazes outside. Dusk is bathing the rock and cactus and ocotillo and all the desert things in shadow. She catches Noam staring too.

"Hmmm, good question," Steve answers. "Give it ten years no one's gonna recognize this place."

"Change is the only constant, my dear."

"Is it?"

"Our guests don't want to hear us debate and philosophize."

"Quite the contrary," Noam says.

"So, did you find the watering hole and the bighorns?" Steve asks.

"Didn't find the water," Noam says. "We were up that steep part, to where the big Joshua Trees are."

"Oh, you were right there. That's the oldest part of the forest. You're lucky you didn't break an axle."

"Yeah, no signal, you'd be fucked," Steve says carrying the plates to the kitchen.

"Pardon my husband's French. It's almost dark. Say give it an hour then we meet back here for that night walk?"

"Night walk? Deadly scorpions," Steve calls from the kitchen. "I pass."

Yuli finds herself jealous of the giddy, affectionate expression that comes over Steve's face in response to his husband's foolery.

She and Noam bring their gear from the jeep into their room. The entrance into their small, cave-like space is a glass door providing an unobstructed view of the property and the desert beyond.

"We going to unpack or—"

Yuli playfully pushes Noam onto the bed and jumps on him, pulling at their clothes, hoping her frenzied kisses will come across as passionate. The connection she felt outside translates to the moment. This is something better than at home. Almost good again, she thinks. She closes her eyes in surrender. An image of the woman walking through the trees is there waiting.

After, lying there naked, catching her breath with him, she can't point to why she feels dissatisfied.

"What?" Noam says.

"You weren't into it, were you? I felt you weren't."

"What? I totally was."

"What were you thinking?" Yuli asks. "Come on, where were you?"

"Here. I mean, at one point I felt *you* weren't really here then I got lost in it all ..."

"Lost in it, huh?"

"I'll show you how into you I am," Noam says. "But we're going to miss the hike."

As they are squirming into their clothes, Yuli is startled by a woman walking towards her but it is only the reflection from the bedside lamp-glare on the glass.

Steve, the guide, knows every inch of the property. Under the stars and moon, the desert is a different kind of gorgeous. Silver leaves, spindly cactus arms, and all the rocks and textures take on new color and shape in the light of night and its shadows. Steve does not deliver on his promise of a scorpion for her to shoot but there are plenty of active long-tailed kangaroo rats scavenging, and one rattler that escapes into a burrow after pleasing them with its namesake warning. Her prize is the tarantula Noam spots on a cactus at the end of the walk near the house.

In the middle of the night, while Noam is sleeping, she returns outside to search for the spider again. The sound of coyotes yipping and barking fills the silence. She is unsure if the pack is coming or going. Noam was right. It was her who wasn't present when they were fucking. She was wondering about the woman out there and envisioning the giant trees lit by stars and all the shades of brown at night in a negative image of the day.

It is not that she doesn't want him, mostly she does. And she thinks she loves him. At least more than she's loved anyone before. The burden is that *this* isn't what she thought being thirty-five would be. She doesn't know what it *should* be, and would say fuck off to anyone who tried to tell her. Though there is nothing wrong, she knows her life is not supposed to be the one she is living. She knows this awareness is a dangerous cage to be in, and one even more dangerous to wake up in with regret years later. She was not lying, the twin thought of the truth she told Noam is that she is also here to decide if she is going to leave him.

A water droplet lands on her, then another. The cloudless sky empties of rain. She wasn't sure if it ever rained in the desert, she knew it must, now she knows the truth first hand. The downpour stops a minute later. She spots the spider on the cactus, touching a droplet beaded on the tip of a thorn with its front legs. She listens for the sound of a flash flood in the canyon she knows must be on the other side of the ridge in the distance.

***

Instead of following the directions to search for the ridge with the watering hole Noam guns it up the incline, again, and she doesn't protest.

He stops the jeep in nearly the same place as yesterday. Everything has exploded into colors. Yellow, pink, and white cactus blooms. Red ocotillo flowers, silver cholla plump with moisture. The tracks she had seen yesterday in the dried earth have been worn smooth by the rain.

"Can we go out there?" Yuli asks. "Make it to the ridge?"

"I was thinking that, too. It's farther than it looks and there are so many rocks. We shouldn't take a chance with the axle."

"Want to walk it?" she asks.

"Hell yeah. I can spot for boas."

"Very funny."

"I thought you'd think so. Hey look at me, I'm a stripper. I think I found someone's pet python."

He takes off his shirt and spins it overhead with his finger. His childish display of jealousy is not attractive.

"Ha, ha. Enough. You're gonna get one hell of a sunburn."

"Then take me into the backseat," he says.

He playfully grabs her and pushes her against the jeep. She pushes back harder than they both expected.

"How about we take it easy, Tiger?" she says. "Save it for tonight, and make good use of this daylight instead?"

"Fine," Noam says. "I'll be a good spotter."

She doesn't like that she's lied to him. She knows it's a very bad sign she can't be honest; that he is not man enough to hear about a school days fling she had over a decade ago. Long before she knew him.

His name was Adam. He was an escort, not a stripper, though he did sometimes bounce at a strip club. They used to come out to the desert, with no money for fancy places, it was just them and the truck and a tent. He wasn't stupid, at all. Yeah, he got high too much, and talk about a dead-end job, but wow did they ever click in bed. With Adam she felt like a dance partner, not a plaything. He wrote her stories, made up just for her, using characters from her favorite books and movies.

One night, in the desert under the stars while they were pontificating on life and the people they would become, Adam proclaimed, "I'm not a prostitute; I choose who I'm with," and told her he was only doing it because he was on the run from his life in Nevada. She never asked or found out quite what he meant by that. The next time she went to see him, he was gone. Gone as in his truck wasn't at his place. Gone as in his roommates had moved, too. She checked and checked again. No one had even seen him at the club. In the pre-internet age, this was disappeared for real. It was just a fling, but the loss of possibility, the loss of the feeling that sex, pleasure, art, and the natural world was what life meant and what life had in store was a real blow. So much was lost along the way of growing up. She hates she cannot tell Noam this.

They push through the heat towards the ridge. Noam offers her water every few minutes and is a good spotter. There is nothing wrong with the moment, Yuli thinks. The moment is quite pleasant. Noam's sweat slicked olive skin glistens in the sun. The cactus and trees and flowers are unfathomably beautiful. Noam is quiet. Quiet is his default state and that's okay. She prefers to think it evidences unknowable depths as opposed to there being nothing to him. She knows he values being in the moment and being in strings of moments with her. She hopes there is more to him than this.

She realizes she is looking through a disturbance in the air, a wall of heat-haze giving everything a distorted shimmer. Through the disturbance, she sees the woman. They are both walking. With her next step Yuli realizes she is walking toward the woman and the woman is walking towards her. They are both converging on the disturbance.

With the thought, she feels faint. Noam gently catches her as she stumbles backwards.

"Wow, you're dehydrated," he says. "It happens fast. We have to drink a bottle an hour. I'm feeling it too—"

"I have been drinking."

They stand there passing a water bottle back and forth. Yuli can no longer see it but she can sense where the disturbance was. Its exact place. She can feel the line.

"How much further," she says. "I want to go."

"Huh," Noam says.

"I want to keep walking. I want to take some shots."

"Okay," he says.

She expected him to protest. "Aren't you going to ask me?"

"Ask you what?"

"What I'm shooting?"

"You're an artist, Yuli, I trust you. This is me being the crew. I'm on the assist this trip, right?"

"Right."

She looks into the distance hoping to see the woman. She knows it is possible to walk out there and… what? Would they cross paths, what would happen? She feels the faintness coming again.

She thinks she should say something to Noam. He is staring at the ridge, his mouth releasing soft mutterings.

"What are you doing?" she asks.

"Um, just writing," he says.

"Now? What were you writing? You don't write."

"Poems," he says. "And yes I do."

"I've never seen you."

"True. They're in my head. I keep them there."

"Really? You don't write them down?"

"Maybe someday. Maybe the ones that stay with me long enough."

"I never knew you did that," she says.

Maybe the reason being a couple isn't to know everything about each other, she thinks. Maybe it is what will be seen together. The uncharted ground, like he said yesterday.

"I want to go back to the room now," she says.

"You sure? Daylight's burning."

"Yeah, I have a job for my personal spotter that needs immediate attention."

For the first time in as long as she can remember she is certain about how she feels.

The sex is the best she can remember, their kisses approaching the lost magic. Something Adam once said to her jumps into her mind. Life is converging and intertwined lines, he'd said. The tough part is figuring out whose story is whose. Is your direction your own? Are you the lead in your story? Or a side player in someone else's? Or are we all nothing at all?

"So, his name was Adam," Noam says.

"Who?"

"The stripper?"

"What? Why would you say that? How do you know that?"

"You were calling his name."

"I was not. Was I?"

"You never told me his name. His name is Adam. How else would I know?"

Yuli doesn't know what to do so she storms out the door and walks around the house to the main entrance. Steve, the chef, is there setting the table and having a cigarette.

"Everything okay, boss?" he asks.

"Um, yeah, sure just came to see if I could beg a smoke."

"You can't. I'm not supposed to and you caught me. Steve's out getting bread. Oh, no, you are *not* okay. What's wrong?"

"How long have you been with Steve? Was it always bliss between you two?"

"Wow, that's a personal question for before dinner. Let's see, you're in my home and sure, I can add therapist to the many lines on my resume. So. No, it wasn't."

"How did you do it? I mean, how did you make it work?"

"I've learned that everything is a choice. There's no magic to love and staying together. No formula either. When it comes down to it, it is a choice to come together and when things get rough to stay together, or not. Everyone I've ever asked—I asked a lot before Steve and I worked it all out—says the same. Fight for him. Drag him to you, or to counseling or whatever. Do whatever you've got to do."

"Right," she says. "You're right, thank you. I shouldn't have run out on him."

"Don't mention it." He holds up his smoke. "And by that, I really mean don't mention it."

Yuli's ashamed, so she decides to take a walk on the trail they were on last night to cool down and clear her head before going back to work it all out with Noam.

On the path she comes across a tortoise crossing to a patch of cactus, going the opposite way of the one she saw yesterday. It is identical in size; she wonders if it is the same reptile. She contemplates helping it across. As she kneels to lift it she sees its shell is free of cracks and scars. She sees no reason to do anything other than watch it as it ambles into the rocks and brush.

An hour later, she returns to the room. The jeep and Noam are gone. She runs to the main house.

"Hey, where'd Noam go?"

"Don't know," Steve, the guide, says.

"Can I borrow your truck?"

"We're not supposed to—"

"Yes," Steve, the chef, says and tosses her a ring of keys.

Yuli knows where to go. Where else would Noam go?

As she speeds on the desert road flanked by Joshua Trees, she wonders is there another Yuli racing toward her? Is it possible that she is the other and out there, there is a Yuli this never happened to? A Yuli who never knew doubt?

When she reaches the incline she guns it, like Noam. The truck bottoms out and lurches, she thinks it is going to flip. It drags on something with a terrible clack of metal on rock, the death knell of an axle, for sure. The truck loses power and slides back down the incline.

Yuli gets out and decides to climb. Hand over hand. There are so many rocks. It takes her a few minutes to cover what in the jeep had taken seconds.

Coyotes are yipping and barking nearby, this time she knows they are leaving for a night of raiding the dumpsters and open cans of Twenty-Nine Palms. Something else is out in the dusk with her. A throaty feline gurgle that can only be a mountain lion breaks the quiet. She's without her camera, without her phone, and feels naked instead of scared shitless to be close to a predatory big cat she cannot see. She revels in the thrill.

Yuli pulls her way to the top and spots Noam. He's already walked far and is nearing the disturbance before the ridge. His lean form is dwarfed by the old trees and the heat-mirage wavering in the air before him. Is there another him out there on the other side walking towards him? Is she going to look through it and see another man walking towards her Noam? Is she going to look and that see the woman walking towards her, is another her?

Their rental jeep is still running. The door is open. Noam's left his boots and his shirt. Something compels her to copy him and to take off her boots. The dry earth feels good. She steps in a moist swath of ground, a place where a flash flood passed. She is making tracks. Tracks that will remain for who knows how long until they're washed away by the next rain.

When she reaches the wavering will she walk through it and keep walking and nothing will happen? Will she switch places with the woman? Will they pass through each other? Will she even know? Noam is right there. A few more steps and he's there.

Yuli sees the woman. The face, the body are visually identical to hers, but Yuli knows the woman is not her. Some spirit, some feeling, the toll of the paths she's walked through the years and the weight of burden's she's carried are absent.

She sees the wavering and can see through it, at the same time. One more step and Noam will reach it. One more second and she'll know what will happen to him. She'll know what is in store for her too.

She senses presences all around her. Animals. All the animals living here. Birds, coyotes, insects. Each one registers as noise in the quiet. She spots a grey coyote camouflaged in a pile of rock. Another at the brown foot of a Joshua Tree trunk. She becomes aware of another and another. There is an entire pack among the trees and rocks. She sees a roadrunner in the distance. Hawks. Lizards. A tortoise emerging from its burrow. Kangaroo rats and hares leaving the cover of brush. A scorpion uncurls itself from its hiding spot at the base of a barrel cactus. She becomes aware of all of them with a speed and certainty Noam could never match.

Bighorn sheep are watching from the ridge. Are their

instincts to avoid danger keeping them away or calling them? From somewhere nearby the mountain lion releases a long yowl, powerful enough to resonate in her sternum. The hot air is full of the herbal mix of everything that grows here. Wind sweeps through the dusk. Yuli's mind fills with the image of a palm tree, not with roots beneath ground, but another trunk and fronds burrowing into an inverted world, that looks almost the same as here, but where she hopes things are not the same as here at all.

A Loch Ness Monster under the Light of the Southern Cross

Staan Creek District, Belize.

Once you're done with the sense of loss and the loneliness and the pain and range of emotions you go through there is something freeing about not mattering at all, about being no one's number one in this world. It's a release. From all the twists and turns. The patterns you find yourself in. All the things, of your own making and otherwise, holding you in place. Time helps. Some days you still wake up raw and hollow, not from your most recent loss, or from any one thing, but from the weight of all of it.

Lena doesn't see this. How could she? Some cuts are too fresh.

There are only a couple of huts here and ours is perfect, stark and empty, a clean slate; the sky, the sea, the jungle, the flowers providing all the color and sound and beautiful things I could want around me.

An elderly lady, dressed for a flight back to New York, is

clamoring about the manatee that has surfaced in one of the sink holes on the property and Lena isn't even interested in looking.

I tell the young Belizean guy renting us the jeep that we're headed to Ihaka's down near Placencia and he says just make sure you don't go to the unfinished condos next door.

"Why?" I ask. "Rough parking?"

He shrugs.

"Everybody knows it's the one place you don't go."

The elderly lady stops directing her even more elderly and dazed-looking husband where to roll their luggage and chimes in.

"Oh, darling, we went past it on our way back from the ruins. Such a shame. It has so much potential. Sleek buildings. Clean lines. Our driver told us it was built by a drug dealer so now no one wants to buy it and finish the job."

"Didn't he say something about a shoot-out and a suicide?"

"They're such a lovely couple, dear, don't rain on their parade. Love, let me tell you about this place where we had breakfast, perfect for you lovebirds—"

"We're not a couple," Lena replies, flatly.

Like me, she never fit in. With dark eyes and light tan skin from her Polynesian mother and a smooth, clear complexion from her father's Scottish side she was always too beautiful to be teased. Mostly I remember her as just… present, a lot like now. Her brother was the one who drew the spotlight. There isn't a touch of grey in her long black ponytail, only a sheen from the sun, and barely a wrinkle on her; unlike so many of the people we went to school with, their bodies gone to hell and faces bearing the signs of their age and then some.

"We're visiting her father," I say with a smile. "I've known them since I was a kid."

We aren't interesting enough and we've lost the woman's

attention to the task of getting her bags into the airport van. I can't help seeing the vast emptiness in her husband's eyes. That and something about the way he stands says he's... lost, he's... just along for the ride and despite paying enough attention to know the drug-deal-shoot-out story he's not really here at all. It's the same with Lena. I don't think she liked hearing her brother's name out loud. I feel the distance between us. And between me and everyone. I had hoped for otherwise but the feeling is nothing new. In the uncomfortable silence I hear the ocean murmuring from not far away, the din of all the living things in the trees, and the call and replies of birds that sound nothing like home.

We hop in the jeep, top and doors off, and I gun it. The heat doesn't seem to bother her nor the bumpy road. She smells like alcohol and I hope I wasn't wrong in pegging her for being a good traveler.

In the fun little airport bar in Belize City, waiting for our puddle jumper, she was enthusiastic about the green cocktails in martini glasses made with pisang liquor. She talked about the war and the stock market with a young couple traveling with their adorable Pekinese, all good signs.

"Glad to be here?" I say.

She only gives a nod.

I immediately wish I hadn't spoken. When someone's mind is in a maze there's not a lot you can do to lead them out.

How long does it take to communicate the events of decades gone by? The scale of disappointments? A day? A week? Even after everything that scarred and didn't heal, I never lost sight of the fact that the world was full of love. I never felt the need to escape. Despite countless ghosts and memories in so many of my everyday places I never felt the suburban streets were harsh or ugly or even painful anymore. No sharp edges. Things just became… worn, and acquired an ever-present weight, un-noticeable on most days. At least the good ones. I was feeling that benign numbness yesterday when I reconnected with Lena.

The road's two lanes carve a path through an incomprehensible mass of wild greenery and trees on either side. I like the heat. And the wind. Lena produces an airplane size liquor bottle, I have no idea where from, and downs it.

In the second my eyes are on her, someone darts into the road. I swerve and manage to keep the jeep off the muddy ditch of a shoulder and moving forward. Lena doesn't appear fazed, so I guess she's alright.

More people emerge from the jungle. They're carrying something above them. Something big. A dead crocodile. Its huge. They're walking with it in some sort of procession. Belizeans. And ex-pats. A couple of dozen people from all walks of life. I slow to a halt to let them safely cross the road.

"Hey, honk for us," one of them calls.

Lena reaches over and smashes the horn, to their delight.

A couple of young men jump on our hood and slap our windshield and give the thumbs up.

"What's going on," I say over the engine and the people. I can hear they are singing. Something mournful.

"We got him. This is the saltie that took the Johnson's kid, Syreeta," a shirtless American guy with long dreads and baby face tells me.

We watch them cross and disappear into the other side. Maybe heading for the beach, I guess. I notice some monkeys in one of the big strangler figs in the tangle of trees just sitting there on a bough eating fruit and watching, too.

"They got that thing in the jungle?" Lena asks.

"Maybe in one of the underground rivers? Or sinkholes. This whole area is connected that way."

I get us moving and before long we've reached what I think are the condos. There's a gateway and long drive that looks like it belongs in Beverley Hills or New Jersey leading past a moat-like canal circling the place. The canals and uniformity of the rows of white buildings evoke every gated community in Florida I've ever seen. The road veers right and a big painted wooden sign comes into view. "Ihaka's." Draped in Christmas lights, it no doubt cannot be missed at night.

I roll into the dirt patch of cleared jungle that is the parking lot and line the jeep up with the dozen or so cars there—new and mostly clean, rentals like ours. A few paces inside the tree line I can see the wall-less bar, the bamboo struts and thatch and two shelves of liquor beneath the taxidermy crocodile exactly the same as we saw it on the TV in 7-Eleven.

And there's Lena's dad. Shaking a metal shaker. Right out of my childhood memories, same dark glasses and not looking like he's aged much. He's in a loose fitting, dark dress shirt and slacks not the plain grey suits I remember him in, when I used to watch him walk from his car to his front door when arriving home from work. I hadn't put eyes on him since the days the Smiths broke up and left us holding tickets to their show at the Ritz. His son's name on the big sign and Lena's tense stare leaves no doubt it's him as if there were any question.

"You okay?" I ask Lena.

"Mmmn, hmmn," she says. "Let's get a drink."

We take seats at the bar. Her dad's still tall and skinny and pasty white. Up close I see there are wrinkles on his forehead and dark patches under his eyes. Lena catches his attention and orders.

"I see you've got Midori. Good. Two melonballs. Extra vodka for me. Hold the pineapple juice for him."

For a second I'm clueless about her order then I remember it was Ihaka's drink, just the way he liked it. He loved those god forsaken concoctions and didn't give a flying fuck if any of his jock team mates summoned the balls to roust him for drinking a so-called girly drink.

Lena's dad puts a plain brown square of a napkin in front of each of us.

"Two melonballs. Got it. Coming right up."

He turns, grabs two highball glasses from the hanging rack, and begins fixing the drinks.

Forget about me. How can it be that he doesn't recognize *her*?

"Fuck this. We're out of here," Lena says and is on her feet.

I know it's been, how long? But not recognizing your own daughter, that's fucked up. Lena marches to the jeep. I don't dare say a word.

"Keys," she says.

I throw them to her and hop in the side.

"How dare he use Ihaka's name for his bar," she says, as we roll past the sign.

She peels out and we're back heading north. She brings the jeep to a dangerous speed then slams on the brakes. She backs up right on the road and turns into the condos.

"Here?" I say.

"I want to see this fucking place," she says.

"It looks abandoned. It is abandoned. It's empty, nothing to see."

She parks up against the big gate and gets out of the jeep.

There's an access door, made out of the same bars, that isn't padlocked and it swings right open.

I follow her. The path to the row of finished houses is flanked by a canal. The water is clean and flowing, looks like rain runoff, draining to somewhere. Hurricane and flood protection, just like Florida, I guess. The canal circles the development and weaves in and out of the buildings. They're a bit weathered but look unused. Unfurnished. No personalized accoutrements I can discern. Until I see a little red light in an unscreened window. A trail cam. It's black housing does not look weathered at all. What the fuck?

Lena's at the last house in the row before a big building at the edge of the jungle. She pulls the door open. Of course it isn't locked. She steps inside and I hurry over.

This one is lived in for sure. There's a wall of books. And a wall with ceiling to floor shelves full of amazing bottles. All different shapes and colors. There isn't one bottle, alcohol or otherwise, that I've ever seen before.

"Lena, I don't like this. We should get out of here."

"You're right," she says.

We go back outside. Instead of turning to leave the compound the way we came she walks toward the big building and takes the path into the jungle. I see there are sinkholes flanking the path where it runs under the trees.

"Careful," I call. "There could be a croc or something."

She doesn't stop. I contemplate whether I should hang back and give her space or follow.

I check out the large building. I wonder if it was a gym or common area. It's got big glass windows, maybe a greenhouse? They're all steamed and it's fogged up in there. Not one of them has been broken.

I go into the trees after Lena.

After a few minutes I find her sitting at the edge of a large sinkhole a couple of hundred yards in. There are no trees above. The sun is going down. It smells like summer.

The surface of the perfectly clear water captures a reverse image of the vine wrapped trees and their countless shades of brown, and the lush green fronds and ferns and saplings all mixed in with the rocky side of the sink hole disappearing into the earth.

As I walk over to sit next to her I startle a foot-long, brown lizard with a triangular crest. Rear toes spread wide, it dashes across the surface of the water, it's long tail disturbing floating water lilies. As it crosses the center point its scales shimmer white and pink and green in the sunlight before it disappears onto the opposite bank. I notice petite white flowers on one of the vines creeping around a robust gumbo limbo tree. And there aren't any mosquitos. I can see why the little town was built here, this is a paradise. Lena downs another airplane bottle of rum.

"I know that sucked," I say. "It's okay to be triggered."

"I'm not triggered."

In the quiet of our silence that follows there is the rustle of the air moving the canopy, the din of sounds radiating from the leaves and branches akin to the buzz of New York's cicadas, yet still wholly new and alien, and a back and forth of bird calls so full about their business that I am certain that this is their world and we are the interlopers.

After a few minutes she gives a solid poke to my shoulder and points to the water.

"What?" I say.

She shushes me, puts her finger over her mouth, then whispers,

"What the fuck is that?"

"Where?"

"There. Right there in the middle."

I ease myself to my feet.

"I don't see anything," I whisper.

There's only the crystal-clear water. Not even a ripple.

She can't hide her disappointment and stares at me as if I'm crazy.

I have the feeling this expression is one I would know well should the trajectories of our lives keep us together after this. It is the opposite look, the reciprocal, of her sated face, the one I saw still flush with heat about to be at rest, seconds from sleep in my bed last night, her disheveled hair transforming my pillow to a thing of beauty when I told her things not only were going to be all right, they were going to be amazing.

It's been one hell of a long day, an upsetting day and she's probably a little drunk and a lot dehydrated. It was only yesterday I rolled by my childhood home on my way back from the grocery store. To feel something. To feel anything besides like a ghost haunting the places that sprung up over the decades in the places I once knew. I couldn't have guessed I'd find myself here today. With her. Feeling alive again just like that, yet feeling so lost.

New York. Yesterday.

I rolled slowly down the familiar suburban cul-de-sac and parked across the street from the house I grew up in.

And I sat there. Thinking.

When you're young you have a resiliency and shrug things off. The young keep going. Unaware that the amount of pain and loss and disappointment one can bear is a finite amount and one day you might find yourself with the last of it left, wondering if you could sustain even one iota more, or if there is strength enough to survive one more heartbreak in you, or if your capacity for love and connection has been worn down to a null possibility.

In the decade since my parents sold it and headed off to fairer shores, I'd made a few visits. To dwell in my childhood memories. Block wide matches of Ringolevio. Games of our own invention played well into the dark of summer nights. The Thomson's house next door.

One of my favorite hiding spots was in their backyard behind their old pool house (there hadn't been a pool since long before they moved in, but Lena's dad used the rickety structure as a shed). It was great because there were two ways out and you could also climb the fence into the Siegel's yard and be on Mimosa Court in a snap if you heard the other team coming.

Lena was a year older than me. Ihaka five years older than her. And little Tavish, in my mind forever the baby, at least a decade younger than us all. Lena's mom and dad worked long hours and kept to themselves and thus Lena and Ihaka were always the last to have to go inside for the night. Lena's Mom worked in a flower shop and her dad worked in a liquor store, we thought they may have owned both businesses but never knew for sure. Both were establishments we never saw, not even on our most far-flung bicycle jaunts. Her dad would arrive home at odd hours. I always thought he looked grim marching from his car to his front door without waving to or acknowledging us kids. We mostly were not allowed inside and had to wait at the door for Lena or Ihaka to come out to play. The handful of times we were allowed in, Mister Thomson was always the one who told us when it was time to leave. One time, big mouthed Chris Eisman asked him since he was from Scotland if he had ever seen the Loch Ness Monster and it prompted an angry outburst, the only display of emotion I'd ever seen from Mister Thomson at that point.

Usually a trip to the pet store was my prescription for being lost in the past, but my bearded dragon, Mister Hieronymus, had bit the dust last week. I'd adopted him, more like saved him, from my ex's kid when we split, over a decade ago. The lizard, with his name bestowed on him by my ex, was the last nebulous connection to a path long gone. And it surprised me how hollow it left me. Not because that I no longer knew if my ex was alive or dead (and hated that I found I no longer cared either way) or that I figured the kid was all grown now and likely did just fine having forgotten me long ago; it was that this cycle and circle of caring for and shopping for the lizard was at an end and there was now one less thing holding me to the earth. The timeless oak trees against the sky of the old neighborhood and caws of the blue jays no doubt the descendants of the ones I once knew I hoped would be a balm.

The door to the Thomson house opened and there was Lena, all grown up and middle-aged and looking divine in a smart black suit, walking out with two people who looked like realtors. I watched them put a wooden 'For Sale' post up on the lawn and thought about rolling down the window and saying hello. How long had it been? Thirty-five years, at least. Had her mom died? I decided too much time had passed and we were too far from the selves that once knew each other so I just pulled away and headed for the 7-Eleven a couple of blocks away that used to be the gas station we bought beer at when we were underage.

Cheating on my health routine with forbidden diet soda and chocolate was my go-to self-care, self-defeating as it was.

Inside the store, a flat screen above the coffee station blared one of those ubiquitous travel shows, a hostess in a sun dress sampling unreal green colored cocktails in a far-flung airport bar. I hated that there was TV everywhere.

A flock of kids who didn't seem old enough to me were mobbing the coffee station, which was fine so long as they stayed away from the fountain soda. Kids were so much different now, with lives stuffed with too much to do I wondered if they even had the time to enact the cruelties I remembered.

I carried my full cup toward the register watching the screen despite myself; the hostess, now in a bikini, had moved on to a bamboo tiki-bar in the jungle—

Someone slammed into me, knocking my cup to the floor in a spray of cola and fizz.

"Holy shit, holy shit, holy shit," the woman said.

"Hey, it's okay, it's just soda."

"That's my dad. That's my fucking dad up there."

It was Lena. On the screen it was her dad, Mister Thomson, behind the bar shaking a metal shaker for the hostess. I had not seen him since he left and from her reaction neither had she.

"Ronnie? Ronnie Greenbaum?"

Here words were slurred. She was drunk.

"After you went to LA, I saw you once on the Jools Holland show and that was it, I always wondered what happened to you."

"So did I," I said.

I thought we were going to laugh but instead we looked to the screen and watched her dad pour drinks beneath a mounted taxidermy crocodile draped in tropical flowers.

"How's your mom? Tavish?"

It was all I could say. There was no way to put my feelings into words, which were that after thirty years what happened to your brother and your dad, I still carry with me and colors my every notion of trust and safety.

"It's just me now," she said.

"I'm sorry."

"Yeah, your folks been gone a while now. Holy shit, I never expected to see you but... I'm glad," she said.

"Really, me?"

"Yeah you. You were always kind. You remember that time after school you stood up to all those assholes for me?"

"Oh, yeah, was that like in tenth grade, wow. I haven't seen you since... your graduation?"

"No. There was that time, I ran into you out East, at the Talkhouse, right before you left for California."

"What? You sure?"

"Oh, yes. I just split from my fiancé and was about to play my first show and was losing my shit in the parking lot. I was about to bail as you were driving up."

"I have zero memory of this."

"Come on. You were so there for me. It's one of the things I'll never forget in this life. You told me how beautiful I was. And how smart I was and that I could do anything. Not just get up there and play that show but anything I wanted with my life."

"I want to lie to you and tell you of course I remember this. But sadly I was probably pretty high."

"You didn't hit on me. You just lifted me up and told me to get myself up there and have the night of my life."

"And you did."

"I did."

"This is the best thing I've heard all day. I'm glad as hell to hear this."

"So. What are you doing here? You're... back in New York. How are you?"

"Um, good. I guess... Feels like a loaded question."

"It isn't."

We laughed.

"I've been back pushing two decades now."

We both looked to the screen.

"What the hell?" I said.

She didn't say anything. She didn't need to. The way she stared said it all. That we thought he was dead or at best that we'd never, ever see him again.

"If we're not laughing, we're crying, right?" she said. "You still drumming? Hey you want to catch up over pizza?"

We went around the corner and got slices. The same spot we used to go when we were kids, the name changed though. After, she wanted to come to my place to put some flowers and what was left of the hornworms on Mister Hieronymus' grave.

In my living room she told me she'd decided she was going to Belize to see her father now that she knew where he was and asked me if I would come then passed out on my couch with flowers still in hand while I was waxing poetic on whether I should or shouldn't.

I was awakened in the middle of the night to her climbing into my bed.

We bought plane tickets online, under the covers. Putting my arm around her felt awkward. She seemed to be right at home curling up against me though.

"Do you remember that one time when we were kids when we almost kissed?" she asked in the dark.

What could I say about that day? A day I thought of often. A day I never liked to speak about, even now.

"How could I forget?"

Were the only words that I could find.

―――――

Lena stands and walks along the bank, glancing in the sink hole every couple of seconds while navigating through the tangle of brush and saplings.

What is it she thinks she sees?

"Hey, I think we should split."

"I want to check it out here a little more. Will you just give me a few?"

"Ok, a few," I say. "Be careful, please."

I take the trail out and stop walking at the big building. Its side facing the jungle is made of two barn-style doors. I pull one open just enough to peek inside. Cool, white mist wafts out and the odor of turpentine and something resinous hits me.

I inch my head in and can see the large space is mostly empty. Up top, a sprinkler wand running along the row of sun roof windows kicks on with a hiss and spray of water. Through the moisture and fog I make out a large, low, rectangular table in the center, running the length of the place.

Something big is on it. All wrapped up in bandages. Some sort of animal? It has a long snout like a croc but the thing is not croc-shaped. And it's the size of a whale. Though it's definitely not an orca or other small whale; its shape is nothing I've ever seen before. Its neck is… long. Too long for a crocodile. One of the cream-colored medical bandages has unfurled and hangs from a thin, triangular flipper.

I step inside. The air is heavy, even more humid than outside and tinged with a herbaceous smell. Beneath the green and floral odor, the reek of something sweet and pungent lurks along with more of that bitter turpentine. At the far end of the table is a cart loaded with odd bottles, the same different colored glass kinds that we saw in the housing unit.

I take another cautious step and freeze when red lights wink on. More trail cams. I breathe for a moment, staring at the clouds of mist glowing pink, then back out. I catch a whiff of something plum-like and resinous as I close the doors.

New York. Long ago.

June smelled like ice-pops and band aids and lawn grass and calamine lotion and hot asphalt in humidity and the pre-adolescent sweat of Lena and I and Chris Eisman and all the other kids gathered for the daily game of kickball on the Thomson's lawn. We watched Ihaka, all decked out in a tux, walk to his dad's old sedan, cradling a delicate flower in a plastic box instead of his ubiquitous lacrosse stick. He returned inside and reappeared toting a clear plastic bag loaded with two big bottles of liquor, one green, one clear.

"Do you think your dad knows?" I asked Lena.

She shrugged and said, "I guess."

A thing such as a prom was a milestone event so far away, so far ahead in our lifetimes we couldn't comprehend it. I didn't think any of us knew the term 'endless summer' then, but with finals done, ours had begun.

"Later, gators," Ihaka called to us with his beaming smile and waved.

He scrunched his tall, muscular frame into the car. Lena always said she couldn't count the number of girls from school that called the house for him. I wondered which one was his girlfriend.

It had been a long time since he played with us. He still seemed to appear out of nowhere sometimes though, like the time he broke it up when everyone was playing keep away with Dennis Clancy's hat after his chemo treatment and calling him Uncle Kojak. I remember when Tavish was born he said they would form a band and be like Alex and Eddie Van Halen someday. I think the real reason I still liked him was because even though our relationship had been reduced to mostly friendly waves, he remained a benevolent force in an increasingly hostile world, and I thought of him as the big brother I never had.

I waved and listened to the flurry of questions bouncing back and forth.

"He's allowed to drive?"

"Is the prom like a date?"

"You think he's going to *do it* with his girlfriend?"

We watched him drive away then divided into teams, teams we'd probably keep the same for Ringolevio later.

After kickball and after dinner everyone was back in the street, along with the fireflies waking up and rising from the lawns and the songs of the first tree frogs of the season in the warm air. Despite the day being like every other day, something felt different, like there was a joke happening that I wasn't in on. Chris wasn't his big mouthed self, directing everyone to take places at base and get set for the game, maybe that was it.

"What's going on, we starting?" I asked Chris.

"Um, yeah, in just a bit. Come on in the backyard, we're starting there."

"What? Base is the telephone pole. We have to start there."

"No, come on, base is at the Thomson's shed, we're starting there."

"What?"

"Yeah, it is, come on."

I followed Chris to the shed. Our whole team followed.

I found Lena and Alice Haninski already there behind the shed. Members of their team appeared behind them blocking that way out. Something was definitely different and it didn't feel like a joke.

"Hey come on, we're already hiding here," Lena said. "Go hide in the Rodriguez yard behind the gate if you want."

"We're not hiding, we're not playing yet," Alice said.

"We're not?"Lena said.

"No," Chris said. "It's Prom Day. Two people have to kiss. We can't start the game until two people kiss."

Everyone laughed. Was everyone in on it? I noticed Matt, Alice's little brother wasn't laughing and he slipped out of the crowd and back into the yard.

"That's stupid," I said.

"No, that's the rules," Chris said.

I did not like his serious tone.

"No one wants to do that," I said. "How are we going to decide who?"

"We already have, Jew Boy," Chris said. "We picked you. Jew Boy and Loch Ness Monster girl."

"Chris, aren't you Jewish too?"

"I am, doesn't matter. You two are kissing."

"I'm not kissing anyone."

Chris scooted back and wrapped his arm around me in a bear hug. Alice held Lena's arms behind her back.

Most of the time the mess of kids went for easier targets. Ones that didn't snap back. The most common attack I got was how it was unfair that Hanukkah was like eight Christmases. I never told them we were lucky if we could afford chocolate, instead my usual retort was "well it's not fair that half my family got the gas chamber and you have all your cousins and aunts and everyone on Christmas."

"Pick someone else," Lena said.

"We already decided," Alice said.

There was nowhere to run. Both ways out from behind the shed were shoulder to shoulder with everyone. I looked at the faces. I knew who were the real low-lifes like Alice and Chris and who were those not brave enough to stand up to them.

I knew I could break myself free from Chris. And I could get myself over the fence pretty fast but then what would happen to Lena?

"Guys, this is wrong," I said.

Chris tried to move me to Lena but found he could not. Then he figured out they could just push her. As Alice forced Lena closer to me she started crying.

"Let her go," I demanded.

Lena's father, with Matt at his side, appeared behind Alice and Lena. The mess of kids facing them scrambled. Past him. Past me and Chris and out behind us. Within seconds it was chaos. Kids hopping the fence into the Siegel's yard. Bumping into each other deciding which way to run. Mister Thompson was only focused on Lena, though. He checked her and after determining she was alright, ordered her to go inside to her mom.

Chris had let go of my arms but didn't run. I wondered if Mister Big Mouth was going to try to play innocent and talk his way out of this.

"Mister Thomson," he said. "We were just playing a game—"

He stopped talking because he could see just like I did that Mister Thomson was all worked up and ready to blow. Chris bolted and jumped on the fence. Mister Thomson was on him in a flash, pushed him up and flipped him over with a fierceness I'd never seen from him before. I heard Chris land with an awful thump.

"What about the Loch Ness Monster now?" Mister Thomson yelled.

I could hear Chris crying in anguish.

Mister Thomson yelled at him from over the fence. I didn't understand the language. Was it Scottish? Or was he using New Zealand language, whatever that was?

I discerned one word of his outburst.

"Taniwah."

It just stuck out to me. I thought it was a curse word. Maybe something he learned from his wife or when he was in New Zealand.

Done yelling at Chris, he turned to me and I thought I was in for it. I was about to run when I realized his rage had turned to tears.

"Why didn't I stop him, Ronnie? It's my fault. Why did I let him?"

In my confusion I thought he was talking about Chris and I tried to explain that nothing had happened. He grabbed me and I shrieked, though his grip immediately softened. He just held me and sobbed. After a minute, I wriggled free and left him there sobbing.

I emerged into the back yard, walked along the side of the house and to the front lawn; and to my surprise found everyone was there, all our parents were out in the street. There was a cop car in front of the house. Holy shit, was I in trouble? I didn't do anything. Why was this happening? Then I saw Mrs. Thomson sitting on the front step crying, flanked by two police officers.

My parents were there on the lawn with everyone. When we met eyes they started crying too. It seemed like everyone was saying Ihaka's name. I thought "oh no what's he done now, he's in some serious trouble" and then I learned he would never be in trouble again. He wouldn't know one day more of this endless summer, or any other. Dressed in a tux, with a flower for his date from his mom's shop and liquor from his dad, he met his end with his drunk jock-ass buddies, trapped in a flaming wreck on his way to the prom.

Lena takes my hand and in the moonlight coming in through the window over our bed, contemplates it with an almost mystical level of attention as if she is telling my fortune.

"What'd you see out there? In the water," I ask.

"You really didn't see?"

She runs the tip of one of her slender fingers up and down my index finger.

"It was nothing," she says.

"Nothing?"

"You saw the lizard?" she says. "The one that ran on the water?"

"The basilisk, yeah."

She moves her finger in a repeating pattern along the back of my hand. It is like she is tracing the path on a map.

"I know what's wrong with you," she says. "I know what's wrong with your life. You like monsters."

She places her finger over her pink lips, telling me not to speak.

"I want to tell you… I'm a monster, too," she says.

In the stillness all the night sounds and lull of the ocean drowns the sound of our breathing.

"One day you'll learn to hate me for it, but not tonight."

I'd forgotten how the feel of softness differs from memory. How a kiss is the one certain way to stop your mind from spinning.

I wake in the dead of night and she is not next to me. The door is open, letting the night air in. I see her on the beach, trudging through the sand. She moves a few paces, then makes a tight turn, then walks some more and turns again as if navigating a maze. She must be sleepwalking.

I remember hearing that waking a sleepwalker was dangerous so I sit on the doorstep and watch. She doesn't stop till the

Southern Cross is in the sky just before dawn. After I am certain she is still, I take her hand and gently guide her back to bed.

———

Under the late afternoon sun, I feel like we're acting like the couple she says we are not. Dozing in the beach chairs. Watching the birds at the edge of the water in comfortable silence together.

Lena takes an icy Belikin from our little Styrofoam cooler. I think she's going to offer me one.

"You know. I get it," she says. "He never forgave himself for giving Ihaka the alcohol. He started working later, then worked and worked and worked and then… then, one night he never came home. We never saw him again."

I remember how Mister Thomson's absence moved from being speculation grown-ups whispered of at picnic benches and dinner tables in the fog of that summer to just being a given. Ihaka's death. And Mister Thomson being gone. Two terrible incomprehensible things that just…were.

"I don't know what to say. I can't imagine what he was thinking—"

"That's…just not what you do."

She takes my hand in hers. It's cold from the icy beer. In the distance there is a little island out there in the blue. I hope she is daydreaming pleasant thoughts about it but I know she is not.

Later, when the sun is low in the sky and it is time to think about a meal I speak.

"Your dad? You want to try again?"

"Mmm hmmm," she says.

So, we get ready to go out. In the tiny box of the shower I picture her moving on the beach in the dark and it makes me wonder if there are walls everywhere, all around us, only we cannot see them.

We arrive at Ihaka's to find Nadine, the gray-haired old, ex-pat hippie who works for Lena's dad, tending the bar. The stools are empty and there's one other couple having drinks at one of the plastic tables under the trees.

"Mister Thomson here?" I ask.

"Marty's day off," Nadine says. "Maybe he'll be in though. Maybe he won't."

I thank her and ask her if she's ever been to the condos next door.

"Don't go there," she says.

"Why? Bad parking?"

She gestures for us to lean in.

"Some days, just before dawn when the Southern Cross comes up. You can see the ghosts of all the people who killed themselves and drowned in the cenote."

"Come on," I say. "Don't give us that shit."

"What? You don't believe in ghosts. Okay, you want the truth? I'll tell you. The place was built by a drug dealer…"

"So?"

"Um, so you want to mess around with someone like that?"

"I thought the story was that the drug dealer is dead," Lena says.

Nadine shrugs, apparently out of fodder for the story.

"What you all havin'?"

"Before I order," Lena says. "About… Marty. I saw him on TV. Is it really as awesome working here as it looks?"

"Before I answer. Tell me, is your boyfriend a good tipper?"

"Well, I am, for sure. Two melonballs, please," she says and puts too much cash on the bar top.

"Well in that case," Nadine says. "Hmmm. Old Marty? Well…he's a good boss but hooo—if you want a good story be here when he takes out his books and starts talking."

"Ooh, talking about what?" Lena asks.

Nadine leans closer again.

"Granted, I've got a lot of explaining to do before I meet my maker," she says. "But only Jesus was meant to walk again after passing through the valley of shadow, know what I mean…"

A sick expression comes over Lena's face.

Mister Thomson emerges from a cluster of big ferns behind the table with the couple. He's carrying a paper box full of green-skinned, spiky guanabanas.

"Lena? I thought that was you, yesterday," he says.

"Dad?"

"I thought I was seeing things. Then you were gone before I could turn around."

He sets the box on the bar, runs the remaining steps to us, and throws his arms around Lena.

"I thought you were gone forever," Lena says, her face buried in his shoulder.

"I thought I was, too."

"I love you. I mean… *I hate you.* I can't even…"

"What are you doing here? How—"

"We saw you on television, Mister Thomson."

"Right. I should have figured that."

"Dad this is—"

"Ronnie from next door, hello Ronnie."

"Sir. Mister Thomson. How are you?"

"Wondering what the fuck you're doing in my bar after thirty years? How are *you*? Don't answer that.

"You're beautiful darling," he says to Lena. "You can't imagine how much I've missed you."

"Really?"

"Ronnie. Nadine. I'd like some time alone with my daughter. Nadine. After that table we're closed tonight."

"Right," I say. "Lena, you okay?"

"Mmmmm hmmm," she says.

"I'll just… go for a walk then."

"I'll come with," Nadine says. "Follow me."

I follow her past the plastic tables into the jungle. After a minute we come upon a storage shed and the bathroom, which is an outhouse in a small clearing overlooking the beach.

"I know you," she says. "You played drums with… don't tell me, it's on the tip of my tongue."

"Okay, I'm not going to tell you."

She rustles through her shorts pocket and produces a box of Colonials and a lighter.

"Is that really his daughter?"

"Yeah."

"You two a thing?"

"No."

Inside the cigarette box are a dozen hand rolled joints.

"Wanna wade out into the surf and get high? Its shallow for a thousand yards."

"I'm hitting the head," I say. "Why don't you go and I'll be there in like… ten minutes?"

I have no intention of following. I watch until I see her enter the water and hope she doesn't see me heading in the direction of the condos.

I arrive at the greenhouse to find the two side doors are open. Inside, most of the mist has dissipated and I can see the table is empty. The thing, whatever it was, is gone.

A slender raccoon-like creature is climbing on a tree where the path to the sinkhole begins. It stops its progression towards a twiggy bird nest and regards me watching it. It's focused on my feet. I glance down and see a spider the size of my palm crawling along the soft earth. I hurry along the path, watching where I step.

From a hundred yards away I can see starlight illuminates the sinkhole. Even in the night the water is crystal clear. Tranquil and still. As I near, I notice a large indentation in the ground near the bank where Lena was sitting yesterday. A single wet bandage hangs from the prickly bark of a small palm.

I carefully move to the edge and stare into the water hoping to see something, a crocodile or anything in there but there is only the reflection of the trees and the stars and the stone side disappearing into the depths.

I move along the circumference of the sinkhole, like Lena did yesterday, brushing fronds and branches away from my face, careful not to put my hands on something sharp or on a snake or spider. Maybe a different vantage will give me a clue to what she was thinking. I picture her on the beach sleepwalking. And sitting at the bar. What could she and her dad be saying right now? With all the years that have passed how much remains of the people that they were? Is it the nature of being a family to always hone in on that?

Something moves on the tree in front of me where I am about to place my hand. As I pull it away I sense motion in my peripheral vision, too. A coiled snake is wrapped around the young hardwood and the cluster of figs and hanging vines draping the thick gumbo limbo. Only it can't be a snake, the white, scaly coil is as fat as my torso. There's a pink and green shimmer about it as it inches around the tree. I see motion across the bank. And behind me. The impossibly long white reptilian-fishy body is looped and coiled around the trees of the entire sinkhole.

A crocodile-like head atop a long neck silently emerges from the water, making no ripples. Yellow fins run along its jaws, the same yellow as the single fin of a crest that unfurls on its head. The long neck raises and shifts moving in line with me. Sentient eyes on either side of its head regard me, like Mister Hieronymus would upon waking up when the heat light came on in the morning. What kind of fish or reptile is such a jewel-like white color?

I know I am in the dark, yet I find I can see. Or I think what I am doing is seeing. Somehow I know there are two snakes above me and a bunch of birds sleeping in nests and countless insects at my feet but I am not seeing them with my eyes. My senses are... confused. Delayed. Mixed up. I can hear all the night sounds but they are muted. I can feel the moist air on my skin and the tree bark I'm gripping only there's an odd distance like I've taken a step sideways off the planet. The thing's face moves closer. A memory fills me.

There's a ring at my door. It's my ex's kid. Wow, what a difference two years make.

"I know you didn't want me to have it. You said I'd never care for it. I did for a while but you were right, Ronnie. Please take care of him. I promise I'll never come here again, please don't get me in trouble. I was going to bring it to a pet store but no one wants a grown-up lizard when they could have a cute baby."

She didn't wait for me to answer; she put it on my step and ran.

When he died, there wasn't anyone for me to call. I wondered what to do with his lifeless body and wondered what would happen, would anyone care when I finally go?

I watch the white coils slide along the trunks, crossing the space between trees, a living, pulsing circle slithering around the smaller circle of the water hole in the jungle floor.

"What are you?" I say. "Are you lost? I won't tell."

A thought blooms in my mind.

"Are you lost?"

Not words. Not a language. Looking at the thing I know as sure as I know when a dog means 'I love you' and a cat means 'feed me' that the thought belongs to *it* and *it* put it in my mind.

I wonder if I can put *my* thoughts in *its* mind?

"Why did you ask that? Are you just mimicking me? Do you understand me?"

The jar of Mister Hieronymus' hornworms fills my mind's eye. Then the worn-down bar of soap in my shower back home. My empty grocery bags. The fuel meter in my car. In the jeep. The half-empty jug of milk in my fridge. My bank account. My tax forms. My lawn in winter. Spring. Summer. My trees in fall. Lena's house. The Thompson's shed. A parade of images of mundane things bombards me. All the detritus of the circles and cycles of the things that measure my life. The days. The weeks. The years. The images come and go so fast all is a blur and I can't see.

"I am leaving here."

With the thought the images disappear.

The white coils are gone from the trees. The sinkhole is empty. The sounds of the night have returned to the right places in my ears and in my head. There's a fat bug crawling on my foot. I kick it away. The jungle is starlit dark again and I realize from its absence the thing in the water had radiated a faint light.

The sound of footsteps and breaking twigs reaches me. Something is moving through the brush. I make my way around the bank to where the path meets the sinkhole. Lena's dad is standing there, a black pistol in his hand.

I feel like I am behind Mister Thompson's shed all over again and he's caught me with Lena. Only this time, things are real. This time I have been kissing her.

"Sir, please," I say. "We're not together."

"My daughter told me, Ronnie. You're lucky I believe her."

"I wish you hadn't come here, Ronnie," Mister Thomson says and lowers the gun.

"Why are *you* here, sir. You must know the rumors. The ghost story?"

"You know that's all bullshit, Ronnie."

"No suicide? No shoot out?"

Mister Thomson paces and I wish he would say something. I glance into the water. It is clear and motionless. I wonder where Lena is? Is she okay?

"I built this place, Ronnie. Me."

The canals. The houses. The strange bottles and books and greenhouse. All his.

"You built all of this, yet it's empty, sir. Why?

"I have my reasons."

"Because of the sinkhole…"

"You saw it?"

I lie and say I have not.

"Come on, tell the truth, Ronnie. Did the Taniwah… speak to you?"

"Speak to me, Sir? No. Um, what are we talking about?"

He paces some more then sits on the ground; the same spot Lena had chosen. He directs me to sit. I'm nervous about how close our feet are to the edge of the water.

"When I met Lena's mother, now this was in New Zealand, I wasn't much older than a boy. In my time, after school you became a soldier or joined the merchant marine. I found myself in a place, a lot like here, near where Lena's mother grew up.

"Something was in the water there.

"It told me I would marry Lena's Mom. And we would have three children."

He's fighting tears. And getting red in the face. Like he was that day behind the shed when he flipped Chris Eisman over the fence and broke his leg. I'm scared of the gun.

"It never told me the pain I would know. That I would… lose Ihaka. When I told my wife, she had a name for it. But she said such things weren't real, like the thing in Loch Ness."

"Mister Thomson. I never got to tell you. I'm sorry about… Ihaka, about everything."

He produces a thick bundle of cash tied with a band from his back pocket.

"I never thought I'd be gone for good, Ronnie. I know how I let Lena down. I know that now. I just thought… I could just find it again. It would know what to do. It would know how to make things right. Weeks became months. Months became years."

I want to tell him it's never too late. Only I don't know if the words are true. I know the weight of years he speaks of. How time can wear on us—how we still might look like the people we once knew yet there is really nothing left.

"Ronnie. Ronnie. Ronnie from next door. Belize is beautiful. Such a beautiful place. Here's what you're going to do. You're going to take Lena around. You're going to tell her, her Old Man is just what he appears to be, an old salty bartender, who invested his money like the wealthy barber did. Tell me you understand."

"Yes, sir. I got it."

He hands me the cash.

"You're never to come here again. Not to the bar. Not to the complex. Not to this cenote. Don't come back. If you do, you won't find me. When you leave me, you will take Lena to breakfast and you will be on your way, do you hear me?"

The name of the restaurant he says is the one the old dazed couple told me about. I stifle my laugh because I realize Martin Thomson is a man used to giving orders. A man comfortable with that gun. Had there ever had been a liquor store that he worked at, at all?

I believe everything he's said about Loch Ness and New Zealand and I also know the stories about these condos are true. Only he is the criminal. He is the ghost. I know what that feels like and I hate that his life and what he has done makes a kind of god-awful sense to me. I have a million things to ask him but I don't dare say a single thing other than, "Yes, sir, I will do as you say, sir."

I put the wad of money on the bed next to our packed bags.

"So that's where he ran off to. To go find... you?" Lena says.

"He wanted you to know your mom never wanted for anything. That her account was always flush, more than flush. He paid for the house, for your school. For everything."

"All these years? She knew?"

"I don't know that. She knew she was taken care of though."

"All these years and I couldn't find him," she says.

It would be cruel to ask if she knew what she was looking for or if she even knew how to look at all so I remain silent.

"Back when we were kids," she says. "Do you think they were pushing us together for a reason?"

I'm careful with what I'm going to say next. There are no reasons. No meanings. Constellations aren't real, they are only the shapes we make of things—

"Oh, don't answer," she says. "Don't worry! I don't think we're soul mates. We're not even a couple."

"Are you lost?"

Why did it ask? Why did it show me the flotsam of my life? It dawns on me after all these years I've never given returning to California a second thought.

"So, all of Belize, huh?" Lena says. "You know where I want to go first?"

I want to feel her lips on mine again. I want the quiet of mind. The abandon. The rush it brings but the charge we felt last night is not present. In its place is an excitement we once knew, a sensation not that unlike the juvenile thrill of sneaking out your bedroom window.

I *am* going to listen to Mister Thomson and I am going to take her to breakfast and then to wherever she wants but first I know she wants as much as I do to see the sinkhole one more time before we go.

The moon is down. The sky is dark. We almost don't realize that Lena's dad is still there, at the edge of the sinkhole, another slender shape among the silhouette of the trees.

I gesture to Lena that we should turn around and go. She refuses. We remain perfectly still in the dark of the tree-covered path. There is nothing left to do but watch him standing there. He must be looking into the water. There's no sign of anything other than lizards and birds and the sounds of their awakening with the coming change to daylight.

Lena's dad shifts and I see he's holding his gun. As he brings it to his head I bring my hand over Lena's mouth. Then quickly get my other hand over her eyes.

Thankfully he lays the gun on the ground. I move my hands off of Lena's face, my face all apologies for the forceful way I tried to shield her.

He sits and takes off his shoes. Then unbuttons his shirt. We watch him slide out of his clothing, ease himself off the bank, and into the water.

He swims to the center. We watch him submerge. And wait for him to surface. After a minute I wonder how long he can hold his breath. After a few minutes more I contemplate if there was any way we could have missed him come up, though I know there is none. He's gone, just like before. As the sky lightens, together we move to the bank and look into that crystal clear water for any sign of him, but find nothing. Just the last traces of the stars before morning.

ghosts of the pantal

1.

Ipanema Beach, Brazil. 2004

The three-story building, indistinguishable from the others built into the sloping hills ringing the city, is the one Rio de Janeiro's unfaithful husbands and their guests know as "the Playground," their playground. In a room inside, the jungle room, a taxidermy jaguar head is mounted on a wall. The big cat once roamed the wilds of the Pantal, now its lifeless stare gazes across the hideaway and through tinted windows to Ipanema Beach where revelers are worshipping the sun. The hillside and bustling hotel strip are the habitats of the rich. There is no middle class in Rio. The crime rate is astronomical. The new government camera system has cut it 90 percent. Still, the city is not a safe place, at all.

On a mountain top in the distance, the statue Christ the Redeemer can be seen, monumental stone arms outstretched, silent and oblivious to everything below; the ubiquitous crime, the business men toasting with iced cachaça, the murderously hungry, the divine samba dancing, the rodizio feasts, the human trafficking all side by side together with every luxury and every human failing one can name. Beneath the jaguar head, New York businesswoman Esme DeMarco and a young Brazilian woman, who Esme's colleagues procured and paid to come, disrobe. The battle between the warmth from the themed room's fire place and the chill of the AC plays out on their skin.

Esme and her brother, Natan, arrived unseen. In a chauffeured car that navigated the twists and turns of backstreets and tight alleyways to the ramp descending into the Playground's garage. An elevator took them, and Esme's three colleagues, up; the building designed for those like them to come and go unseen. Automated locks keep those inside in and those outside out. Esme thinks the entry is fun, something out of a Batman movie.

Esme's colleagues are in the Playground's other rooms, with women of their choosing. Lunch and discussion of their International Monetary Fund project was rushed short to maximize time. Natan is in the kitchen, where the servants are waiting to bring food and caipirinhas when summoned. An armed guard stands watching security camera feeds with professional stoicism.

Esme has already forgotten the woman's name. She does not know if she speaks English or Portuguese. She doesn't care. The young woman shudders when Esme reaches to touch her. She likes the way the fire reflects on the curve of the woman's calf. There's something wrong with her foot, Esme notices. The angle does not look… correct. The young woman places her hands on Esme's shoulders then slides them to her neck.

"Stop," Esme says.

It is not her thing.

"Stop," she manages to spit; then finds she is gasping for air.

The young woman does not stop. Esme's vision is fading and the room becomes black, dark as the jaguar's lifeless, glass eyes.

2.

American Airlines Flight 88. New York to Rio De Janeiro (18 hours earlier)

"Excuse me, may I trouble you to switch seats?" Natan asks the woman next to him.

"That your wife up there?" the woman says.

Natan thinks the woman is beautiful and stylish. He notices her pronounced Adam's apple and masculine, well-manicured hands.

"No, not my wife. My sister," he says.

"Oh, I like your sister. I like that she dresses up for a flight."

"We, well she, has an… engagement, right from the plane."

"An engagement? Oh, *that* kind of business trip. I see."

"You could say that. I'm not along for the party though," Natan says.

"Such crocodile tears, my dear."

"I just got back in a relationship, one I've been fighting to keep. Don't know why I'm telling you this, even if I wasn't, that kind of party's not for me."

"You never partied with me, handsome."

"I'm sure you're up there with best."

"Up there? I am the best. I mean. I was. I saved my money. Started my salon in the Village. I do hair for runway shows too.

It isn't much but it's *my* dream. In *my* studio, no one cares if you are a boy or a girl. It's all about the art. I swore I would never go back to Rio."

"Yet here you are."

"Here I am. My first and only time back. My mother. She's come down with… there's something about you doll, I never talk about my life."

"I get that a lot."

"Bet you do. You're not the only one with an eye for seeing things as they are. Your sister's a CEO or some shit but you, you're a pro. How much to kill my son of a bitch ex—"

"I get asked that, a lot, too. I'm a farmer now."

"A farmer?"

"A sunflower farmer."

"No such thing."

"Yet here I am," Natan says.

"I know men like you. I can spot you a *mile* away. You're a killer."

"150 acres in the Catskills, says you're wrong. As does a family of porcupines. And an old bear we all call Papa Honey. Who's been eating from the apple trees on my land probably since you were in diapers."

"A real farm? You grow shit?"

"The apples and blueberries have gone wild. I only have luck with sunflowers. I told you I'm here for my sister."

"I get it now," the woman says. "Some advice for you, handsome. Use protection—don't kiss. Absolutely *never* kiss on the lips."

"I'm not here for—"

"The advice is for your sister. Just telling you straight. Seems like your first time."

"You gonna switch seats, or what, my friend?"

"Or what. I'm comfortable already. But I like you. So, one more thing. Beware of red headed women."

"Um… thanks?"

"In my country it is safer just to flat out avoid them."

"Safer?" Natan asks.

"Kuru'pir."

"What?"

"You don't speak Old Tupi…"

"No."

"Didn't think so. Where I come from there is nothing but monkey shit and jaguar skin, and your own skin, know what I mean…"

Natan is about to reply when he sees the serious demeanor that has come over her.

"You are handsome and a charmer and I seem to like telling you things," she says. "You're a watch dog, I get it. So, in your… engagements… watch out for—"

Her voice cracks.

"—for the red hair, yes. If her feet are facing the wrong way, if you want to live, stop whatever you are doing, leave and run like hell."

"That's quite the… advice. You've got me all wrong though."

"Do I?"

The woman closes her eyes and turns her head. Natan notices her hair is red. Dyed though. Does that count? He glances at her feet just in case. For the rest of the flight he keeps an eye on Esme as she sleeps, as he promised her husband and promised himself he would. His sleep is fitful and burdened by the knowledge that the days are growing short that he can keep her out of trouble and snares of her own making.

3.

Rio de Janeiro. (2 hours after landing.)

Esme's old friend from graduate school, Elias Machado, lives in one of the lovely hillside homes with his kids and new fiancé. He is hosting Esme and Natan for their 48-hour trip celebrating his impending second marriage. Over the years, working on their various projects and investments, Esme and Elias have been to the great countries of the world; yet as far as Natan knows, they've only seen it mechanically, with their architect eyes and technical minds. Elias has never been to the Amazon or the Pantal, the great natural wonders of his country, despite the project he and Esme are working on.

Esme and Elias have done all the things "right". They've succeeded on their smarts and strength and boot straps. They've built wealth and live in ways universally commended. What they share beyond their mutual love of numbers and logic and the precision of their trade is something they can't name and don't even know is a thing—an emptiness and inability to feel. Natan sees it. *He* knows it is a thing even if there isn't an English word for it. He's seen his sister struggle; seen her feed that emptiness with subterfuge, deception, and sex. He's afraid for her. He knows the empty things feed on you too. That there isn't much of her left. That is why he is here.

Elias Machado's servants take Natan and Esme's bags. Other servants hand them cool drinks before they are off again. Within minutes they and Elias and Elias' new fiancé are on the luxurious hotel strip where they rendezvous with their three business colleagues and their wives. There is a round of kisses and hellos then the men (plus Esme) and the women separate into two groups. As the wives enter the first boutique to begin their shopping a large SUV with blacked-out windows turns the corner. Esme and the men and Natan pile in. The SUV speeds away. Past the coconut vendors, the volley ball players, and the telenovela film crew filming on the beach. The vehicle turns into an alley. It navigates the twists and turns and takes the ramp into the Playground's garage.

4.

The two prostitutes taking their break in the Playground's kitchen are wearing only white towels. The guard insisted Natan wear only a towel, too. He complied to avoid making a problem.

After snorting lines of cocaine and picking at a plate of spiced chicken, the women take turns making advances on him, which he refuses.

"It is our job," they say.

"This is my job, too," Natan replies.

"Are you gay?"

"I'm not gay."

"Are you married?"

"I'm not married."

Natan hears them decide in Portuguese that he is gay. They return to doing lines to the delight of the guard who watches them as if they are the most interesting television show. Behind him, on the screen, the camera feed shows Esme being choked by her naked plaything. Natan grabs a kitchen knife, secures his towel, and runs to the jungle room.

5.

As Flight 88 speeds towards Brazil, Natan slips in and out of memories that become dreams as he falls into fitful bits of sleep. Natan's grandmother, Grandma Rivka had a cabana in the Catskills where he and Esme spent summers in their youth and later on in life. He sees Grandma Rivka tending to her field of sunflower seedlings one June when he was a young man, one of the last times he saw her.

"So fragile. So fleeting," Grandma Rivka says. "Your sister says why bother. I say, what a miracle seeds are. What a miracle this Earth is. These human bodies. Extraordinary cosmic miracles? Machines of divine will? What do you think, Natan?"

"I don't know."

Natan is at the farm to hide while trouble blows over. Grandma Rivka doesn't like it when he uses the farm, and her, this way. Yet she allows it.

"Your sister never comes."

"She doesn't... understand this...aspect of the world."

"You two will either become the worst of us or you will become great forces of good for humanity. I am counting on you to turn your sister around, Natan."

"How do you know, Grandma? Why shouldn't I just stay here and grow things, with you?"

"Would it matter if I said because I see it in the stars? Would it matter if I said I love Esme, I love you both. That I want to believe that there is a meaning to the world? And that meaning is us and what we do."

"It doesn't seem fair."

"What? What doesn't seem fair?"

"Life. Everything."

"Nowhere is it said that life is fair or is supposed to be fair. To think otherwise and to try to impose fairness on the world not only is a falsehood it is to invite sorrow."

"When you put it that way it makes me think, why do anything at all?"

"We do things because we want to. As for the rest, because we love each other. Now are you going to help your sister like I told you?"

"I will. It still sounds to me like there is no meaning.

"There is meaning enough, my boy, there has to be."

6.

The woman on the plane next to Natan thinks of the small village in the Pantal where she was born as she drifts into sleep. There was something about the man next to her that inspired her to speak of the aboriginal language Old Tupi and all the things she left behind when she moved her life to Rio and then New York. Her life in Rio she does not allow herself to think of, not even in dreams.

How long has it been since she spoke of the red-haired things called the kuru'pir, the forest spirits of the Pantal. The things that can look like people except their feet are turned backwards. As a girl she once saw a kuru'pir use its back turned feet to create a trail of footprints to lead a group of poachers deeper into the woods, to be killed.

As she grew up, the Amazon Rainforest River basin burned. Development threatened the Pantal at every turn. She learned the worst dangers no longer have to be present to do their harm. And she knows the kuru'pir have come to the cities. Doing the things and haunting the places she does not allow herself to think of. They have become good at disguising themselves. Why she felt she should warn this American man, she does not know. She decided she was much too tired to say much more.

She slips in and out of a memory of a jaguar she saw as a child; the big cat gracefully entering the water and swimming across a gentle, flowing river. She falls into sleep and dreams of the forest spirit and the poachers and how it ended in blood and flames.

As Natan is running to the jungle room, a flash of pity for himself washes over him. It is not fair that his fears have come to pass. He hears Grandma Rivka's words in his mind, that sorrow comes from trying to be an instrument of justice and it dawns on him how many of his sorrows have been born this way.

In seconds he is in the room. Esme is being dragged across the floor and has gone blue. The naked woman has her by the neck in a choke hold. Natan sees her backwards facing feet. Without thinking, he is on them. With brute force he frees Esme from the woman-thing's grasp. His instincts come alive. The woman on the plane was right. He is a killer. He pushes Esme's former plaything against the window. Esme has dropped to the floor and is motionless.

"Go ahead, kill me," the woman-thing says. "It is what you do. It will not save her."

Esme is more than oxygen starved. She has turned an unnatural sickly blue.

"A bargain," Natan says. "Take me. Trade me for her."

The word, the strange foreign word, the woman from the plane used, blooms in Natan's mind.

Kuru'pir.

"Take only you?" the kuru'pir says. "Not good enough."

"Do you value… your life?"

Natan hates the threat. He hates that he means to follow through on it.

"*You* and them," the kuru'pir says. "All four of them."

"My sister lives? And you take five of our lives? How is this fair?"

"Your life is spared. You will serve me. They will die."

"Why kill them?"

"You will kill them. Then you return with me to the Pantal."

"You want me to spend my life… in the Pantal?"

"You will give 20 of your years," the kuru'pir says. "It is a place of jaguars and flowers. You will kill. You will feel free."

Natan thrusts the kitchen knife into the kuru'pir's chest.

He drops to the floor and checks Esme's pulse and her breath.

The kuru'pir bursts into flames. Esme's colleagues and the guard rush into the room.

"Which one of you brought her?"

"How is she burning, she's nowhere near the fireplace? What the hell is going on?"

"It's him, the brother! I told you I didn't want him here."

"He saved your damn life. I saw it all on the camera, she was coming for us next."

"Is Esme going to live?"

"She has to live," Natan says.

He compresses her chest and breathes air into her blue lips.

"You have to live," he mutters as he tries to start her heart. "The price I paid. The price we paid. You are going to live and be the woman Grandma Rivka knew you could be."

A spurt of dark blood jets from Esme's mouth.

"You have to live," Natan cries.

The jaguar head does not hear his demands. Nor does the monumental statue visible on the mountain in the distance. If they have noticed these happenings they give no sign; just like the dwellers of the neighboring hillside buildings, and those fighting to survive in Rio's streets, and the sand-coated beach goers reveling in the cloudless, sun-soaked Ipanema day, they remain oblivious to it all.

Tiki Bar at
The Edge of forever

Long Island, New York. 1986

The Tiki Hut's pink neon sign is a beacon in the night to the Friday night grown-ups coming from their breathless, non-illuminated lives. From our vantage in the Dairy Barn parking lot, we've got the perfect view. June's first fireflies hover at the edge of the street light out front of Tom's Hardware and Richie's Stationary, the Deli, and the soda shop on the corner where we gather to get our smokes for fourth period. They're closed and dark except for the ever-present glow of the Galaga console leaking through the Deli's window. How can it be there are only two days of our routine left?

A couple my parents age, laughing and almost giddy—on shore leave from suburban existence, open the Tiki Hut's black front door. It's made of the same opaque glass as the window. I catch a blast of something obscenely bouncy before it closes behind them and they are gone.

The echo of firecrackers going off in a nearby cul-de-sac reaches us.

"Hey, Ihaka put a tape in to kill the quiet," Sarah says from the back.

Despite the linebacker's frame and rock-star black hair he's grown into I'll always see him as the kind boy next door. His glazed-over stare disturbs me.

"These are all the ways America eats itself, right," I say, hoping for a reaction.

It's the sort of thing that usually gets him going. But he remains a ghost in the front passenger seat.

Dairy Barn's lights go off. David's spindly frame appears a minute later, Ihaka's lei still around his neck. With his almost-moustache, shock of curly hair, and old Hawaiian shirt he looks a lot like the manager he likes to complain about, mostly for the offense of not letting him play Rush tapes during his shifts.

The fresh lei was a graduation gift from Ihaka's grandma, who's been sending them for as long as I can remember. Those leis were the one thing generous Ihaka would never take off, yet he gave this one to David yesterday just like that.

"Hi Wendy, I'm home," David says in his best Jack Nicholson impersonation.

A hint of gunpowder and the sea is in the humid night air. Along with the reek of Dairy Barn's dumpster. David hops in the back seat with Sarah and proceeds to go through my tape case.

"Tangerine dream, more tangerine dream… I can barely read your writing, Melissa, you *are* going to be a doctor."

The Tangerine Dream tapes were gifted to me while sleeping out for Jones Beach tickets last year. A woman old enough to be my mom and high as can be gave them to me and told me to put them on when in bed with a boy. I dig the band though her very-stoned burst of generosity I remember with a strange sadness because it's as close to any big sister advice anyone's ever given me.

"…Kitaro, The Police, The Cars, Melissa, really? Gag. Okay, Master of Puppets—"

"Give it here," I say and put it in.

Usually Ihaka has to wait his turn for it. Kirk Hammet is the only Hawaiian rock star I know of.

"Turn it up, Mel," David says. "Hey, Ihaka. Flask please."

Ihaka mechanically hands him the flask. It's full of his notorious green mixture of Midori liquor.

"Drink up," David says. "I'll drive tonight."

"Poison to me."

"It's the last week of school, come on."

"Sugar is death. At least for me. And everything becomes sugar. Speaking of which, I totally forgot to take my shot."

I ask Ihaka to hand me my bag at his feet. As I take my insulin kit out of my bag red and blue cop lights flash on in the dark corner of the lot. I stress, but see it's Mr. Millman, our neighbor from the block. He walks over with his flashlight trained on me.

"Melissa. Ihaka, kids," he says. "Anything going on here that's not supposed to be?"

"Nope. Just picking up David, Mister M. Realized I forgot to do my shot."

I can feel David and Sarah squirming. Our pot is safely hidden in the glove box, in the first aid kit.

Mister M shines the light around. He's worried about us. Once upon a time it was only the City that ate you alive. He knows we go to the beach. Everyone's heard about the bodies found out East. It's all over the evening news.

"Two more days and you are high school graduates," he says.

It's his way of saying be careful. After he departs Ihaka abruptly gets out of the car.

"Hey? What's up with you," I say.

"I don't feel like going to the beach."

Lauren, the new girl at school has stepped out of the Tiki Bar and is standing outside having a smoke. She's the daughter of the new owners.

Ihaka crosses the street and goes to her.

"What's with him?" David says. "He's known 'friends come first' since like sixth grade."

"I don't think it's that," I say.

I start the car, pull around and double park in front of the Tiki Bar. Ihaka's nervous. Finally, a reaction.

"Hey, guys, this is Lauren. Lauren, these are my pals."

"Hey," I say. "We're gonna cruise the causeway and pull over at one of our spots, Ihaka, so you know where we're gonna be. You both can come with though."

Lauren is ordinary. She's dressed all in busboy's blacks and smokes with the intensity of a grown up. This is the closest I've ever been to her. Despite her looks I can tell there is nothing ordinary about her. Nothing I can articulate, maybe she spends too much time around grown-ups.

"I gotta get back to work, thanks," Lauren says. "You want to come in sometime? I'll ask my folks."

She flicks her smoke and opens the door.

There's a blast of air-conditioning and shitty music again and then everything goes black, all-encompassing black. An after image of fireworks only in a thousand shades of darkness swallows me.

Then I'm behind the wheel. Ihaka is getting back in the car and something about the way he moves tells me he's shrugged off his pensiveness. I've missed something. Missed a few seconds.

"Gang's all here again, woo-hoo let's go," David says.

"Okay, let's go," I say slowly, trying to shake off my disorientation. "Just gotta take my shot first."

David takes a swig from the flask and passes it to Sarah.

I listen to them cheer each other on as I ready my injection.

You are what you put inside you. They just don't grasp it yet. Ihaka cranks the stereo. The thrashing rhythms wash over us.

I come home high. I pass Mom's best friend in the driveway who does a sloppy cheerleading thing when she notices me. They of course have had too much wine.

I head for the kitchen and hunt the fridge for a snack.

"Sweetie," Mom says. "You're excited for the prom."

It's a statement not a question and I'm betting it's to try and mask that she's lit. I can smell the cigarettes she "doesn't smoke" on her from across the room.

"I could care less, Mom. Ihaka and the gang want to, so you know to the Prom it is."

This sends her into quiet contemplation, so I speak before she can launch into some lame Hallmark philosophy.

"Mom, hey, how long has that Tiki Bar place been there up by the soda shop?"

"Oh dear, well, let's see, we moved here in '72. It was there back then."

"You and Dad ever go?"

"No?"

"No," she says. "Things were tight. We had work. And we had you. There wasn't much else…"

A stray thought about Ihaka's "Hawaiian" grandma jumps to mind. I remember Ihaka saying she's from New Zealand originally.

"…but when I was a girl, your age, back when I lived in Brooklyn, I went to the Mai-Kai a few times."

"The what?"

"It was the big deal place in the City. The well-to-do kids had their sweet sixteens there. It cost eleven dollars. That got you got a fancy drink. Dinner. And the tropical show. Ooh, it had sexy head-hunter-guys dancing. Sort of like…Chippendales—"

"Mom! That's awful. I'm going to pretend I never heard that."

I know Hawaii only from Brady Bunch re-runs. Curses and idols. Luaus and palm trees. Hula girls. One of Dad's friends went there on a trip he won for being salesman of the year once. I always knew Ihaka's feelings about Hawaii were something… intense. Something in the depths of his personal world unknown to me. As Mom rattles on about Don Ho I wonder what it must really be like to be different like him. Being in Hebrew school was sort of like that but I had Ronnie Greenbaum and the Seigels on my side when people called me a dumb blonde or a stupid Jap. Does Ihaka have anyone that understands him or even sees him at all?

———

After school I give David a lift to Dairy Barn. His manager isn't there so he pops a tape in and the steady, low, opening notes of Subdivisions I've heard a billion times starts in.

"Enjoy yourself, Bozo," I say.

"You'll be back," he says in his best Schwarzenegger voice. "No, seriously, I'm off at 8, come get me on the way to the beach."

Instead of going home, I drive across the road and park in the lot behind the Tiki Bar.

I put my face down on the steering wheel and allow myself to cry because here with no one around, I can.

The Tiki Bar's back door opens. Lauren exits hauling a black trash bag in each hand. After she throws them in the dumpster she sees I'm here. She motions for me to roll the window down and comes over.

"How can *you* be fucking sad," she says. "You're like miss number one cheerleader, everything's perfect."

"It's not—"

"Sorry, that was obnoxious," she says. "I didn't mean it that way. I know there are a million reasons to cry. You know this is my parents place, want to come inside and get wasted?"

"I don't drink."

"We have awesome coconut ice cream. It's for this new frozen drink. Wanna raid it with me?"

"I really shouldn't, but yeah, just this once, okay."

Without the cloak of night and artificial light, the bar's back hallway looks like someone's basement. Old wood paneling. Old everything and a sense of being stuck in time. The passage opens into the dark main area where the smells of dry beer and lemon floor cleaner hit me. It's even more humid than outside with ghosts of cigar smoke and cigarettes everywhere. A five-sectioned mural adorns the wall above the shelf of liquor behind the bar. The center section is a portrait of a Hawaiian Queen in formal attire, hair up and regal sitting on a throne. The panel to her left is of a tall ship anchored off a beach full of idols and Tikis. The panel to her right has a bunch of Hawaiian guys in grass skirts, holding knives and spears to the neck of an old-fashioned fancy looking white guy. The two outer sections are of local people in Hawaiian shirts, each of them holding up a tropical drink.

So this is the place? The location of so many stories of debauchery from my friend's older siblings? It's a freaking dump. Being an adult must suck.

Lauren disappears into the dark.

"This is my first time inside a bar," I say.

I hear her flip a switch. Strings of Christmas lights crisscrossing the ceiling wink to life, illuminating a wall adorned with license plates and a patchwork of photographs. Layers of faded polaroids overlap crisp glossy prints. All are shots of people in the Tiki Bar. The wall across from me is done up with paper Halloween skeletons draped in plastic flowers. A lone structural column is covered with plastic skulls and the husks of dried-up real flowers.

Lauren goes behind the bar and serves up two highball glasses full of ice cream.

"I mean, I can make you a fancy float if you want," she says. "I like it like this."

I plant myself on a bar stool, take a small amount onto my spoon and I put it in my mouth. The painting behind Lauren is staring down at me.

"That's Queen Lili'uokalani," Lauren says. "And that guy's Captain Cook."

"Who?"

"Captain Cook was the explorer dude that pretty much bullied Hawaii around. They eventually sent him back to his ship in pieces though. Queen Lili, she was the ruler of the Kingdom of Hawaii before it was overthrown."

"Who are all those bozos?"

"Probably our neighbors, right? You know it's Senior Prom for Eisenhower High, tonight, right? Want to work a shift?"

"It is? Are a ton of kids coming?

"No. Their parents will though, dad says. They come here until it's time for their kids to come home or pick them up from wherever."

"I can't. We're going to the beach."

"Didn't you go last night?

"Yeah. It's what we do. Where else is there? You can come."

"I gotta work."

I take another mouthful of ice-cream. The Christmas lights blur. Blackness gathers in the corners of my vision. I hear the mumble of a crowd. One of the bony hands of a skeleton on the wall moves.

"Okay, I've had enough."

"You barely touched it."

"I just had more sugar than I eat in a month. I'm diabetic."

"Oh, shit. I didn't know—"

A door on the wall of photos swings open. A man in jeans and t shirt tromps across the floor.

"Dad, you're early. This is—"

"She the new busboy?"

"No, she's my friend—"

"Mai-Tai," he mutters.

Lauren grabs bottles from the shelf behind her and beneath the bar and begins fixing a drink. He's bombed. She's scared of him. The situation is... revolting.

"Um, I'm gonna go, thanks Lauren."

Why would adults want to come here when they could do anything in the world at all? The bottles are pretty and the drink Lauren is making is colorful and bright but it's all poison, pretty looking poisons. I never want to come to a bar again.

We're given the cold shoulder and are run off of our first choice of beach spots by a bunch of rich, North-Shore, surf-shop kids. I take us to our next choice, one of our Plan-B spots. A bunch of the ever-present little straw-brown bunnies flee my headlights as I pull over on the shoulder. I gun it in reverse into a little gap nestled in the dunes, perfectly out of view of both sides of the road and nosy cop-eyes; the State troopers are not as kindly as Mister M.

It's Sarah's turn for a tape and she's got some live Doors on the boom box.

I hear David and Ihaka talking as they start the fire.

"...after I graduate? I'll probably be in Hawaii by the fall."

"That's far. You've never been there."

"Hawaii never gave up its independence. It was forced into becoming a state. The Kingdom is still a real thing. You don't have to be part of the US. There is a choice..."

There's a huge splash in the waves. Then another and another. Dolphins are jumping just off shore, heading west, parallel to the coast. Sarah and Ihaka clink paper cups at the sight of them.

"Here's to all the fools," Sarah says. "All the fools who are so close and don't even know dolphins are here and that you can do this."

"And hey, to our last night," David says. "Our last night

before the last day of school! We should sleep here, on the beach."

"We have to make it to the bleachers by midnight," Sarah says.

It's a tradition for seniors to "sleep out" on the bleachers on the last night. Mostly it's become an annoying game of cat and mouse with the teachers and the cops though.

David takes out our pot, shields a joint from the wind to light it, and takes a deep pull.

"There could be anything out there," David says, looking out to the ocean.

"And there probably is," I say. "Like sharks or a monster."

"Dude, your dad is from Scotland, right," David says to Ihaka. "Didn't you tell me he saw the Loch Ness Monster once?"

Ihaka sprays green alcohol from his mouth with his laugh.

"He totally did," Ihaka manages to say while cracking up.

After he collects himself, he passes the joint.

"Dad is being totally cool," he says. "We're all set for the Prom. He totally hooked me up with a bunch of bottles from his store."

I'm happy to see him acting like himself again. Sarah's house party and the Prom is going to be a shit show but all things pass. I head into the dunes to pee.

Something moves in the beach grass. I expect to see a bunny fleeing at the sight of me but a child steps from the growth into a patch of moonlight-illuminated sand.

"Oh, hello," I say. "Are you lost?"

The little boy does not have a shirt on. He can't be more than two or three. He's calm. Too calm for a kid alone in the dark in the middle of nowhere.

"Are you okay?"

Looking past him I see the silhouette of someone on the dune about a dozen yards away, just standing there, motionless. The breeze blows the grass framing the person shape. I squint and all the colors of the night-time sea appear in the blackness—an infinite amount of grays all muted in shadow.

There's another splash. The dolphins are throwing a fit of clicks and whistles.

The kid takes a wobbly step forward and falls on his face. His back is red and raw, there is a steak shape of missing flesh carved out of him. He has to be on drugs to not be screaming in pain. The cut is clean and too precise to be anything but intentional.

The figure on the dune shifts its weight, a barely perceptible movement and the moonlight catches on the long knife I realize it is holding. Blackness creeps into the periphery of my vision, threatening to take me. My ears rumble. My throat goes dry. I fight to keep conscious and try to glance the figure's face. I see… Lauren? No, she's not that tall. Is it the face is of her drunk and sloppy dad? He raises his hand with the knife and then he's my dad holding my insulin kit out to me. I think I'm going to scream only I'm looking at myself. It's me. I'm holding the carved out cut of the little boy's flesh. My teeth are sharp, triangular shark teeth too big for my mouth. I bite into the raw steak. A car crash fills my mind's eye. A body flies through a car windshield and is impaled by thick chunks of glass. All goes black.

"Mel? Mel, snap out of it!"

I've fallen in the sand. David, Sarah, and Ihaka are helping me to my feet.

"I… saw the killer."

"What?"

"I saw him."

"No, you didn't," David says.

"Wait, how do you know what she saw," Ihaka says.

"If she saw the killer we'd all be dead."

"Did you forget your shot, again Mel?" Sarah asks.

"I did have too much sugar today, but I swear."

"Let's look around," Ihaka says.

They scour the area and look through the grass. They find nothing.

"There's no footprints here," Sarah says. "Nothing at all."

"I know I saw something."

"I'm on your side," Ihaka says. "I'm on your side. And I'm on your side," he says to David and Sarah. "It's the four of us back-to-back. Forever. No matter what happens. Okay, that's what I know. That's what it's all about. That's what I wanted to tell everybody tonight."

"I'm spooked, man," David says. "Is she okay?"

"Mel, you okay," Ihaka asks.

"I… guess so."

"She's okay, so here's what we're gonna do. We're gonna get high. We're gonna put on some Tangerine Dream for Mel. And listen to the waves for a bit to mellow out, then we head over to the bleachers for the last night of high school, okay?"

"Okay," David and Sarah answer.

I say okay, too. Though I'm not okay. The body I saw go through the window was Ihaka. I think about going home and telling Mister M about the kid and everything but we're so high and what good at all could come of it now?

Ihaka and I sit in his car with the windows rolled up, our place for important conversations. In the rear view I see neighborhood kids run past, playing in the afternoon sun.

"What do you mean you're not going," Ihaka says. "This is totally last minute, Mel. Why? Because you saw something, no you *think* you saw something last night."

"Just trust me. I saw you... getting hurt. Why is it so important? Please don't go."

"I need to belong somewhere."

"The prom is going to make you belong?"

"No, but you're pretty and can fit in anywhere."

"Fitting in is just an illusion. All that shit's just skin deep."

"Even if it's all fake you can still have it if you want. I'm going tonight to feel that, just for once. Please don't tell me you think there's anything wrong with that."

Through my front screen door I watch Ihaka carry the alcohol his pop gave him from his house into his car. The kids have stopped their game and are staring at him in his tux, like I'm doing. They resume their play as he drives away.

"What's wrong?" Mom asks.

"I'm afraid I'm never going to see him again."

"College doesn't start until August. You have all summer and then there's always Homecoming and Thanksgiving..."

She's right. It's just the stupid prom and we'll be back on the beach tomorrow.

"… your father's been working hard. We're going to be able to get you one of those new insulin pumps."

"Um, right. Thanks, bye Mom. Be back later."

I cruise over to the Tiki Bar and try the back door. Lauren's there in the hallway carrying a tray of washed glasses.

"Hey, you came!"

"I did."

"Oh my god, do you want a cocktail? Let me make you one."

I follow her in and she sits me down at the bar. The place is full. In the night, with the lights and people the "shithole" feels… different.

"People will tell you otherwise but three ingredient cocktails are the way to go," Lauren says.

She pours pineapple juice into a metal shaker.

"Pineapple juice, with lime juice and rum is the best. The secret is fresh ingredients but the real secret is aeration."

"Besides tasting the green stuff from Ihaka's flask this is the first I've ever had."

"You like it?"

"I don't taste any alcohol."

"Good!"

I hear the sizzle of a grill and the smell of something cooking reaches me. In the corner of my eye I spy a drink on the bar next to me, the unmistakable bright green of the Midori Ihaka uses. I turn and see it's Ihaka there, right there sitting next to me. Long red welts run down his face and neck; the angry wounds disappearing beneath his shirt. I realize the place is full. A crowd is pushing against us. Hands grab Ihaka. Fingers dig into his cuts and pull. His flesh peels away and I realize what is sizzling.

"Mel, you look pale," Lauren says. "Hey are you okay?"

"I don't think I should have had this drink," I say and fall forward into black.

———

I wake to the sounds of electric hums and beeping. The room is stark white. I'm in the hospital. I don't know what time it is. Mom is sitting in the chair next to my bed.

"Oh dear, you're awake. I was so worried about you," she says. "What were you thinking? You know you can't drink alcohol."

"Where is everybody? Is the prom over?"

I don't like the look on her face. A flash of the bar patrons with their hands coated in Ihaka's blood races through my mind.

"There was an accident," Mom says. "David is here. He's in stable condition. Ihaka... oh honey, he didn't make it."

———

One year later.

There's a fresh lei on Ihaka's grave.

It's late in the day. I didn't expect to run into anyone, but Sarah is here. I haven't seen her in forever and we talk.

"I never see David, either," she says. "I heard he's living in the city or something. Oh Mel, it's so sad, Ihaka never got to go to Hawaii."

"Hawaii wasn't just a place to visit for him," I say.

"Well, yeah. You know what I mean."

She points to the pump strapped to my waist.

"Oh, you've got that now. Good, you don't have to worry so much about the sugar."

The darkness isn't from sugar. It comes all the time now. She won't understand.

"Um, did I tell you, I got in to SUNY Binghamton?" she says to put something in the awkward quiet. "I'm transferring in the fall. We're totally going to stay in touch."

"Totally. We totally are."

The lie comes easy. She leans in and we embrace. I move my hand to her lower back, and rest it there, above where her kidney is.

We're not slipping away slowly, painlessly, the way people do. We're already gone. Some things, like Ihaka, are just gone and there is only before and after. We're in the after only she doesn't know it.

I'm in busboy blacks. Lauren's getting the bar top polished and ready for happy hour. WLIR is on the radio. Lauren's dad will put it back to dinosaur rock when it's time to open.

"Hey, Laur, I haven't been to the beach in so long. We should totally go."

"You know I've been living here, how long, over a year and I've never been. I don't even know what to do?"

"I'll show you."

"Okay."

"Promise?"

"I promise. Not tonight, though, but I promise. Hey can you get the clean glasses from the kitchen hung up and ready?"

"Got it."

The DJ gives the traffic and weather and an update on the latest bodies that were found. Then it's opening time and the whirl of night begins.

———

After our shift, Lauren and I go outside and have a smoke. I ask her to change her mind and come to the beach tonight. She refuses.

"How about coming to Hawaii then," I say. "You ever been?

"What? Hawaii, no, that's a million miles away, why?

"I don't know. I want to go. You know, for Ihaka."

"Really? What difference its gonna make to him now?"

"I don't know. I just know it does."

"You should do it then. Go get a plane ticket."

"Now?"

"Yeah, now before you change your mind."

"You're right. I'm gonna go to Kennedy and get a ticket."

"Whoa, you're serious? Am I gonna see you tomorrow for opening?"

"Yeah, of course. Unless I run away to Hawaii."

———

The neon sign in my rear view is a beacon in the night. A lure calling to the breathless. An irresistible, invisible hook to snare the empty hearted. Ihaka knew it's what you put inside you that counts, sadly he wasted his time with that green booze he put in his flask. That was the way he liked it, with no pretty illusions or props.

I'm not going to get a plane ticket. I know what's really

calling to me. I stop at home and nab a shovel from the tool shed. I drive to one of our old back-up spots off the causeway, pull over and reverse it into the dunes.

No tapes tonight. No campfire. I know Lauren's going to love it here though.

In the sand under the moonlight, I dig.

where the jaguar king lives in the dark heart of the wood

Stann Creek District, Belize. Winter 2011.

I t is said that the Jaguar King lives in the dark heart of the wood. Watching over all the cats.

The wood's proper name is the Cockscomb Basin Wildlife Preserve and Jaguar Sanctuary. 150 Square Miles of tropical forest. All five of the cat species that dwell in Belize can be found there. Jaguar, Puma, Jaguarundi, Margay, and Ocelot.

Sunset Rick is an American ex-pat. He runs a two-unit vacation place, Sunset Rick's, in the little beach town not terribly far from Cockscomb. He's at Rosalinda and Enrique Alvarez's farm, which borders the eastern edge of the preserve, picking up his order for the week. The pre-dawn sky is still a glistening carpet of stars, illuminating the clearing where the Alvarez's vegetables are growing. Rick looks to the jungle, a living wall teeming with layers and overlapping layers of buzzing and clicking that looms over the farm. He walks to his pick-up truck, bags of produce and dairy in hand, and scans the shadows and spaces between tree trunks for motion.

The guests due in to his second cabin, June and Andy from New York, are arriving in the afternoon. The thought of flying, even on one of the puddle jumpers that are the only planes that land on the air strip, reignites a little flower of unease in his beer gut belly. It has been decades since it has been his job to keep one of those rumbling metal behemoths in the air. Circling to and from the fail-safe points, day in, day out. Armed with a nuke and extra fuel. And it's been decades since he crashed the little plane he had here out in the jungle, the last time he ever flew at all. He's grateful for the fragrant smell of wet earth and flowers and green and the hint of smoke from someone's trash fire in the damp almost-morning air. A morning doesn't go by that he does not at least think about kissing the ground and small swatch of beach where he's made his home. He doesn't tell guests the Air Force was where he got the name Sunset Rick. He doesn't tell guests he knows how to fly at all. He does tell them he spends his time drawing and watching for birds. And for big cats, if he's lucky. He's always on the lookout. Jaguars are tough, if not near impossible, to spot. Most visitors and locals alike will never, ever see one.

A shape moves across the Alvarez's field. Black on black. Just a shadow? Or is something there? He knows the jaguar he calls Cygnus likes to venture out from Cockscomb during the night to rummage in garbage for easy pickings before returning at dawn. Rick holds still and squints and yes he sees her, right where the green jungle meets the farm. She's there. Just inside the line, just inside the boundary of the preserve. Where it is illegal to harm her, illegal to shoot any jaguar. She's trotting along, openly, brazenly, not concealing herself as she is so capable of doing, as if she knows the boundary and knows the rules, somehow. Maybe she knows he'd never, ever even think about shooting her. Maybe she knows Enrique Alvarez would love to blast her. As would several others who live nearby who do not share his awe and appreciation. These people think twice before shooting. Not only to be sure their quarry is outside the border. They know Sunset Rick isn't the only one watching. They've heard the stories. The Jaguar King is out there. Watching over the cats. Protecting them. Even avenging them. Rick has been here twenty plus years, one full year before Cockscomb was founded, and while he has his notions, he can't say for sure if all the stories are true. He's also never seen a jaguarundi; yet he knows that doesn't mean these most reclusive of the cats are not real.

Cygnus halts. Turns her head and looks Rick's way. She can smell him. Knew he was present long before he had any hint of her. Rick wonders if she's contemplating the Jaguar King, too.

A raucous toucan call, the first sign of day, punctures the nighttime cacophony. The jaguar bounds off, her spots and sleek, feline contour becoming one with the tangle and brush as she flees the coming morning for places where daylight cannot reach.

June and Andy watch as the little Cessna, they and their luggage deplaned from just a minute ago, reaches speed and lifts into the air at the point where the dirt strip of a runway ends at the Caribbean Sea. Sunset Rick is watching them from the shade of a rusty tin roof held up by four poles at the corners that is the "airport."

He swings open a hinged section of the rusted remains of something that once upon a time was a barrier and says, "Welcome."

Andy doesn't like the way the old ex-pat looks June up and down as she's hunting for her smokes, but he's used to it. She's in a t-shirt with Duran-Duran's Rio album cover on it, half tucked in to a pair of black denim cuts offs. Bruises from iron-deficiency, in various stages of fading, mar her pale legs. Her short shock of hair that was once punk during the days when she purchased the t-shirt remains short now for efficiency, not style. Endless hours at the shop and time with her niece and every iota of sleep is what counts; though she feels she cleans up nice on the date nights Andy every so often persuades her into. She lights up a clove cigarette, a real one, contraband Andy provides for her, somehow, even though it has been years since Obama banned them. Andy doesn't want her to smoke, yet he keeps her flush with them because her money is tight and he knows how much she loves them. She takes a big pull, inhales like her life depends upon it, then realizes the men have already loaded the luggage.

The three of them fit easily in front of the truck. The windows are down. Belize's heat is palpably real; the November snow and all the crushing minutia they've left behind is a ghost unable to dwell in it.

"First time here, you two?" Sunset Rick asks.

"I come to Belize a lot," Andy says. "Well, used to, back before I met June, I mean. Never made it this far down. Always wanted to. I told myself I would, one day, you know, come back with the woman I love."

"Good old love and romance, I remember that," Rick says.

"I remember it too," Andy says. "This one… protested, but she's here. We made it."

June smacks Andy's tattooed bicep.

"I run a business. And have… a daughter," she says. "All I

need right now is to be eaten by a jaguar or get some tropical disease."

Rick reaches down with one hand, his other never leaving the wheel, and produces a can of beer. He glances at Andy and June to see if they will dare to voice disapproval.

"Yeah, we do have jaguars," he says. "Scarce on diseases though. Plenty of beer. Want one?"

"Can I smoke instead?" June asks.

"Sure."

He swigs his beer just as they hit a patch of bumps.

The road is an unpaved swath cutting through untouched jungle on both sides broken up only by the infrequent clearing or sign indicating the presence of one of the few area businesses.

"A paved road is on the way. Supposedly. Someday its really gonna come. Along with cops. And rules. Well real ones. For now, we're still free here though. *For now*. There's no AC in the cabins, you'll want to get the ceiling fans going and—"

"It's perfect," June says.

Rick sees her face light up as she takes Andy's hand.

"It's absolutely perfect here. I see what you mean," June says. "You were right. I *can* see myself staying here forever."

Andy is painfully aware she didn't say "*us.*" A small thing considering all signs of the nicotine starved, sleep-deprived, uptight, worried bundle of nerves he spent the long day of travel comforting has disappeared into the tropical heat and sun.

"Why the change of tune, sweetheart?" Rick asks.

Andy braces for June to blast him for the patriarchal endearment. But no. There's only that faraway look on her face. The one she wears when she's in the place she goes when in the grip of her lowest lows, the place he can never reach her.

"There's a jaguar," June says. "Nearby."

"What?" Andy asks.

"I can... feel her. I... see her spots. She almost all black, you can just make them out. You see her when she moves, then she's gone into the jungle like... oh I don't know how to say it. We have to find her. I have to see her."

Andy and Rick exchange an inquiring stare, each expecting the other to offer an explanation.

"I guess this means we're going after all," Andy says. "I knew there was a reason I loved you."

"I'm down for going right fucking now."

"Easy cowboys," Rick says. "You don't have to go far to see a jaguar. We've got one around here, exactly like the one you described. Damn if I know how you did that. Hell, you near picture perfect described the jaguar I call Cygnus. She comes out of the preserve every night. Why they get a taste for our garbage is beyond me."

"Andy's always wanted to go. That's why he planned this whole trip, to take me."

"You heard the lady."

"Is there anywhere around here we can rent a car?" June asks. "Or, maybe do you think we can use your truck?"

"You're my guests. After you lovebirds settle in, I'll do my best to be of service."

Rick knows the Jaguar King doesn't like outsiders. He wonders what's he gonna think of these weekend-warrior-hipster-has-been-wanna-bes. Stupid question. He knows the Jaguar King doesn't care for humans, at all.

———

The two guest houses at Sunset Rick's are right on the beach. Separated by a lush, greenery-lined walkway winding through the property to the house by the road where Sunset Rick lives with his wife.

Andy has come because he is thinking of asking June to marry him. He hasn't asked yet. Partly because he believes she'll never go for it; after what she's been through, she's said she'll never belong to a man or anyone, ever again. And partly because he's told himself the only time *he'll* ever surrender to love again is when he finds a woman who'd live out his dream with him—a dream of going far enough south to find the jaguars—a dream of finding a place to stay forever, like Sunset Rick has done. For the longest time this standard insured he'd never love and thus never could be hurt again. He knows he's been running from himself, with Belize being the place he runs to most. To lick his wounds. Collect himself. To find himself in connections and companions made on the road. In travel families he hoped would become families for real yet always crumbled. So many of his hopes always seemed to be going south—to find jaguars. He always yearned to be south bound himself and for a family for real. One that would last.

June is here because she hates herself. The self she's become. She hates pretty much everyone, Andy just less so than most. She knows Belize is where he used to run away to. She's not sure if it was running from the law or something in his head or his own kind of Peter Pan syndrome. She knows something about running away. When her sixteen-year-old daughter overdosed on pills and almost died, she lost custody to her piece of shit ex. It wasn't that she let Anna-Lisa use, she just didn't police her, she didn't think pot and pills was a problem. Javier didn't police her either, three months into living with him Anna-Lisa was drunk behind the wheel, learner's permit in pocket. The crash killed her and two of her high school friends. And then Javier was out every night. Her so-called friends saw him all the time in his restaurant in Astoria and never failed to report back about how nice and how popular it was. Did they think this was supporting her? She knows what Andy doesn't—that you don't have to go far to run away. Most of the time, she is just… numb. From the work and hours keeping her studio afloat. And when there isn't that, there's Andy. He's kind to her. He wants her, sometimes it seems like he worships her, sometimes it seems like he even listens to her. Surrendering to this kind of numb is new, sometimes she thinks maybe it could be something real and she's learning how to be good with that.

She knows it's *not* good that Andy's always running away, at least for now he wants to run away with her. These little islands of time he steals with her, sometimes feel good enough; at least as good as all the other intoxicants she's ever tasted.

Andy is asleep five minutes after they fuck. She is glad for the sex, which back home often falls victim to the stress and the fighting and the catastrophe de jour. When they are fucking, she feels alive. Lit up, everything ailing her is just a shadow. She watches him, his hand on the little note book he thought he'd scribble drum notations on, post-sex as he often does. She understands the drain of the travel has sapped him, yet this leaves her alone with her thoughts—the last place she ever wants to be. At least she can smoke in peace without his disapproving silence. She flips through the guest book on the kitchen counter. Line after line of names of happy couples and how much they enjoyed their stay. The only one of interest reads: "Going to Cockscomb? The best guide is a quarter mile up the road from the Alvarez farm—Frankie and Ivy." She dresses in a sarong and goes outside. The sound of gentle waves a hundred yards away greets her along with the tang of marijuana on the air. She ducks onto the fern-lined walkway covered in trees and plants of all kinds and flips open her pack of smokes.

She trips. There's a fat, black power cable on the ground she didn't see. It originates a few yards away, plugged in to a shiny red powder-coated generator. A bearded man in a beefy, mechanized wheel chair is tending to it, a wrench in one hand, a smoking blunt in the other. A small black house cat watches from the safety of a cat carrier at one side of his chair. A square oxygen machine on wheels with plastic tubes is on the other.

"Watch your step there, neighbor," the man says.

"That you? I smelled you from my cabin."

"Guilty as charged."

"Something tells me Mister Sunset Rick doesn't mind you and your cat smoking up in his garden. He's so cute, can I pet him?"

"Oh my cat doesn't partake. His name's Larry. It's not safe around here for little ones—"

"So, no petting, in the carrier he stays," a female voice says.

A tall woman with a mane of jet-black hair is walking towards them on the path. She's cool and collected, dressed in a black tank, black capris, and worn in Doc-Martens. June is immediately conscious of the fact she's a sweaty mess.

"I hope his smoke isn't bothering you," the woman says. "He always smokes when he is setting up."

She has a European, accent, Russian maybe? A bass guitar slung on her back. June hates her already because she's thin and fit and half her age. Pretty as hell without a stitch of makeup. Two sleeves of bright, colorful tattoos she would kill to have. The kind of woman she knows Andy fell for before her.

"We were just getting ready to play," the woman says.

Is she blowing me off? June asks herself.

"Um… don't mind me I'm just having a smoke. Then jaguar hunting, hopefully."

The woman kisses the man on the forehead. "You got this?"

"Yeah," the man says. "Go. I'll have you powered up in a jiff."

"Ciao," the woman says.

June watches her walk to the beach, playing her bass as she goes. A half a mile off the tranquil shore, there is a tiny island. Crowded with palms. A wooden ship, an old one with sails, is anchored off it. June ashes her clove.

"Want one?"

"Nah, bad for the lungs. Want some of this?"

"Hell yes," June says.

The man hands her the blunt. June takes a deep pull, then glances at the oxygen machine, confirming it is off.

"That your ship out there?" June says, exhaling a mouthful of smoke.

"I can neither confirm nor deny. A real beauty though, right?"

"Really? Okay. Who the hell comes to Sunset Rick's with their cat. *And* a generator. Guitars. *And* the boat from a CSN album cover?"

"It does look like that one, right?"

He tells her their names. And the name of their band. She doesn't retain a word. She recalls giving him a fake name. She wants nothing to do with the person she is back home. Those ghosts have caught up to her and all she can think of is how did her life come to this. And how jealous she is of this guy and his girl.

"…we were staying a bit up the coast at Francis Ford Copolla's hotel. Not. Recommended."

"Copolla's place? Sounds fancy."

"I don't mind fancy. I can get used to fancy. Staff is not cool. Who doesn't like music? You and your man like music, right? Rick's place is the best."

June worries that the sleep she was so looking forward to has just gone out the window.

"Rick does seem cool," she says. "I think he's going to lend us his truck."

"Right. You said jaguar hunting?"

"Yeah. Not hunting-hunting, but yeah."

"Rick told you about Cygnus?"

"He did."

"He must like you then. Don't let his shit-talk about the Jaguar King give you pause."

"Jaguar King?"

"As in, fuck with the jaguars, the Jaguar King's gonna come and get ya, Jaguar King. Big black jaguar? The jungle boogeyman?"

"No. Nope. Didn't say anything like that."

"No?"

The man motions for his blunt back and takes a hit to break up the uncomfortable pause.

"Oh, never mind. They're just stories to scare people. Jaguars are so… exquisite. Aren't they? Obviously, you agree. I know you do. Probably why I like you already. Cats, I have to say… are most important to me. They're not to be trivialized, not to be fetishized. Or forgotten or used and abused. Sunset Rick knows this too."

"Shit, don't know if that means Rick likes me or not after all."

"Ah, he loves ya. Now, I gotta get Natalia her power going. Things might get loud, you said you two like music…"

"We do but… what the fuck?"

The man gently places his wrench and blunt on the ground.

"Come here a second, please," he says.

"Uh, I gotta go."

Larry the cat gives a tiny yelp.

"Aw, no, we're cool. I gotta tell you something, quiet."

June cautiously steps closer. When she's a few steps from him, he speaks.

"The "fuck" is, this is for Natalia. She… doesn't have a lot of time."

"Oh," June says.

"Oh, is right. This is what she wants before she goes." He gestures to the ship. And the generator and the two amplifiers on the dock at the beach where Natalia is plugging in. "So, this is what she gets."

"Oh, listen, I'm really sorry."

"Don't be. It's been a good life. When it's time to go it might as well be here, right?"

He puts the blunt out and returns the oxygen tube into his nose. There's static then a single, deep bass note reverberates from the shore.

Marcus S. Nelson was a biologist from New York who specialized in big cats. His friends called him, "Markie." Every summer for most of the 1980s he'd come down to the Cockscomb Basin working on the wildlife corridors and big cat territories with the people who went on to found the preserve. The year before the preserve was founded, he hired a local pilot to fly him over the area to fine tune the map of the terrain. The small plane hit the tree tops and crashed in the jungle. The wreckage is still out there; no one had a reason or the resources to cart it away. Markie's body was never found. And he has not been seen since.

June parks Rick's pick up on the dirt road just outside Enrique Alvarez's farm. The sun is almost down. A group of a dozen Mayan women are walking to the road trying to keep in the shade. Andy's leaning on the truck eating an obscenely big American-style burger they picked up at the beach bar down the road from Sunset Rick's. The women are trying not to, but they cannot help but stare at the two newcomers, out of place with their new clothes and tourist food.

Where the road turns onto the farm it narrows to barely one car-width wide. Rick told them the guides live and run a visitor center not far past the Álvarez's just inside Cockscomb.

"Will you let me drive?" Andy says. "The going looks rough."

"It does. That's why I'm driving."

Andy puts his trash in the back seat. A rifle is there on the floor. He says nothing of this as June drives into the jungle. After a few hundred meters, the trees and vines meet above them, covering the road in a canopy alive with birds, and motion, and insects and butterflies that flit back and forth between outbursts of white flowers. The air is moist and heavy. Full of pollen and musk and loam, yet undeniably… clean. Andy spots a couple of chickens and a rooster strutting towards the farm. He fingers the ring he has concealed in his shorts pocket.

"June. You know I love you, right?"

"Um, yes dear," June says and laughs. "What do you want now?"

The roar of a motor and chug of un-muffled exhaust breaks the dusk-time lull. A huge, dirty truck is barreling towards them on the road ahead. June pulls the wheel sending the truck off the road and into the forest. Andy slams against the passenger door as the other truck steam rolls past without stopping. A trio of men, rifles slung on their backs, sit in the open bed, grasping the rusted side for hold. For the first time ever in Belize, Andy is frightened.

"What the fuck was that?" he says.

June tries to back up, but the pick up's wheels spin. June throws it into drive and the truck moves forward, rumbling over ferns and saplings and brush onto an embankment sloping into a stream. An animal trail leads into the forest on the other side. June stops and inhales deeply.

"Hey wait a sec," Andy says. "Over there, what's that?"

On the trail on other side is an animal walking towards the stream. It is twice the size of a large house cat, with a super-long tail. Its center of gravity is low to the ground.

"Is that an otter?" Andy says.

"Looks like a…weasel. Only… bigger."

The animal halts and looks across the stream at them. It has a cat's head. Dark grey fur.

"That's not a jaguar."

"No way," Andy says.

The thing rolls on its back, exposing its belly.

"Damn trusting thing, whatever it is," June says. "All that noise didn't scare it off. It must like us."

"Likes you, my dear," Andy says.

The stocky, cat-like thing pads to the water and takes a long drink. It looks across the stream at them again then turns and pads back on the trail into the trees.

The odd beast is on their mind when they roll up to the lone wooden building in a clearing a quarter mile up the road. There is a satellite dish atop the high roof. A hand painted, wooden sign reads "Welcome Center."

June is eager and knocks while Andy is still in the truck putting on bug spray. A short Mayan man opens the door. Inside, is a single large room, with a high thatched ceiling and a fan moving the air around, a layout common to the area. There are two long, picnic-style tables that appear intended for guests. A woman and a child sit at the far end of one of the tables. A flat screen is mounted in the corner near them, showing a weather report. Another younger child is in front of a laptop computer at the other table.

"Hi," June says. "We're the two that just called an hour ago. No one answered. We also sent an e mail. About going in to Cockscomb."

"I am sorry," the man says. "We are about to have dinner."

"Would after dinner be okay? We've come a long way."

"It has been a long day here."

"For us too. I gotta tell you," June says. "And to top it off these guys in a truck pretty much ran us off the road and we saw this thing down at the stream like a big cat-faced otter, any idea what that was? You live around here—

"Jaguarundi?" the woman says and comes to the door.

She ushers June inside and to a poster on the wall that shows drawings of the five cat species that live in Belize. She points to the picture of the jaguarundi.

"Oh, jaguarundi, yeah, that," June says. "I never heard of it. We're here to see jaguars."

"You saw a jaguarundi? Now, where?"

"At the stream, just up the road. Not more than ten minutes ago."

"I have lived here seven years and not seen one yet."

"She's lucky when it comes to cats," Andy says from the doorway.

"Why do you want to see jaguars?" the man asks.

Anna-Lisa's face in the emergency room blooms in June's mind. All blue and air-starved. The stale air of her dark-room fills her, the taste of oil and chemical and sweat, and the tired hum of outdated equipment running down the years. Compassionless voices of people she knows slur into one drone about their days, their husbands, their fabulous lunches. The crack and the ring the first time Javier's hand met her face follows. And her body's memory of how good and how awful it felt to punch him back.

"I just have to see one," she says, softly.

She's conscious of how ugly and loud she must seem to have come knocking at this hour like this. That's not the woman she wants to be.

Andy has his wallet out and open. She doesn't have the

words to stop him. He's always been generous to her; it is his way. For once, just once though she wishes he would let her handle things and that she had the words to express this without rage.

The woman takes the money from Andy.

"Okay, wait outside. Until we come for you," she says. "After we put my children to bed my husband, Sam will take you."

———

Sam is barely as tall as June who stands at about five six. His face is round; a little moustache beneath his sloped Mayan nose. June's not sure if he's older than she and Andy, yet she recognizes he moves with the deliberate gait of the elderly, overworked, and those preoccupied with a great burden. Something she knows too well. He retrieves a tree branch from the damp path for a walking stick, turns on his long flashlight and leads the way into the jungle.

After an hour with him she likes that he is quick to smile and thinks his pensive eyes are kind but she can't stand it that he ignores her when she says she hears things in the jungle on either side of them. Andy hasn't outright shushed her but has asked her to stop bothering the man and it is maddening that neither male will listen.

"This is the part of the forest where the secondary growth ends and the old growth, the primary growth begins," Sam says. "The trees in this area have never been cut. You can see they are bigger. With more space between them. The battles for sunlight have been won and lost long ago."

He taps on a bark-covered vine as thick as his arm that is wrapped around a fig tree wide as a small car.

"In an emergency you can cut this and find water," he says.

The vine spirals around and around the tree and all the way into the dark heights above where bats flit in arcs and tight turns chasing insects that the humans do not see from the ground.

A six-foot-long black snake, thick as the vine, slithers onto the path a few paces ahead. It rears up, tastes the air with its tongue, then resumes its journey across the path, disappearing into the trees.

"What kind was that?" Andy asks.

"A Fer De Lance," Sam says.

"That sounds poisonous," June says.

"It is," Sam says. "Do not be afraid. If you see a snake again, get behind me."

"Afraid, fuck no," June says. "I'm kicking myself I only have my phone with me. Getting ready, things were so crazy. I didn't even pack my camera. Are we going to see it again?"

"Let's hope not," Sam says.

Andy wonders what getting behind Sam is going to do. Does he kill snakes with that stick? June's pre-trip concerns about coming here that he dismissed as no problem are back in his mind.

"I think I hear something," June says. Again.

"The Fer De Lance likes to take sleeping birds," Sam says.

He walks to a tree with low hanging limbs and points to a bird sleeping in the leaves.

"Some do not sleep in nests they just sleep. Sometimes snakes and owls take them."

June marches in front of Sam and points.

"Out there to our right," she says.

Sam shines his light to where June has pointed.

"A peccary," Sam says. "You might call it… a big pig."

"How do you know?"

"The eyes," he says. "Look there."

He shines his light in the ferns and plants. Hundreds upon hundreds of pink and orange dots are illuminated in his beam.

"Every animal's eyes are different. They all respond to light. Those are spiders."

June and Andy shine their beams at the low greenery too.

"Those are all spiders?" Andy asks.

"Yes," Sam says. "Every one of them. If we find a jaguar, I will tell you to turn your light off. Some animals freeze. Jaguars do not like it."

Andy bends to fix his laces. A small, brown snake is curling its way around the tree trunk he has grasped to steady himself.

"That one is harmless," Sam says. "Careful, there are things if you touch that will make you itch."

Sam resumes walking and gestures them to follow. Andy follows a few paces behind and June a few paces behind him.

After a few minutes Sam stops and bends down.

"Here are jaguar prints," he says. "Fresh. Look. They were made tonight. Here is where a jaguar reached the trail. And next to her was her cub."

June snaps photos with her phone. Sam walks with his head down and stops after a few paces.

"Here is where a big male, wow look how big, crossed the path. Maybe he was following them. Maybe he wanted to see who was in his territory. Now shine your light that way and look."

There is a shape a dozen or so yards into the forest. At first, June thinks it is a car or bus covered in jungle before realizing it is a plane, like the one they flew in on. Smaller trees and vines have grown in and on and around it.

"Long ago before the preserve was founded one of the men working to protect the cats crashed here. You can see where we lost the primary growth trees and the newer trees have moved in for the sunlight."

"Do you think it was left here because they were afraid of the Jaguar King?" June asks.

"Jaguar King?" Andy says.

"He's the one who kills you if you fuck with the cats," June says.

"Where'd you hear that?"

"When you were sleeping. I met our neighbors."

"They cool?"

"Do you like music?"

"The Jaguar King. He is not real," Sam says. "A story to protect the cats. How would we take the plane away even if we wanted to? Nature wastes nothing. Given time."

"Okay, I'm not fucking around. I *really* heard something this time," June says. "Something is out here with us."

"There are many, many jaguars in Cockscomb," Sam says.

"How many—"

"Guys, shut up! There. In the tree."

Sam shines his light where June is pointing. Then immediately clicks it off.

"Lights off," he says. "Off. Turn them off now."

With the flashlights off, the darkness is near complete. Andy thinks he's hearing everything sharper. The insect's buzz. The whir of frogs. His heavy breath. The rustle of the jungle.

There's a deep grunt. Then a chuff, chuff, chuff coming from the right side of the path, above them.

The noise changes to a guttural growl that sounds… like an annoyed expression. The stillness breaks. Moving air hits Andy's face. Something hits the ground next to him with a solid thump.

His spine comes alive. A place inside reminds him he is prey. That he is meat.

There's a jaguar on the ground. Next to him. Rumbling and growling.

He hears its steps on the moist ground. Hears it breathing. Something soft brushes his arm. Its tail? The darkness explodes into motion, the sound of paws on dirt and broken brush and cracked branches. The jaguar is bounding away. Andy's senses have it pinpointed as it bolts into deeper darkness.

They stand there for a long minute. Listening. There is only the sound of human breaths and the jungle. Andy reaches to hold June's hand. She does not let him take it.

Sam flicks his light on. Andy's not sure if June has been laughing or crying or both.

"…that was probably the big male who's prints we saw. He is gone now. Jaguars are naturally curious…"

He realizes that June is crying. He touches his cheek and realizes tears are streaming down his face too.

The return hike to the entrance is in silence. Midway, June stops and listens to the jungle. Sam and Andy stop too. When they near the starting place June's stride slows and her eyes go far away. Andy reaches to put his arm around her. She smacks him in the bicep.

"I told you I heard something. It was following us the whole time," she says.

"You were right, you were right," Andy says.

"I wonder what it's doing now," June says.

"The jaguars like it in the center of the preserve," Sam says. "Humans don't go there. The jaguars know this."

"Can we go?"

"It is two days in, two days out. We were lucky to come this close to one tonight."

"When was the last time you took someone?"

"Years ago."

June thinks of the names Frankie and Ivy in Sunset Rick's guest book. Did their moment of vacation bliss last?

"You said you moved here. Seven years ago?" June asks. "Why'd you come? The jaguars?"

An owl passes overhead.

"The jaguars, I like. Yes," Sam says. "I think Cockscomb needs me. No one wants to live here. Especially young people. Everyone good moves away."

"I heard a road is coming," June says. "Do you think that will be good?"

"How does one answer these things," Sam says. "I don't want here to become like everywhere else. I know change will come though. And Cockscomb will grow. Maybe it can grow up to be wonderful."

The owl has landed on a low branch. It cocks its head and looks at them.

Dawn is still an hour away when they pull away from the Alvarez's farm. This is the point in their date-night pattern where they would have sex. No matter where they were. In the back seat. On the side of the road. In the Guggenheim Museum restroom. Tonight, she is glad he is too tired. She knows there is something wrong with him. His energy has been too low and he passes out too much, even for him, and not just from working.

"Promise me you will see a doctor," she says.

It is rare that she says anything. She's asked him so many times she has stopped bothering. She does love him. At least the him that he used to be. The him that he sometimes can be. That he sometimes sort of is. He's passed out and does not hear.

A big green snake crosses the road. It is at least ten, maybe fifteen feet long, its body longer than both lanes. She is glad to enjoy the experience of seeing it without having to filter it through their shared existence.

The sun is almost ready to come up when June parks the truck back at Sunset Rick's.

———

There's bass and drums coming from the beach. The playing is surprisingly gentle. And not as loud as she had expected. She gets Andy out of the car and walks him to their cabin and into bed.

There's no way she can sleep. Her mind is racing. She steps outside the cabin and lights up a smoke and asks herself if she wants to get high with the neighbors. She decides she does, as she finishes her clove.

She watches Natalia at the edge of the dock, playing her bass, her form just a silhouette in the night. Her man is slumped in his chair, asleep with a guitar in his lap. Rick is in a chair further back. An audience of one. Looks like he is asleep, too.

June hears drums. Real ones, yet she does not see a drum kit.

The sound is coming from across the water. From the ship. Natalia's long, sliding bass tones and the sparse, deceptively simple, open beat—plenty of room in it, are meeting halfway. Blending perfectly with the sound of the waves. And the sounds of the end of night and the coming morning. It might be the most beautiful thing she's ever heard.

Larry the Cat is out of his carrier. He's on the beach where the dock meets the shore, chasing small crabs.

To June's surprise, a jaguar is crossing the sand towards the little house cat. Creeping low and steady. It's lithe form unmistakably female. Black spots barely visible on black fur. This was the one she envisioned when they landed. Neither Natalia nor Larry see it. They don't know it's there. The jaguar rises from its crouch and changes its trajectory, heading for the water away from the humans. Larry notices it and bolts for the dock. The big cat trots into the gentle surf. And into shoulder deep water then it is swimming. Towards the boat? Towards the Island? Only her head is visible.

June puts the clove out and decides she's going to tell Natalia a jaguar is near and that her playing is beautiful.

There's a man standing a few feet from her in the darkness of the path.

"Holy shit, Rick. You scared the shit out of me."

The man is tall. Old and lean. Long, thin grey hair. No beard. There's some sort of dark ichor or dry blood all around his mouth. He's barefoot. And wearing only tattered remnants of shorts. This is not Rick. This man is feral. His hands are covered in that same dark ichor as his mouth. There's the smell of musk. The smell of the jungle. His long limbs do not seem right, there are long pink raised scars where bones were broken and improperly set.

June instinctively steps aside to pass him. The man matches her step, placing himself in her way.

"Who are you?" June says louder than she intended. "What do you want?"

She knows she should be afraid. She finds she is only curious.

"I want you to come with me," he says. "You know where."

His voice is gentle and cultured. With a hint of a familiar accent. Erasing the notion June had that he would be mute.

Sunset Rick has heard her. He's up. Crossing the beach. A rifle in his hand. The feral man and June watch him near. When he is a few paces away he lowers his weapon.

"Markie?" Rick says. "Is that you? Are you for real?"

Sunset Rick has not seen his friend since he crashed the plane out in Cockscomb. Since he saw him crawl away, battered and bruised into the dark heart of the jungle that day. He'd always wondered and had his notions of which of the stories of the Jaguar King could be real.

The Jaguar King extends his hand for June to take it. June wonders if it will be hard and rough. Or if her hand will pass through it as if is nothing.

The decision to find out, the decision to close her fingers around his, to follow as he asks, is not a decision requiring contemplation at all.

June did not return home. When Andy awoke that morning, she was gone. Her possessions in the cabin not disturbed. He has not seen her since. Sunset Rick claimed he had not seen her. He cooperated, but was of little help in the investigations that the Belizean police and the American authorities undertook.

Years rolled on.

Some days more than others he thinks of June. He thinks they really could have been something. He's not sure he understands himself fully, he's still a major work in progress but thinks there was a chance and June could have found themselves, found some meaning, together. They were just finding out about the part of love that is making choices and building something. He doesn't think he's ever going to know about that now.

He walks back to his side door after throwing out his trash, the 3am sky and cold night uncaring of what he wonders about in quiet moments like these. Something moves at the foot of the driveway. The place inside him that came alive when the jaguar jumped next to him comes alive again. The feeling of being powerless in the night, sometimes so far away, so readily returns.

The sound is the neighbor's cat. It is walking, perfectly balanced atop the plastic fence, leaving the scene of the crime of the knocked over trash can he now has to clean up. June's empty-eyed far-away expression fills him. Sometimes he thinks he can feel her, that she's standing still as she does, with that faraway look on her face, and she's out there, somewhere, somehow, in the dark heart of the wood.

The fourth Bell

The fourth bell's pitted metal left me no doubt the crusty old thing had to be from a ship wreck. It wasn't only larger than the dozens of other bells on Terrence's work table, it was categorically different.

I had returned from the hospital last night to find Terrence had moved his work area, and Gerald's massive ten-foot square tank, right smack into the middle of our living room and I still wasn't used to it. Early evening sun streamed through the ceiling to floor glass windows, turning the views of our sprawling property and the Long Island Sound beyond into giant rectangles of dirty, orange-tinted light. The room was full of wonderful things from the life Peter, Terrence, and I had built. Without Peter, the way the cavernous space dwarfed everything only added to the oppressive weight on my chest. Terrence was my best remaining friend on this earth; my brother, my partner, my creative soul mate, my chosen family, and I knew he was all torn up inside just like I was, but nothing I did or said seemed to reach him.

Gerald floated motionless in the center of his tank. His eight sucker-covered arms dangled in what I took to be boredom and resignation but his eyes were alive and watching us. Flags, a Ouija board, waterproof maps, chess pieces, and children's blocks with letters on them littered the bottom of the tank. Terrence picked up one of the smaller bells and held it to the glass. Gerald remained motionless. I know Terrence wanted a response but the only sign Gerald was even alive was the minute ripple traveling along the thin fin-like skin on the contour of his pink-grey head.

Terrance slammed the bell on the table and huffed through the pages of one of the oversized old books held aloft in front of him by one of the mechanical arms from our last project.

"I don't think he likes you very much," I said as diplomatically as I could.

"Of course *it* does," Terrence said without looking up. "Doesn't matter anyway."

I hated his refusal to use Gerald's name.

The sunlight cast August's glow on the miasma of mechanical parts, tools, and equipment that covered every available inch of table-top space in the room. A dust-filled ray illuminated the nest of spider-like mechanical legs, wire-laden circuit boards, and other disassembled pieces and remains of our last project that surrounded the tarnished World War Two era dive bell languishing in the far corner.

Gerald gracefully brought his arms together and jetted to the bottom of the tank. He gathered the letter blocks and brought them to the side of the tank nearest Terrence. I marveled at how adeptly he tumbled them over and over with the tips of those four-foot tentacles. He could turn any color or squeeze into the tiniest space, though this usually meant he was all fed up. He glanced at me, then put the last block into place; his tablespoon-sized eyes saying everything I needed to know, though they didn't need to.

D - I - E T – E - R - R – E - N - C- E, the blocks spelled.

He waited for Terrence to look then quickly changed them to read "Hi Terrence."

If Terrence noticed, or even cared, he didn't show it. He struck at the seven bells he had arranged in front of him with a thin copper rod. I expected their sounds to be sharp, or at least cleaner, but each tinny ring sounded as if it had traveled from far away through some muffling impediment. Peter's face sprang into my mind. His tortured face, sucking in those last gurgling breaths. Closing my eyes never helped.

Terrence fervently struck the bells again in a different sequence.

I hated that he had moved Peter's worktable into the living room and claimed it as his own. The table had always been covered with the latest schematics and plans the three of us were working on. The old books and all the bells were new additions. The largest bell, the old crusty one, sat fourth in Terrence's current lineup and felt like even more of an intrusion than the rest of the miasma.

Terrence brushed his sandy hair out of his eyes and squinted as the mechanical arm moved the book he was trying to read closer to him. Despite the beginnings of worry lines and creases, his face was still boyish and had never lost that rascal charm. After the crash, he'd taken to wearing vintage rock t-shirts and old jeans. He had been planning to dress like that at Peter's funeral until I informed him in no uncertain terms that I'd drag my ass out of the hospital if I had to and dress him properly myself, but there never was a funeral. At least not one that we were told about. Peter's "long-lost" family had come out of the woodwork upon the news of his death and promptly set about trying to lay claim to his share of our fortunes. There was no way we were going to let those vultures get their hands on anything of Peter's. Cutting us out of the funeral and not even letting us know where they had buried him was their way of punishing us.

Terrence claimed his new-found wardrobe was his version of Einstein's same-black-suit-everyday thing. I knew it really had to do with a yearning for when the three of us were young and together and everything was easy. Today he had on a Rolling Stones shirt. Peter had loved the Stones. Terrence couldn't even name four songs by them.

"You know, it wouldn't hurt to *try* being—"

"It's not a pet," Terrence said. "Pampering isn't going to help figure out which seven bells I need."

"Need for what?"

"To make it right for..."

He knew if he said, "Make it right for Peter," one more time I was going to slap him.

Peter was gone. Terrence hadn't been right there, forced to watch his pained last moments of life, unable to help like I had. Maybe if he started being nicer to those of us left in his life it would help, otherwise he wasn't making anything right.

Gerald moved the planchette around on the Ouija board and changed the blocks so they spelled incomprehensible phrases.

"What are you doing, Gerald?" I asked.

He ignored me.

"See what I mean," Terrence said. "At least when Peter was spacing out, we still knew he was still contributing to the plan."

The plan. It was always all about a *plan* for him. Ever since we were kids, Terrence was at his happiest when embroiled in some *plan*. Peter, Terrence, and I, the three little geniuses. All grown up, out of school, and in this great place of our own where we made one plan after another happen. Without Peter, we weren't the same, nothing was. I know that's the way things go. Everyone dies in the end. Everything changes, but Terrence wasn't right.

He worried me. And he hadn't even been the one who watched Peter, trapped upside down in the car, in that ditch. Gasping for air. Drowning out in the middle of the desert. I hated this was how I remembered him.

Gerald tapped the letter block "S" against the glass. I knew it was his shorthand for "smile."

Terrence scowled.

"I know you don't want to hear it, but think about it. Maybe if you were nicer, he might just decide to help," I said.

"Nicer doesn't matter," Terrence muttered. "I don't even think he knows."

I didn't know what Terrence was after with his books and bells. But if Gerald didn't know, I had no doubt he could figure it out, one way or another.

No one could replace Peter. Not even someone as special as Gerald. With Gerald, I thought we would be three again and that maybe things would sort of feel the same. He could pick the exact scores of cricket matches in advance and had something to do with a new project Peter had been dreaming up right before the crash. Peter's Australian contact had no shame and demanded an exorbitant sum to part with Gerald, but money was never an issue. We had all the money we could ever want, but no amount could give Terrence and I what we wanted most.

I last saw Peter in New Mexico. I try to remember how happy he was that night, out in that desert canyon testing our latest project. He had pinpointed the spot as having the largest concentration of Gila Monsters, and we had carefully driven off the road and found our way in. From the front seats of our rented SUV, we watched our rover walk on its mechanical legs, maneuvering around the bases of tall cactus and granite outcroppings of rock like one of those robots fire departments sent into burning buildings. The rover's top was loaded with antennae and dishes pointing up that detected cosmic rays, its underbelly crammed full of temperature sensors to track the fat nocturnal lizards Peter had come for. Night air tinged with the clean scent of desert brush and dry earth gently blew through the open windows.

A smile bloomed on Peter's face as he watched the data come up on his tablet. He loved the mandala patterns it formed. Seeing him happy was a rare thing. Too often, his face was solemn and stern. That's when I knew he had his birthplace, Mumbai, on his mind, which had been happening more and more lately; all his recent paintings depicted the far away city in one way or another. I knew his family was out there somewhere, but that was all. Any direct mention of either subject caused him to shut down.

I wanted to remember him overcome with joy, that joy particular to an inventor seeing his invention manifested for the first time. The joy as he watched the rover move over the sand and listened to the whir of the motors in its joints and grind of metal on metal as antennae and sensors rotated.

"It's working," I said. "It's locked onto some star now for sure."

"It tracks all celestial objects, not just the stars," Peter said. "I can't believe how many lizards it detected already."

Peter hunted in the back seat for his water color pad and aquarelle pencils. He set his tablet on the dash, propped the pad on the steering wheel. Instead of sketching, he began writing in his distinctive flowery handwriting. I glanced at the pad and saw something about cricket match scores, and a phone number next to the words Darwin Australia. As usual, he was on to something new even before what we were working on was complete.

The data coming from the rover bloomed into a mandala on Peter's screen. The shape was a graphic representation of how the movement patterns of the nocturnal Gila Monsters corresponded to all those celestial objects in the night sky, even the ones we couldn't see with our eyes. I couldn't see it yet, but I knew there had to be an application for biology or maybe astroscience. Peter came up with the ideas, Terrence handled the lion's share of building them, but it was my job to figure out who we could sell them to and for what.

Peter was no help. He said he had dreamed it up so he could use the shapes of the plotted data in his paintings but now he was sketching an octopus and what looked like a dive bell next to his scrawl. All his inventions ultimately were born from his desire to create art. We all loved him for that. His purity. The integrity with which he created. I worried that Terrence secretly resented him for it as well.

I noticed the breeze had ceased. Something kinetic waited in the stillness. A fat rain pellet splattered on the back of our rover as a rumble I felt in my chest punctured the night's quiet. Before I could voice my confusion the dry earth transformed into spattering mud from the downpour that had not existed a mere second ago. The rumble became a roar. Something hit our car. A wall of water. We were in a flash flood. Foaming, roaring, spraying water lifted us and sent us careening along the canyon floor. I saw one of the rover's mechanical legs in the maelstrom and managed to click my seatbelt as we spun end around end. The water took us where it pleased, knocking us against cacti and brush until we lurched to a halt against a boulder. Peter's tablet flew into the windshield. We strained against our seatbelts. I felt the current pushing, tilting, willing us with its elemental force in the other direction. Something gave and we spun free of the boulder. Down became up. My stomach heaved. We flipped and dropped into a ditch on the side of the road with a crunch. My head hurt. The window was spider-webbed. We were upside down but alright. I looked over at Peter and we both cracked a pained laugh. Then the water poured through the windows. The way we were titled Peter was lower than me; his hair and fore-head already submerged. I struggled to break free of my belt and reach him. I tasted my own blood and the belt held me fast. Water rose to above his nose and he began to gasp for breath. The water stopped before it reached me. I waited there bleeding, trapped upside down with my drowned friend. Sometime in the night the water receded. It wasn't until morning before someone found us.

Gerald was tapping on the glass trying to get my attention. Terrence was in the middle of speaking. I tried to banish the image of Peter's lifeless body hanging upside down with his head underwater.

"…I just need to pin down the locations," Terrence said. "I feel like the bells know. They call to each other."

"Terrence. They're bells."

I expected rage or sarcasm for questioning him, but before me was just my friend. My sad friend wearing a t-shirt of a band he didn't know or like. My friend who was struggling just like me.

"I don't know how I know," Terrence said. "I just do."

One of the old books on the table was open to a page with a drawing of a boy reaching into a man's pocket. Beneath it was another drawing of a hand reaching into the silhouette of a man's head. Hand drawn staves annotated with music notes and notations surrounded the drawings.

I glanced at the fourth bell. I didn't like the way it made me think of a ship wreck. Ship wrecks meant drownings.

"How do you know you need seven?" I asked. "And how do you know you have the right seven?"

D – O N – O - T L- I –S – T – E –N, Gerald had spelled with the blocks.

"I'm not incompetent," Terrence said, that awful rage surfacing again. "Are you going to trust the octopus over me? Are you going to question everything I do or do you want to help?"

"You know I want to help. I'll always help you. What do I have to do?"

"Okay. Good. Just listen. I'll try to show you what I mean."

Terrence struck the seven bells again with that copper rod. The sounds were hollow, even more muted than before. Terrence bobbed his head and kept looking back and forth from me to the bells. After a moment it was clear nothing was happening. For Terrence's sake, I really wanted whatever he was doing to work.

He muttered something about Peter always getting it right

and went back to flipping through the big book the mechanical arm was holding.

A tiny shadow moved across the work table. Then about a dozen rounded, almost triangular, fish-like shapes followed. Only nothing was casting them. Gerald jetted to the corner of his tank nearest us. He rolled and unrolled his arms while patterns of green and purple pulsed along his skin.

The little school of shadows moved back and forth on the table then disappeared. My ears filled with the rasp of dozens of whispers all speaking at once. Then there was only one voice. Peter's voice.

"Do not go to Lin-Kasai," it said.

I waited to hear more but there was nothing. Terrence continued to flip through his book in frustration. Hearing Peter's voice had me shaken.

"I can't figure out if I should look next in Argentina or—"

"You didn't see or hear any of that?" I asked.

Before he could answer, the items in Gerald's tank lifted from the bottom. A cloud of blocks, and chess pieces, and map markers swirled around Gerald floating motionless in its center.

"Are you doing that?" Terrence screamed at him.

There was no way for Gerald to spell no. I could feel his fear. Everything ceased moving and fell to the bottom. Gerald quickly began arranging them. He marked a location and a route to it with plastic pawns on a map of Long Island.

"Hmmm. A change of heart?" Terrence said. "What's gotten into him?"

"Go easy. He almost got pummeled by that cloud of stuff flying around in his tank. Did your bells do that?"

"I think so. They all have neat tricks. I just can't figure out exactly what they are."

"Neat tricks, huh?"

Gerald was messing with his blocks again. I expected another round of Die Terrence.

I W- A- N- T T- O H -E- L- P, Gerald spelled. W- A- N- T T- O C- O- M- E

"But you can't," Terrence said.

I wanted Gerald to come with us too. Terrence had begun a dialog and addressed him directly. That was something, and at least some kind of a start. I'd take it.

It took us all night to find the place. I don't know why. It wasn't terribly far away. An industrial park in Hauppauge. I'd been in a nearby park last summer where they manufactured the blades for a hydrofoil we had created. This whole area was deserted. We walked through an alley that led into a square formed by the convergence of several alleys. A circular fountain that had gone dry long ago remained in the square's center a lonely reminder that people used to frequent here. A garbage dumpster partially concealed a door on the other side.

.We walked across and rolled the dumpster away from the door.

The words "Silversmith and Ironworks," adorned the wall in faded black paint.

The opening refrain of the song "Gimme Shelter" blared from Terrence's pack.

He fished his phone out of his pack. Gerald filled the screen. His suckers were alive with motion as he formed words with the blocks.

"Who is filming him?" I asked. "How's he calling you?"

"I don't know," Terrence said. "He's using the arm? Doesn't matter. He's just trying to piss me off."

Gerald moved his head right up against the camera so his eye filled the screen.

"You can't come," Terrence yelled and turned his phone off.

I hated watching him like this. He pushed the old door open and I followed him inside. Light streamed in from the doorway and spaces between the rows of boarded windows high up on the left wall. Empty black iron cauldrons big enough for a person to bathe in and discarded dirty white molds were in a heap in the center of the floor. From the look of the thick layer of dust and all the debris no one had passed this way in ages. Terrence picked up one of the molds. Inside the block of dirty plaster was a concave half-hour-glass shape.

"A bell," he said. "They're all molds for bells."

I found something profound about the empty shape. I knew if I could just corral my thoughts I could share them with Terrence. What I was driving at was something he needed desperately to know. But I found no words and couldn't form a cogent train of thought.

Terrence was picking up molds and inspecting them. I crossed to the other side of the floor and into a small square room that was once an office area. A map of the world covered its back wall. Different colored pins marked towns and cities. Lines were drawn in marker between them indicating supply lines or delivery routes or who knows what. One lone pin was marked at the tip of South America. Lin Kasai was written in black marker next to it in a familiar scrawl.

"I think you ought to see this," I called to Terrence.

A star had been drawn around the pin on the town of Playa Portencia. The map indicated it was not far from our home on the

North Shore, in fact it showed to be only a few beaches over. Granted I spent most of my time working but I'd never heard of it. Next to the star was written,

"You'll find me here. Bring the bells."

The handwriting was unmistakably Peter's flourishing scrawl.

Peter's parents had buried him but wouldn't tell us where. That was all I knew to be true. Everything else, the handwriting on the map and Gerald sending us to the foundry there had to be an explanation for.

Playa Portencia was a fishing town, a real throw back to what life on Long Island used to be like. Too few of them remained. The fishing boats were out for the day, except for a large freighter on the horizon, bound for some port unknown or maybe heading into the Seaport in the City. A hot wind whipped spirals of sand along the asphalt parking lot. Terrence and I trudged to the rocky shore, the bells snugly stashed in his back pack. Salt-water tide pools were everywhere between the rocks of all shapes and sizes covering the beach. At the shore, about a dozen wooden docks stretched into the water. Three quarters the way across was a square concrete foundation the size of a child's desk. It looked like the base for a statue or monument.

Someone bumped into me as I maneuvered on some rocks to avoid dipping my feet in a tide pool.

"Sorry," I said.

He looked nothing at all like a fisherman; he was older than me, but young and oh so thin. His shock of dark hair was flipped to one side, like a fifties rocker.

"I wasn't looking, sorry man," I repeated.

He pointed to the freighter just barely visible on the horizon.

"That's the Amaranth," he said.

I called to Terrence to look. He was already at the concrete bent down and reading from a placard set in it. I looked back to the skinny man but he had vanished.

"Here lies Peter Ramacoord. Beloved son," Terrence read.

"It also says that this is a historic site. A merchant ship was claimed by the rocks here long ago."

He stood there in silence. I wanted to ask him if the name of the ship was the Amaranth but he was having a moment; thinking about Peter, I hoped, which was what he had needed to do for so long. Then he placed his pack on the concrete and took out the bells. A thin silver flute. A small brass one that looked like the kind they rung for a butler in the movies. The old iron one he placed in a groove in the concrete as if it were made for it.

For some reason this made Terrence laugh. It was the first levity I'd seen in him for a while, but it was a nervous laughter. I didn't like it.

"Terrence, what was the name of the merchant ship?"

"I had it right all along," he said, ignoring me. "I was just in the wrong place."

I moved so I could read the placard myself, but then he rang the first bell.

I winced; part of me expecting an explosion of sound or something. There was nothing. Terrence fell to his knees, his body shaking as if responding to something physical. The fourth bell rocked back and forth in its concrete cradle. I could see it and all the bells vibrating, but I heard nothing.

I noticed a faint ting, an almost imperceptible sound, like the first patter of a sparse rain on grass. Someone was standing at the shore by one of the docks, sketching in a pad. I knew that pose. I knew those black jeans and that tattered t-shirt. Peter.

A realization was dawning in me on how this had come to be. The idea was just aching to be born in my mind, along with my thoughts about the molds in the foundry, something about the distinction between the living and the dead and between the past and the future, but I could not grasp it long enough to give it voice.

"Reach for it," Peter said. "Let all misconceptions and misunderstandings fall away like negative space and see the creation."

Though he was by the shore, I heard his words in my mind clearly as if he were right in front of me. I wasn't sure if he were speaking to me or about something he was drawing.

"I've got it," Terrence shouted to me. "I've figured it out. They're not bells, they're keys."

He didn't see Peter.

The wind whipped the waves into spray. The ephemeral vortexes of mist unlocked my answers. I knew what I had to say to Terrence. I knew how to make this all right.

"You always were the smart one," I said. "I knew you would figure it out. They're not keys to open. But to close. We're here to say goodbye. To lock our memories, our love for him in our hearts. That's the way things go. That's what we do, that's all anyone can do when you lose—"

"No. The bells *open* doors. I figured it out. We figured it out. Just think of what we can do with this."

"Terrence, I really think we should stop and think this over."

"No," he said. "I have all the bells and I know what to do."

A big wave rolled in and erupted into a cloud of spray and foam. The water gurgled and became a patch of bubbles. When it cleared, something big was there. At first I thought it was a boulder or dislodged seaside rocks, but it was metal. A brown metal orb patched up with different colored metal plates, climbing from the sea on eight robotic legs. Our rover's mechanical legs. It was our dive bell. Gerald's head peered from the glass porthole in its center. Seawater sluiced off its sides as it stood on four legs. The other four waved in the air, pincers at the end clacking open and closed.

Terrence laughed and I wished it were with the amazement and joy I felt. His face looked anything but happy.

Gerald had no voice. No blocks to spell with but the meaning of his suit's out stretched arms was universal. Stop.

Terrence looked at him and smiled. He held up the fourth bell and said, "No."

"I'm sick of you," Terrence said. "You *think* you're Peter, but you're not. And I'm not surprised. I knew you were building it. I let you."

Gerald moved toward him. His mechanical legs whirring and clicking as he inched closer.

Terrence raised the fourth bell higher. Its crust fell away revealing a finish that was solid black. Its odd gloss looked like it would shine and reflect light, but it didn't, it was as if it were a piece of night cut in the shape of a bell. I knew I couldn't let him ring it.

I ran to him and grabbed for it. Terrence pivoted. I slipped on wet rock and fell into a tide pool. I heard a crunch, crunch, crunch and the whir and hiss of motors and hydraulics. Gerald had closed the distance from the shore and was upon Terrence, reaching for him with his mechanical arms.

Terrence rang the bell before Gerald's arms could restrain him. I winced again, but I heard no sound. Gerald snaked two of his arms around Terrence's waist and lifted him. With his two others he tried to pry the bell from Terrence's grasp. I knew the strength of those motors. He should have been able to snatch it away like that, but was unable. Terrence held on.

"He only wants to help," I said. "He knows you need to stop. You treat him like he's nothing."

"He is nothing," Terrence cried. "Nothing like Peter at all."

"Of course he is nothing like me," a familiar voice said. "He has way too many legs."

Peter had come from the shore. Terrence saw him now. They stood side by side in their black jeans and rock tees. A smile grew on Terrence's face. We were all together again.

"You're back," Terrence said. "You've come back to us. I knew you would."

He was all choked up and fighting not to cry.

"No. I'm not back. I've only come for these," he said. "They're much too dangerous to have around."

Peter reached for the bells. As his hand neared them one by one they disappeared. Something changed. I couldn't pinpoint what. It was the relief akin to the removal of an annoying background hum or the fixing of a flickering fluorescent light. It was hard to say what was different but I felt the relief from a pressure I hadn't realized was present. Only the fourth bell, the bell that Terrence held, remained. I knew it, too, needed to disappear. I knew once it too was gone the weight I'd been carrying around would be lifted, and danger would be averted.

"Don't do this, Peter," Terrence said to Peter. "Don't you miss us?"

Peter smiled. Terrence smiled too. Seeing them standing

there next to the mechanical hulk Gerald wore, smiling together provided some comfort. This was my family. Things were going to be all right again. Everything was going to be okay.

Terrence closed his hand around the top of the black bell and thrust it at the glass face plate of Gerald's dive bell. Gerald's arms grasped for him but Terrence pounded, pounded, pounded away.

The plate cracked, spider-webbed, and broke open. Water poured out sending Gerald onto the rocky beach. He convulsed on the rocks, his tentacles reaching for a tide pool. Terrence put his foot down, blocking Gerald's path to shore. He pushed the empty shell of Gerald's suit and it fell.

"Do something," I screamed to Peter and ran to them.

Peter only reached for the fourth bell. As his hand neared it both he and it disappeared. Gerald crawled for the shore. I ran into Terrence and did my best to tackle him. He met my charged, punched me, and flung me off him.

A big wave crashed on the shore and enveloped Gerald. As it pulled back to sea, Gerald was gone. I stood and ran for the water and dove in. I hit my head on rock. Sharp edges cut my hands and arms. I tried to swim. The current took me. Waves battered me. I pulled myself forward. With the last of my air I called for Gerald before everything went black.

I woke up to the all too familiar blips and chirps of a hospital room.

"Don't worry," Terrence's voice said. "I'm with you. I'm working on something to make this all right."

I meant to protest but whatever drugs they had me on took me.

After my concussion healed Terrence returned to take me home. My stitches itched and I wanted them out. The living room was back to the way it was. No work table. No tank. Nothing to indicate Gerald had ever been with us.

"I'm working on something," Terrence said gently. "When you are up to it do you want to go visit Peter's grave?"

"Gerald's gone," I said.

"I'm sorry," he said. "I think I can find him."

He was happy. He was embroiled in a plan again. Angry as I was, there was some comfort in seeing him content. But I knew he was wrong. No memorial, no visiting of Peter's grave, no machine Terrence could dream up was going to help this time. Gerald was gone. Peter was not coming back. The water had taken everything.

The Hand of Fire

Tel-Aviv, 1984.

The ancient stones of the subterranean chamber were cold and damp despite the dry heat of the afternoon. Grainy sunlight reached in from the narrow entrance Jeffrey Stein had slipped into moments before when his parents weren't looking. He thought the archaeological sites were much more fun than the city of Tel Aviv, as shiny and cool as it was. The people from the tour said this place, King Herod's Tomb, was empty cleared of all artifacts centuries ago, but Jeffrey was drawn to it as if something remained inside waiting to be discovered. He ventured into the near dark and thought he saw something move in the corner. He wished there was more light than just the slim patch of sun.

Jeffrey's elbows tingled and his forearms trembled, much like when all four ghosts were closing in on his Pac-Man and the twists and turns felt out of control. The shape he *thought* he saw in the corner moved. A tattered figure wrapped in robes and rags ambled toward him.

Jeffrey froze. He eyed the path to the stairs but couldn't run away. Mummies were supposed to be in Egypt, and they weren't even real.

"Take my hand," the figure said.

As it spoke, a blue light, sharper than any video game screen, glowed under its dusty wrappings.

Sweat dripped from the strands of Jeffrey's dark black hair poking out from under his sun hat. His brown eyes were wide open.

"Ephraim Ben-Moshe. Please. Listen to me."

It spoke slowly and deliberately, not at all how Jeffrey imagined a mummy would sound.

But it didn't sound anything like a bum or a street thug or some other kind of person Mom and Dad had warned him about. Which it had to be; even though it knew his name, his Hebrew name, like one of the old rabbis or stinky-breathed people Dad said were his uncles at his bar mitzvah.

He tensed to fight and pictured himself locking its arm, kneeing its groin, and kicking its knee like his dad had taught him. He trained with Dad every day, even on vacation. But this was no playground bully.

Jeffrey bolted for the light. A quick turn and he was back in the main room, bounding up the steps to the entrance gap in the stone blocks. He jumped over the rope with the hanging sign that read KEEP OUT in Hebrew, Arabic, and English.

He breathed in the smell of arid ground and roasting falafel. The members of the tour group were taking pictures of the dusty white-robed man near their tour bus who was selling food and pictures of his camel. He saw his father's familiar loafers storming towards him.

"Jeffrey, this isn't back home! When your mother tells you to stay close…"

"I'm gonna kill him, Moishe," his mother's voice sounded from not far away.

But he wasn't worried about being scolded, or grounded, or not being allowed to float in the salty Dead Sea like they had threatened. An image of the thing inside the tomb lingered in his mind's eye. The echo of its deliberate, steady voice made the back of his arms and legs tingle and filled him with the uneasy sensation that he had been here and done all of this before.

Jeffrey followed his mom and dad through the crowded seaside plaza. All the bright lights and sounds and smells of the pizza places, falafel joints, and ice cream parlors surrounding the open-air square converged on him; everything so clean and new and beyond state of the art that it felt like the future, not what he had imagined Tel Aviv to be. The newest music videos from back home, and even movies still in the theatres, blared on shiny TV sets hung high for the viewing pleasure of the carefree families, groups of teens, and tourists gathered around the rows of pristine plastic tables eating and laughing and enjoying the warm evening. Jeffrey looked across the boardwalk to the long, wide beach and the Mediterranean beyond.

He doubled over from a sharp pain in his chest. An image of haggard soldiers standing waist deep in the waves beneath a burning red sky eclipsed all else. A single arresting thought came to him, "This is the sea you swear to push us into."

"You okay?" his mother asked.

The image disappeared as swiftly as it had come.

"It's nothing," Jeffrey muttered.

I won't let that happen, he thought. And it surprised him how the thought had come from nowhere.

He remembered the crunch Jimmy Boden's jaw made when he had punched him in the face. He remembered when the kids at school caught him and how he fought and fought, even though they all piled on him.

"Stop daydreaming and stay close," his dad said. "This isn't New York."

High above a fighter jet streaked through the blue, followed by a rumble and a whine. Jeffrey barely discerned the split-tail and retractable wings of an F-4 Phantom. The staple of the revered Israeli Air Force. Before the Russian Migs came to Syria, the Phantoms were the fastest planes in the region. Back home Rabbi Berger had taught him the names and armaments and speeds of all the planes during his private preparations for his bar mitzvah. He wasn't sure why the rabbi would tell him these things along with the tunes and language he needed to learn to lead the Saturday morning service. Other kids he had asked had received no such instruction. He didn't care, studying planes had been loads more fun than the lessons.

His mom and dad stopped in front of a pizza place and scrutinized the menu displayed in the window.

"Pineapple?" his mom said.

A round of laughter rose from the throng of kids gathered round the television of the adjoining ice cream parlor. They wore striped Benetton shirts and Sasson jeans, their hair combed neat and stylish in ways Jeffrey never could achieve. He thought of his corduroys and Rob Roy shirts and shrugged off the memories of his classmates teasing him. Here, he was merely funny looking and different. Any laughter his way wouldn't be for being a Jew. Or for not looking Jewish because of his brown skin.

These Israeli kids ignored him as they ignored everything else but each other and the ice cream parlor's TV. On the screen wind blew trash around a dark, dirty street to the sounds of ominous synthesizer chords. Trashcan lids rattled. Blue sparks flashed and gave birth to brilliant white lightning and then the naked form of a man. Jeffrey recognized him as the big guy from the Conan movie.

The girls giggled and another round of laughter and comments in Hebrew arose.

"Dad, what's going on with that man?" Jeffrey asked, just as he would if they were at home watching movies on a rare Saturday afternoon respite.

His dad had been watching too. He kept his attention on the screen as he answered. "He's from the future."

"Why? How?"

"He was sent to fight his enemy before he grows up."

"Moishe, don't let him watch that garbage."

"It's *just* a movie, Rachel."

"Well, *just* stop watching and help us pick toppings."

While eating his pizza, Jeffrey thought about what he would do if he could travel through time. Would he go forward to after school so he could get out of the schoolyard and halfway home before he could be ganged up on? Maybe he'd go back to when the jackasses were in first grade and then beat *them* up. Maybe he'd give them a scare instead and a message not to bully him; a message they'd remember and understand when they grew up.

His mind drifted to the images of the Old City of Jerusalem he knew from postcards and history books. The ancient Wailing Wall of the Great Temple, the glistening copper top of the Dome of the Rock, and the Temple Mount. Tomorrow they would drive there. Along the way they were going to stop at some archeological sites. Abraham's Well. King Herod's Tomb.

Jeffrey rubbed the back of his hand. He thought saw something white there, like an after image of the sun.

A kid playing the Zaxxon video game near the parlor door yelled and slammed the side of the bulky console. The screen went blank.

"I never beat that robot before. Now I have to do it all over again," the kid yelled.

Jeffrey watched the screen turn blue then restart several game levels earlier.

"Dad?" Jeffrey asked. "In the movie, if the bad guys are going back in time, why don't they do it again and again until they get it right?"

His dad sipped soda through a straw and swallowed. "In this movie, the good guys broke the machine. But in real life, you can't send matter back in time, physics doesn't allow it."

"I know," Jeffrey said.

As part of his training, Jeffrey's parents had taught him about math, philosophy, great military battles in history, along with physics and Einstein's theories. Jeffrey knew because of relativity that it was possible to at least go forward in time. Just travel at the speed of light for one year in a direct line away from the earth and come back. You'd be two years older, but everyone on earth would be long into the future. It didn't work backwards, though.

"What about energy?" Jeffrey asked.

"Impossible. It's all impossible," his mom answered, chomping a pizza crust.

"Don't tell him it's impossible," Jeffrey's dad said. "You're going to stifle his mind. What about that professor, the one in the wheelchair who says particles can jump out of black holes? That's supposed to be impossible."

"Okay, there are theories, but it's all nuts to me. The numbers don't add up, and even if they did, technology is nowhere near able to do it. It will never be."

"The world is not all about technology," Jeffrey's father said to Jeffrey as if consoling him.

"Then how did we land a man on the moon? Prayer?" Jeffrey's Mom said.

"Maybe. That's how it started, when President Kennedy declared…"

"Well, we're not going to send a man traveling through time on the power of prayer."

"Not unless God wanted to," he said.

"What if enough people wanted to?" Jeffrey asked. "Rabbi Berger talked about what is possible with enough force of will."

Gunshots and an explosion filled the screen to the delight of the circle of teens.

"It's just a movie, Jeffrey. And we're talking a lot about it for one you won't let him see," Jeffrey's father said to his wife.

"It's rated R," she said.

"And the world is rated?"

"We didn't come to the Holy Land to watch this kind of stuff. Just think, this time tomorrow we'll be in Jerusalem."

The kid smacked the Zaxxon game again.

Jeffrey's hand moved to his chest. An image of the pizza place as a gaping, smoking, bombed-out ruin filled his mind. A slick of blood, so much blood, covered the tiled floor. Since being on the trip the visions were coming more frequently. Back home he'd been burdened with visions of burnt-out buses.

Smoke rising from the ancient buildings of the Old City. A fiery, red sky over a stark desert. And crying people. So many crying people. He hoped there was something wrong with him and what he was seeing weren't glimpses of real things. The notion that what he was seeing could actually be real made his stomach queasy. He'd fight any schoolyard bully. They came one at a time and didn't want to get hurt themselves. But how could he fight an enemy that surrounded you, attacked all at once, and would just keep coming and coming?

The alien thought made his stomach feel worse. With his finger he traced something on the back of his hand and stared at it blankly with the uncomfortable feeling of having something to say stuck on his tongue just out of reach of memory.

In the Pac-Man maze, the computer never tired, Jeffrey thought. The ghosts would chase you until you lost or walked away. Jeffrey pictured himself slamming the machine like the kid playing Zaxxon. If you could reset the machine, you could wipe the slate clean. To fight again. To live again. To try again. It wasn't winning, but it wasn't losing.

"What's my little warrior thinking now?" his father asked.

Jeffrey heard the question simultaneously spoken by the creepy man from the tomb.

Jeffrey turned, expecting to see him, but there was only the white sunlight sparkling in the Mediterranean waves and children bounding along the beach followed by jubilant, barking dogs.

Hot, mid-day sun baked the tour bus. While his parents and the tour group milled around a table of trinkets, Jeffrey carefully inched towards the unimpressive pile of ancient stones that was the entrance to King Herod's Tomb. The narrow entranceway, a gap between the grey blocks, was irresistible. A rope hung across it with a hand-written sign that read KEEP OUT in Hebrew, Arabic, and English. As he ducked under the rope, he felt an electric tingle on the back of his pushing him forward, pushing him to explore.

He waited until his parents were preoccupied by the guy selling falafel and his photogenic camel, then slipped into the cool damp darkness and hurried down the stairs.

He stepped out of the square of sunlight from the entrance, ventured a few steps into the tomb and halted. Dirty robes, bloody bandages, tin cans, and cigarette butts were strewn along the floor. A whiff of ozone lingered in the musty air.

He held his nose and turned a corner, but he didn't want to go too far into the darkness of a room that once had dead people or something in it.

Something rustled in the darkness of the room. Was someone else down here? A stray dog, or another excited explorer maybe?

"Hello," Jeffrey called.

No one answered.

A faint blue glow emanated from the corner of the chamber across from him. Jeffrey rubbed his eyes. As his vision began to adjust, he made out that the room was large and square and empty except for the rubbish.

Something moved. In the corner a pile of rags and robes were moving. They rose from the floor and assembled into a tattered, human shape.

"Take my hand." The voice came from the shape.

Jeffrey thought he should be afraid but found that he just wanted to watch.

It ambled toward him. He couldn't make out a face but saw

that the source of the blue glow was light leaking from the dusty wrappings.

"You will be safe with me," it said.

Jeffrey eyed the path to the stairs but instead of bolting stood transfixed.

"Ephraim Ben-Moshe. Please. Listen to me."

He felt the surge of adrenaline but still did not run. The thing reached out its hand and grabbed him. He knew he should struggle but only focused on how his wrist felt so cold.

"Yes, yes," it said. "You remember I told you not to run. We've been down this path before. So many times. I fear this may be the last. Come with me to the desert."

"The desert? What? Who are you? Why are you doing this?"

"No, no, no. You have to remember. We're running out of time. You're going to die, again. You need to listen—"

Jeffrey twisted his arm to break the man's grip. He gathered his breath to yell for help as blue light spilled from beneath the man's displaced wrappings.

"Jeffrey? Are you down there?" his father called.

Something about the blue light was so familiar.

"Yes, yes. Please remember," it said. "There isn't time."

Jeffrey stopped struggling. He allowed the man to turn his palm down.

"Next time you will remember everything. You must. You must come with me."

He traced on the back of Jeffrey's right hand with one bandaged finger. A glowing letter, a Hebrew letter, appeared there.

Jeffrey's father called for him again. People were descending through the entrance.

The robes and rags collapsed to the floor. The letter on Jeffrey's hand faded then disappeared.

Jeffrey's father stormed through the dark.

"Here. I'm over here, Dad."

"When we tell you to stay close…"

"Dad, there was this…"

He wanted to say, *There was a man dressed in rags who told me I was going to die*, but he held his words.

His father gently lifted him and touched his forehead with the back of his hand. "You feel warm. Water. Get my son some water," he called.

His dad slung Jeffrey's arm around his shoulder and helped him up the stairs. Looking back, Jeffrey saw what looked like a man hovering above the pile of rags. He was naked and appeared made of light like one of those afterimages you see when you look at the sun. Glowing blue Hebrew letters danced over his body. Then the man disappeared, the light winked out with him, and the chamber returned to black.

Jeffrey drank the Capri-Sun juice pouch even though he didn't want to. The silver bag was like an astronaut's drink; another fascinating thing they didn't have back home. He knew he should hydrate. He told himself that once the body feels thirst it is already dehydrated but didn't know where the thought came from, which disturbed him. His dad insisted he skip the rest of the days' activities. Thus, the tour bus had to go directly to their Jerusalem hotel, their next destination, to drop him off. Everyone else wasn't very happy about the turn of events. He didn't blame them. He still wanted to see more old sites.

"We should have never come, Moishe," Jeffrey's mom whispered.

"You knew this time would come when we took him in," Jeffrey's dad whispered back.

"The years passed so fast."

"He's not safe anymore, Rachel."

Jeffrey wondered what they meant.

The bus pulled into the lot in front of the hotel. It looked just like one in New York, only a lot less crowded and there were palm trees. The lobby was populated by impeccably dressed staff of many ethnicities attending to a group of priests in heavy robes and another group of somber old Jews in dark suits with long curly strands of hair. A bellman approached and took their bags to the elevator on a shiny gilded cart.

The elevator was made of glass, and Jeffrey could see the mysterious buildings of the Old City as he rose. He even glimpsed the big soccer stadium in the outskirts of the New City.

The bellman wheeled the cart out of the elevator and led them to their room. He put the key, a strange plastic card, in the slot in their door.

"Do you think we can see everything from our room?" Jeffrey asked.

"One way to find out," his dad said.

Jeffrey pushed through the door. The world exploded into booms. Jeffrey thought "firecrackers," then his chest erupted into a ball of heat. He looked down and saw he was soaked in blood. A swarm of faces buzzed over him. Strong arms held him. Knives arced past his face. It hurt more than any schoolyard fight. He struggled and screamed and screamed, though all he could hear was the voice of the ghostly man from the tomb saying, "You're going to die."

His name is Avi Ben-Avram, Jeffrey thought. The realization he knew the man's name, that he was certain of it, filled him with a blooming sense of wrong along with the blinding pain. With the last of his strength he screamed, not in pain, but from the sense someone was cheating, like someone had jacked up an arcade game instead of letting it play out, only a million times worse. He tried to struggle but found he could not lift his arms. There was so much more of the world to see, and a sense of something dreadfully important he was supposed to do pushing him to fight, but instead he knew he was about to die and then the last of his life left him, again.

The entire bunker shook from the explosions above ground. Red wine sloshed from an ornate silver cup onto the white table linen. All that remained of the leadership of the State of Israel remained in this bunker carved deep into the Negev's ancient caves. Avi Ben-Avram pictured the ruined buildings of venerable Old Jerusalem. The modern architecture of Tel Aviv had also been reduced to rubble. The last remnants of the army were scattered and hunkered down in positions that would soon be overrun.

So this is it, Avi thought.

Time after time he had been sent for the child. To save him from their enemies. To bring him to his purpose. When he failed, as he did again and again and again, he was sent again and again and again. He would go as many times as they would send him. Israel had to remain. But now that sense of infinite time, of infinite tries was gone.

Between his full dress uniform and the mask and gloves, all of him was covered. He yearned to feel the metal of an Uzi and the sand and the hot desert sun again. But he knew his purpose was here now. The old instinct to touch his wife's hand overcame him. Rachel glanced at him, her face a stoic mask he knew too well. She had agreed when he told her what he wanted to volunteer for. She too knew the future was more important than any one family, as much as the idea pained them.

Grand Rabbi Yavin Baram sat across the table from her, his long face and grizzled smoke-grey beard betraying no sign of the direness of the moment. He poured wine into silver cups, passed the first cup to Rabbi Lubof, who in turn passed it to General Bela, then to retired Admiral Charles Francis Wesson, the American. It went around the table to Rachel. She passed it to him. It was empty. Empty like the space beneath his uniform and gloves. Nothing of him left to take the wine. All that remained was the energy that once powered his body, now held together by force of will, the prayers of the Grand Rabbis, leaders, and remnants of the nation. He was a point of focus keeping that energy in the shape of a man. And he was what Israel needed to save and steer the child.

Avi accepted the cup. He pictured the words of the prayers dancing beneath his glove. Light spilled from beneath his sleeve causing the cup to cast a double shadow.

Another explosion rocked the table. Stones fell from the tunnel's mouth leading out of the bunker. The rock hewn passages beyond were crowded with carefully stacked Torah scrolls salvaged from the ruined temples of Tel Aviv and Haifa, from Yaffa, Rehasim, and Oranim. How could it be that these places are gone? he thought.

Muttered prayers carried from the darkness of the passageways. Avi pictured the rabbis, their long hair and beards and robes rustling in the shadows as they prayed in the near dark.

They kept the prayer, the chain of intention unbroken and his energy tethered. When the last of them ceased, he would be gone.

"The next time we sit at this table, may the Hand of Fire be among us," Rabbi Baram said, his voice filling the cold, rocky chamber. Its strength helped Avi believe.

Amens rang around the table.

After the blessing they would send him back again before they were overrun. This would be the last time.

He tried to conjure a memory of his extended family. Like all the lives he'd known that were lost to wars, they were distant fires, burning still but somewhere far away, their faces too hazy to discern. His only clear thoughts were of the future. Faith and duty. This was all that was left for him. They knew. It was why they chose him.

"It's not too late," Lubof yelled at the American. "You can do something to make this stop."

"The President is praying for you," Wesson said calmly. "He is confident God's will shall be done."

Prophecy. Revelations. All we are to the Americans are sacred cows, thought Avi.

He recognized the detached look on Wesson's face. Everyone believes their beliefs are the right ones, the only ones, he thought. But our truth must be true, look what has become of me. How else could this be?

"You are going to die here with us," Lubof said to Wesson.

"It is written that the Lord said the Children of Israel will end in flames and then His son will return again," the Admiral replied, more to himself than to anyone.

Avi knew the prophecies. The world ending in ice and fire. Their enemies had tried and tried but no nuclear fire had come to Israel. They had smuggled warheads on barges into Haifa's harbor. They had lobbed missiles into their cities. One was even built in a Jerusalem basement. Every device did not ignite. Each had been carefully inspected and dismantled with no reason found for the failures. It was as if the Hand of God reserved the right to light holy fire. Israel's own nuclear arsenal remained hidden. But they were useless. All their tests failed. They bluffed the world that any attack on Israel would be met with nuclear destruction with their policy of neither admitting nor denying their "arsenal." A program began deep beneath the quiet desert sands to find the one the scholars called the Hand of Fire. The child. Ephraim Ben-Moshe.

Christian, Arab, and Jewish mystics gathered in secret, studied separately and together. In the Old City. At the Vatican. In New York and Chicago. The Dead Sea Scrolls, Lost Gospels, and ancient Arabian writings foretold his coming.

All were in agreement that a "Hand of Fire" someday would come to determine their fate. Only *he* could end the long conflict of the region. Only *he* could bring the "cleansing fire." The dissent was over whether this meant utter destruction and who or what this hand was. Kings and Presidents and holy men and government leaders wanted to destroy such a game-changing figure. Others wanted to protect him. The Rabbis identified him as the child Ephraim Ben-Moshe.

The boy had been taken to America to grow up in safety. Avi pictured the glowing letter he had traced on the boy's hand. He *was* just a boy, yet he had been hunted and killed, rescued and saved, time and time again.

Rabbi Baram chanted the final passage of the prayer. The notes of the ancient melody were arranged in mystical intervals, each sound, each space between holding cosmic significance.

Avi noticed the glisten of held back tears in Rachel's eyes

even though they'd had so many goodbyes. These were tears for lives that would never be.

The table shifted out of focus. The cavern and everyone in it blurred together into an indiscernible swirl. Avi felt the cadences and descending progressions of the hymns circle, pulling on his phantom limbs and chest, drawing what was left of him out of the chamber and into the tunnel. Then time parted like the sea for Moses. He fell into a swell of prayer and the current took him.

———

Something moved in the darkness. Jeffrey's elbows tingled and his forearms trembled. A man wrapped in tattered robes and rags ambled from the shadows toward him.

"Take my hand," it said.

A blue light, sharper than any video game screen, glowed from under its wrappings.

Jeffrey eyed the path to the stairs and readied to run. The figure shrugged off its robe. Spirals of unwinding wrappings and linens fell to the ground revealing a man of glowing blue light.

Trains of Hebrew letters slithered around the man's arms and legs and all over, trembling and white and ablaze like starlight.

"Come with me," the glowing man said.

An image of the letter on his hand rushed back to Jeffrey.

Footsteps scuffled on the chamber stairs.

"Are you down there?" Jeffrey's dad called.

A heartbeat passed. In a wink the blue man appeared in front of Jeffrey, so close he could read the white letters crisscrossing over him like living bands of tefillin.

"There isn't time," the man said. "We've been down this road before."

Jeffrey knew him.

The man gripped his hand and traced a letter on his palm.

His name is Avi Ben-Avram, Jeffrey thought. How do I know that?

Letters lifted from the man's arms and snaked themselves onto Jeffrey's arm. He wanted to scream, but he only watched the letters flow over his body and deliberately wind around him.

Trails of words raced over him, moving faster and faster, then too fast to be seen, all the letters, all the words becoming one shining armor of light.

"Hope at last," Avi said.

"I heard something. Maybe he's down here," Jeffrey's father yelled. "Is there a flashlight in the bus?"

Jeffrey felt inspired and excited and scared all at once, a feeling akin to the resolve that filled him when he realized there was no escape from a schoolyard fight as everyone closed in.

Images flooded in. Stacks of Torahs in caves. Rabbis praying in the near dark. Missiles leaving silos in the desert sand.

Jeffrey's father tramped down the steps. A flashlight beam crossed the dusty rays of sunlight.

Jeffrey followed Avi into the darkness then paused just long enough to catch his father's eye, Avi's light from behind spilling around him in a blue corona.

Jeffrey's dad watched them recede but did not follow.

"He's gone," he said to himself.

Jeffrey heard the chamber fill with voices but did not look back. With each step more memories returned. The chamber led into vast spiraling labyrinths beneath the desert. He found he knew the way. He kept running. A sense of calm washed over him along with the feeling he could run the maze forever and the ghosts would never catch him.

Avi took Jeffrey into the isolation of the Negev with its caves, mountain hideaways, desert tunnels, and archeological sites forgotten in the sand. He answered the boy's questions with training. He taught him prayers, the secret meanings of words, and histories of things that had not yet come to pass.

Jeffrey found that the video games and music that he once thought he missed no longer mattered.

"Take me to the future," Jeffrey asked during one of his geography lessons.

"There is only one way," Avi said.

Jeffrey had a hard time understanding nuclear fusion and fission, at first. And an even harder time believing that nuclear fire would not ignite in the land so many held onto as holy. The end points of all the complex lessons were simple and always the same. He was prophesized to be the one, the only match that could ignite Armageddon.

One desert night after a marathon session of geography during the quiet passing into dawn, Jeffrey watched a kangaroo rat hurry to and from its hiding place in the base of the wall of a ruin of a Roman outpost. He thought of his parents' sacrifice. How they gave up the comforts and blissful ignorance of American life to take him in. He watched Avi standing on a rocky ridge nearby, motionless but for the prayers spiraling over him. The hopes of people like them and their sacrifices. That is what matters, Jeffrey thought as he fell asleep under the lightening sky. A nation. A future. A chance.

He awoke to find a bundle of newspapers tied with string near him in the desert sand. The sun was up; heat hovered above the night-cooled ground, but there was no trace of who had made the delivery. The articles detailed the regional conflicts. Murders. Bombings. Military atrocities. The ebb and flow of escalations and retaliations between Israel and its neighbors. Five years passed this way. Training. Studying. No outside contact but for occasional drops in the night.

Day after day they trained in seclusion. Moving from place to place in secret. Jeffrey's young man's body transformed into an adult and was sculpted into that of a soldier. His mind sharpened and filled with the ways of sages and military tacticians.

One dawn, when the shadows from the newly arrived sun were just beginning to grow, a lone Israeli soldier arrived at the mouth of the mountain cave that was his most recent of ever-changing homes. The young man had a message and was visibly shaken by its brevity.

"It has begun," the soldier had been instructed to say.

Jeffrey had seen the planes overhead. From his visions he knew what came next. He hoped he could find another way. A way out of the certainty of ruin and blood. He rose and went to prepare himself. The day had come. It was time to go to the rabbis in the caves.

War raged. Israel's enemies learned from their past mistakes. They learned to put aside their differences. They learned to fight together. They learned they could deal with each other once their common goal was achieved, their shared vow to drive Israel into the sea.

Battered Israeli soldiers retreated into the Mediterranean, their weapons at chest level in an attempt to keep the last of their rounds dry. Missiles arced from the red sky into the waves throwing up showers of hot metal and steaming water. Approaching tanks grumbled behind the bombed-out seaside condos and crumbling promenade that had once been the gem of Tel Aviv.

Waves red with blood flowed through Avi-Ben Avram, his form making the stained water glow sickly pink. He could do nothing but watch the commanders attempt to rally their men to reach the shore. They knew this was their end, but they did not want to go down in the sea.

Bullets passed through him. They did nothing. He felt nothing. He would continue to exist until the last shred of belief of the last person praying him into existence ceased. Until then there was hope, however slim. The Hand of Fire would determine what would come to be. It might be that the land could still be saved. That some might survive. Soon he would know.

Artillery fell from the sky to the beach. When the smoke cleared, red foam frothed atop the waves, washing blood out to sea.

Dark purple wine sloshed in Rabbi Baram's goblet. His hand shook, but not from the explosions above.

Avi led Jeffrey Stein, Ephraim Ben-Moishe, The Hand of Fire, into the cave. Together they crossed the chamber and stood at the table across from him and the leaders and other rabbis, priests, and imams. Tall and lean with stringy hair and dark, weathered skin he looked like just another desert nomad.

"You are he?" Rabbi Baram asked. "You look nothing like I expected of the boy whose life we predicted and charted."

Jeffrey did not reply. He held out his hand.

Rabbi Baram held out the case that contained the ignitions for their nuclear arsenal.

"Did you do as I said?" Jeffrey asked.

"Yes," the rabbi said.

Avi nodded in confirmation.

Jeffrey took the case and without fanfare or another word returned into the tunnel from which he came.

Avi and Jeffrey emerged from the networks of tunnels into the bright desert sun, the glare making Avi's glowing form difficult to see.

All the lines of the past had come to this, Jeffrey thought. Hundreds of paths. Thousands of lives. No matter how they twist, they all come to the same point, to this moment.

"If I do this," Jeffrey asked. "How will I be remembered? A hero? A savior? A madman? A villain?"

"Does it matter anymore?" Avi said.

Jeffrey opened the case, revealing the electronics inside. The codes had already been entered. The protocols followed. The warheads ready and armed. All he had to do was turn the key and press the center button to send the arsenal airborne.

He pressed the center button.

Across the desert hundreds of missiles shot into the sky in

clouds of sand and smoke. Jeffrey didn't know where they would land. They had not been aimed.

The divine hand would do as it chose; be it with duds that would not ignite or nuclear fire.

"If they are right, tell me they will all restart someday," Jeffrey said. "Tell me they will rebuild. That they will begin a new history."

"May God's will be done," said Avi.

Jeffrey felt no sense of accomplishment or relief. Only the emptiness that came from knowing he had completed his purpose and that *this* moment was all there was, that *this* was how it would end for him. He had outrun the unstoppable enemy and done the impossible. Now at the end of the maze it didn't feel like winning. It didn't feel like anything at all.

Glowing letters of prayer danced around Avi's form. Missiles sailed in the heavens above. Jeffrey watched their exhaust trails spread out across the sky, like fingers from an outstretched hand.

phantom constellations

Anza-Borrego Desert, California. 1992.

"Once you visit the desert you never look at the sky the same again, no matter where you are," Chase says to me. "You'll see."

"I believe you."

And I do. After the bluff ahead the world is nothing but unblemished, powder-blue.

In the rear-view I watch her attempt to pass her cigarette to Harrison. She's so high she misses that his attention is captured by the almost-dusk-time shadows of all the cactus and brush on the sand and winding road.

Her not-dyed blond hair and light eyes come from her mother's side. Her mom met her dad when she was stationed over in Miramar, she told us last night over rolled tacos in the joint across from the Photo-mat where she works. Her height's from her mother too, she said. Skin color and distinct nose from her dad. Along with the knowledge of all the things that make Southern California, Southern California—the beach, the desert, the food, the drugs. You have to try the tamales Dad brings up from his abuela in Mexico, she told Harrison who wasn't enamored with the "taco-sticks," at all. She taps his leg insistently causing the cigarette head to fall. Neither notice. Har's framing the endless open-space and sky moping that he's out of film, I can tell. I wonder if he's going to start in on that how-nothing-ever-goes-right-for-him business again. Maybe he'll recognize that finding Chase was something going right for him, above and beyond the free film. She says she loves him. If she doesn't really see him, does she even really know him though?

Moon's trying to open the passenger window. The child lock has her stymied—her inept fumbling the opposite of my first glimpse of her last night back at Chase's place. I didn't believe my eyes—thought I was looking at Chase standing in the doorway, silently watching me, though I'd just watched her lustily "retire" to her room with Har. Was this Chase's twin? So the same in so many ways except for the glaring opposites of Moon's dark hair and alabaster skin.

"Oh, okay, we're here. Stop here, stop here," Chase says.

Beyond the metal rail separating the pavement from the unfathomable drop, the view is unimpeded for miles and miles and miles. Myriad nuances of color and every shade of brown and white and gray. Winding roads snake through border towns to the edge of the wild spaces; everything washed out and hazy from the heavy sun almost ready to set—the lone shape burning in the perfect sky.

The plan is to watch it here before heading off down into that view to have a campfire dinner and night under the stars.

Moon's figured out the window and has it open before I have the truck stopped in the parking spot. A blast of hot air sends the chemical note of her sunscreen along with the aroma of sage and brush and ozone at me. I cut the engine. Without the AC blowing we realize we are surrounded by… stillness. All four of us are taking it in. The motion of birds on the scrub and the gentle breeze doesn't break the sensation. Moon adjusts her light-blue half-shirt and white terry cloth shorts and slides herself halfway out the window. I gently touch her leg and tell her to be careful. She responds with a flirtatious wriggle of her hips.

"Its amazing out here," she says. She makes eye contact with me in the side mirror, sticks out her tongue and taps the tip twice with her slender, manicured index finger. "You want to? You really should join us."

Her silver-sparkle-polished nail catches the sun.

"I'm good," I say. "Still good. Still the one driving."

Sixty-eight days sober and counting is better than good. Taking care of myself. I agreed to this jaunt because I'm taking care of them.

I eye the white gift bow I've left on the rear view. I'm done letting people down. Every day since I've been out has been work and studying. Switching the NY plates for California is the final thing left.

"Holy shit, look! Look at that!" Chase says.

Moon twists herself to see. Harrison is up against the window.

"What the hell," he says.

The occupants of the two other cars are out and at the rail gawking at a long white line of a cloud that has just appeared out of nowhere in the sky. The first thing I think is that's one of those ropy, high-the-hell-up-there clouds. But aren't they always in big groups? This one is hanging low right in front of the sun.

I watch the line… bending. And… inflating. In seconds it's become a bow arcing over the valley.

We pour out of my truck into air alive with kinetic certainty.

The bow folds over and over and becomes a puffy mass. A storm cloud? A giant undulating herald of desert rain? Whatever it is its forming and reforming its contour with the impossible speed of a time lapsed photo; glowing oranges and pinks and reds, all the setting sun's colors emanating from it. Brighter than any fireworks. It's all so surreal because the angles don't seem right for the reflection or projection or whatever the hell I am looking at.

"Hell of a thunderhead," one of the other onlookers says.

"Ha. No thunderhead, look at the sky. Folks over at the air force base are laughing their asses off right now."

I hear the words but there is only this feeling of... stillness. There is only the feeling of... desert air alive with a coming storm? There is only a wave of... comfort...my bones telling me everything is all right. There is only the shape...that is no shape... that is the cloud.

"I want to stay this way," Chase says. "I want to live this way, right?"

Before I can decide if she has made a statement or asked a question, I laugh in recognition that I know exactly what she means.

Across the lot I hear the word "right" spoken by the other people.

Moon hands me a boxy disposable camera, one of the green panorama ones from the supermarkets. "Take a picture of me, get it all."

The cloud is a convex half-sphere. A wave. A giant tidal wave rolling towards the bluff.

Moon poses, slightly lifting one long leg and holding her

back-length hair in a messy bun. Chase and Harrison are staring into the sky, standing alarmingly still.

There is nothing wrong here, I tell myself. There is only beauty. Beneath the feeling of peace, part of me is screaming. I'm the life guard. I'm the adult here today. Fuck this.

I manage to wrangle all three of them back inside the truck. I hit the button to send up the windows and crank the air. I fumble my keys into the ignition, and that's when Harrison pushes his door open, beelines to the guard rail, and climbs.

Harrison has put the rolls of black and white film up front and is scouring the Photo-mat's aisles for a frame Nehru's tasked him to procure as a prop for his shoot.

"Do you believe in love at first sight," the counter-girl says to me absently as she watches Har shop.

On her name tag "Chase" is hand-written over "Chelsea".

I'm in my blue work clothes. My name's embroidered on my chest. Came straight from my shift to some bar on the Pacific Beach strip to meet Har, who came to see me. First time since I got out. When they gave me my stuff back with it there was a letter he'd sent to Mom and Dad's back home. He'd scored a real job. A good one as an assistant to a director on a real Hollywood movie they are shooting nearby in Ocean Beach.

Har comes to the counter with a frame and actually introduces himself in a rare display of extraverted-ness and boyish charisma.

"How much?"

"It's yours," Chase says.

"Really? Is this because I'm the only one here without a name tag?"

"For you, doll, yeah really. Anything. Take it. And take the film."

"Whoa. Guess this means I'm gonna have to keep the dough Nehru gave me."

"Who?"

"My boss. Nehru Casteltinni." he says.

I wince at how pretentious he sounds. Chase remains starry-eyed.

"I'm about to close up. Want to go for tacos? You can use the dough for that. Cool?"

"I've never had," Har says.

"What? You've never had Mexican food?"

"We're sort of newcomers. From New York," I say.

Chase locks up the place. We're close enough to the beach to smell the ocean on the night air. Har steps into the street.

"Hey you can't do that, that's jaywalking," Chase says.

She leads us to the corner where we cross the four-lane road then double back to the taco joint. Har disapproves of this route but remains quiet. He must like Chase. I hope he doesn't go off on how unfair he thinks he's being treated by Nehru.

I notice we're the only white guys as soon as we're through the door. Chase and Har are rambling on like they've known each other forever, oblivious to the glances from disapproving faces.

We sit at a linoleum-topped table. Chase orders and within minutes three iced-teas and three plates of fried rolled tacos topped with loads of guac are in front of us.

"Why does this iced-tea taste like... fruit?" Har asks.

"This is California, baby," Chase says.

Har pushes guacamole around with a fork and I realize what a big baby he is and wonder why people ever fall into his orbit.

"Taco-sticks" and iced-tea is a bust so, food unfinished, we load into my truck, both of them hopping into the back seat. Chase directs me down the Five to Chinatown, to please Har.

"San Diego's so clean and tiny compared to New York," I say. "And no traffic."

Neither reply. They're kissing. I interrupt with a cough when we hit the city.

"This is Chinatown?" Har says.

"Well, Old Town is more picturesque," Chase says.

"What's Old Town?"

"All Mexican food," I say. "You wouldn't like it."

The entrance to the Chinese place is flanked by two dragon statues covered in aging golden paint. Inside is dimly lit and inviting. We dine on Kung Pao chicken and black tea, real tea, to Har's liking beneath a ceiling mural of an inky blue sky crowded with stylized old-fashioned golden stars.

Chase clicks her worn chopsticks together, wooden ones, not disposables.

"Oh, how many stories those chopsticks can tell," I say.

"See," Har says. "My buddy here's a poet. You can't teach that."

"Oh, so you're in film, too?"

"No, I'm a plumber. On my way to being a master plumber. I'm studying for the exam to go to school to get my MBA too."

"He's being humble," Har says. "Only reason he isn't a film maker because he's too busy being the real deal. Life. He's living it for real."

"Wow, who knew? Two New York guys here in California," Chase says. "Why'd you come out, Harrison?"

There's a pause and I can feel Har's gears spinning, thinking about back home.

"I came here for rehab, not college," I say, so Har doesn't have to answer. "It was my ticket away from brutal New York. I'm an addict. The place got me into a trade, so I stayed."

I think hearing my naked truth out loud puts a scare in Har. Up until six weeks ago he was living in his mom's basement among impossible clutter. His screenplays and story boards and VHS tapes stacked among the detritus of his broken family living above, all the broken things not thrown away, only accumulating, poison anchors adding weight to lives already sinking, sinking, sunk. Just thinking about the numb silences and wrenching screaming matches and worse has my stomach unhappy.

"I'm a nomad," Har says.

With a glance he instructs me not to counter him with the truth.

"I'm really actually a vagabond. A traveling bartender—but I took this job shooting this film."

"Right, your film."

"Well, it's a Nehru Casteltinni film. Ya know, my boss, so it's kinda his film but he's all coked-up and partied-out so I'm setting most of the shots and doing all of the leg work. I'm sure the producers are going to credit me. I didn't even think the fiend was going to give us this time off for Thanksgiving week. So hey, my first time in San Diego first chance I had to visit my man here."

He pats me on the back. For a second I believe him, that he's okay, living out our childhood dreams of making movies. And that he's going to ride into the sunset for the both of us.

"Oh, you have to come to the desert then if this is your first time here! We all have to go. Let's do it! My Dad used to always take us thanksgiving time."

After dinner we wind up back at her place, a little low-rise, cute but in disrepair, in a cluster of similar low-rises a couple of blocks from the beach, back in Pacific Beach near the Photo-mat. The main room we enter into has a surprisingly stuffed book case, a coffee table with a full ash tray and a TV hooked up to Sega. I don't see a couch but there are lots of big pillows.

Chase takes Har by the arm and leads him to a door to the right of the kitchen area which comprises the far wall opposite the entrance.

"We're going to retire and get to know each other better, she says. "You gonna crash here?"

They don't wait for me to answer.

I go to the bookcase and decide what I'm gonna do. It's full of astrology books, self-help stuff, new age titles, and a ton of fantasy paperbacks. I pick up a bottle of fancy-looking perfume from among the stacks.

As I smell the cap, I realize someone's watching me. I turn and see a woman in a black silk robe with long black hair and pale skin leaning in the doorway opposite the one Chase and Har disappeared into. For a second I think I'm looking at Chase. A dark-haired, ethereal, poised and confident Chase. We stare at each other silently.

"Hey boss," the woman finally says, then shuffles to the fridge.

There's a big yellow sun on the back of her robe. And from something about the way she closes the distance I can tell she's using. There's a sound from her room. Someone's in there with her.

"Smells better on my skin," she says.

Everything about her—every motion, the way her gaze lingers is saying, "Do you want to join us?" Maybe it's just me—projecting—maybe it's just my wanting playing tricks on me.

Joining her would be oblivion. Joining her would be to taste the sweetness of nothingness. The sweetness of lost time. Cool heat eclipsing my mind's questions. Will I pass the exam? Will I make master plumber? Will I get into the union? Will I ever start my own shop? How long until I take over the insurance payments on the truck to show my folks I'm not a waste.

"I said it smells better on my skin. I never understand why boys like video games so much."

She's still speaking as she returns to the darkness of her room. I distract myself by looking away and recounting multiple choice questions in my head. I don't glance over even after I hear the door close.

Sometime in the night I'm woken by someone walking past me. I've passed out on the pillows. An older woman in a black pencil skirt is buttoning her white business shirt on the way out the door. I drift back to sleep.

I wake again after what feels like only minutes to someone kicking my side. A different woman is standing there. California is the land of beautiful women is the first thought my sleeping self manages.

"I warned you already," she says in a thick Russian accent. "No staying the night. Now I'm going to have to shoot you in the face."

My eyes are blurry but I think she's holding a gun.

"Um, I'm Chase's friend I've never been here before."

She *is* holding a gun. And a lit cigarette in her other hand.

"Seriously. My friend is in there with Chase now. We met at the Photo-mat."

"Oh, you have New York accent. And that is your New York truck?"

"Yes, yes."

This seems to satisfy her.

"All you American boys look the same."

She takes another disdainful look at me. Then trudges to the fridge for a beer and disappears into Moon's room.

———

In the morning all is chipper and cheer and sunshine. I don't see a reason to mention my night time encounters. Whoever they were, they're gone and Chase and Moon are a flurry of cigarettes and coffee and scrambled eggs. Chase calls Har "Honey" and "Dear" and "My film maker." Moon calls me "Boss."

"We've been up early, loaded your truck with supplies," Har says.

His smiles seem for real. We're going to the desert. He feels like my dear old friend again. The guy from the block I grew up dreaming with. It's been so long since I knew what it felt like to do something just for the hell of it.

———

Not far outside of San Diego, all the small towns, and windmills and aqueducts have me realizing that these West Coast cites really are built on desert.

Peter Gabriel's song San Jacinto is on the radio. Three fighter jets in formation soar across the sky perpendicular to the road. Chase says this is quite a common sight. And adds, "Mexico's like ten miles, that way. My Dad knows the routes the drug planes fly, low and close to the mountains to avoid radar."

"Oh yeah, can't *wait* to meet your dad," Har says.

Chase punches him playfully.

The back seat is their honeymoon palace and they have the cliched glow of those who have just slept together for the first time. At least Chase does. I see hints of the stress of the shoot on Har's face. In a day or two he'll be back to it. And I can tell his plum job isn't as plum as he's making it out to be. I want to help.

"So, I was wondering if you are going to ask about your contract," I say gently.

"That's not how it works," Har snaps.

The radio fades in and out in a pattern that sounds like morse-code.

"Well, I think that's how it works," Moon says to me, softly. "You're a good friend for telling him."

"I don't want to upset him."

There is an uneasy silence as we roll past the last buildings of some small town and are again flanked by desolate scrublands.

"Without rules. Without boundaries, I'm just a whore," she says.

"I can hear you back here," Har says.

"Then you hear me talking about myself," she replies. "I'm not a prostitute. I'm an escort. The difference is I choose. I choose *who*. I choose *what* I do. Or if I do anything at all. You choose who *you* want to be, okay?"

I'm worried Har is going to pop. And what am I doing? In a car with a girl we met at the Photo-mat and her escort roommate who uses. Would Har kill me if I came up with some excuse to call this all off?

"Nehru does treat me like his little whore," Har says calmly.

I hear all the hurt he's felt in his entire life in each of his words. I know he's grateful that I'm not turning around, he knows I'm thinking about it.

"Okay," Chase says. "Two more miles or next town whichever comes first and no more talking business, okay? Hey, Moon. You ready?"

Moon takes out a square of white paper perforated into tabs from her tiny purse. There are dozens of little yellow suns printed on it. She and Chase open their mouths wide and say "ahhh" through their giggles. Moon tears off two tabs. They each place one of the tabs on each other's tongue.

"You with us?" Chase says to Har.

"Nah, I'm good," he says and laughs.

I recognize this laugh. It says 'oh look what craziness we have got ourselves into' and is a further check to make sure I'm not going to rain on his parade.

"The desert is the best," Chase says to me. "I love it there it even when straight. This way it is so much better though. First time in the desert I think you guys should."

"You in?" Moon says.

The last time I ever used I didn't OD, I took a bad needle—who knows what was in it. I was feeling cold and numb and managed to call my dad before flopping down into a tub of running water to try to warm up. Mom and Dad standing over me, fishing me out, was the last thing I remembered before the emergency room where they restarted my heart.

"I'm taking care of him," is all I manage to say.

"Thought so," she says and rolls down the window. She slips

her sneakers off and joyously sticks her legs out the window into the wind.

———

Har climbs over the guard rail onto the rocky outcrop before the drop as the cloud rolls over him and then us.

For a minute all is smoke. Like inside a plane breaking the cloud layer. Then it is gone. Impossibly fast. We open the doors and check the sky all around. The valley. The mountain pass we came from. Nothing. Just the sunset's last rays dying in a perfectly clear sky.

One of the onlookers is having a smoke. The thick wisps strike me as obscene. We run to the guard rail. Har is perched on the crumbly ledge, clutching his knees, with nothing separating him from the drop.

We help him over the rail. He's crying.

"You okay—"

"Give me all the drugs," he says.

"Right on," Moon says and opens her little purse.

"Come on, no," I say.

"Yes. All of it," Har says.

I snatch the square of paper from Moon.

"Careful how you touch that," she says with a giggle.

Har snatches it, rips off a corner and stuffs it in his mouth before I grab it back and return it to Moon.

"Did you see that shit," he says.

"Welcome to California, baby," Chase says and the girls laugh.

Great, now I'm babysitting three people.

We head down the mountain into the desert, there's nothing else to do.

Chase and Moon are hyper focused on all the boulders and cactus we pass as we descend. A coyote that darts across the road changes their giggles to a round of intense whispers. Har is telling us in great detail and in one long, long never-ending sentence how he's going to make breakfast for dinner over the fire. I can't stop thinking about the cloud. Is this the way people deal with… happenings like this or is it just the drugs?

We roll past a rectangular bank of showers and restrooms into the empty campsite. Who wants to be outside in the cold for Thanksgiving? With the sun gone it is hard to believe the day's heat was ever with us.

There're spaces delineated for dozens of cars, each with a roof-sheltered picnic table and fire pit. With no other buildings, no lights except the stars, the landscape is a sprawling city of cactus and rock etched into the warm, glowing sky.

I'm impressed that Har and Chase loaded my truck with an iron pan and eggs and pancake mix. Along with water, and firewood, and two tents. No sleeping bags though.

Breakfast for dinner is a masterstroke. And then without cleaning up, Har and Chase disappear into their tent they've set up in their own camp spot a few spaces away.

Moon and I clean up and set up our tent next to my truck in a spot with a view looking out on the star-lit silhouettes of desert plants against the rocky hills ringing the camp site. Inside and zipped up it is still cold; we have no jackets or long pants. I retrieve the wool Mexican weaved beach blanket I keep my truck and we huddle under it.

Moon rolls over and faces me. I'm very aware of the softness of her skin touching mine. Her leg gently draped on me. Her shallow, steady breath.

"This is nice," she says. "My girlfriend doesn't kiss me anymore."

"Russian girl? Carries a gun."

"Yeah—"

"Met her in the middle of the night. She threatened to shoot me in the face."

"Oh. She's like that. Possession is part of love. Isn't it? The last part to let go…"

"You're letting go? She won't let go?"

"I don't know. Sometimes when things are over and you're still holding on the only things left to grasp are the shadows. You know, you could really do good as a plumber. I could run the books. I have these great business suits."

She presses tighter to me. It is good to be warm. To be held. I like that her face—her lips—are so close to mine. It isn't that I don't want to kiss her. A kiss is never just a kiss. With it comes all of her. And all the reasons the addictions have her. Someday, I'll be alone and look back at this moment with regret, I tell myself as I roll out from under the blanket.

"Long day. I'm hitting the shower."

"Watch out for rattlesnakes," she says.

I retrieve the roll of quarters from the glove box in my truck and cross the empty campsite.

I have enough coins for little packets of soap and shampoo and leave my clothes by the vending machine in the vestibule. I put the rest of my quarters in the box next to the faucets; warm water cascades onto my sand and grime and dried-sweat coated skin. There are droplets of white light glistening in the rivulets. I look up to see if this is something to do with the light fixture.

Someone's in the vestibule with me. Moon. Standing in the doorway, like last night. Only naked. Her hair is tied up.

"Can I join you? Save water and all? I brought towels, from Chase's bag, ha."

I was hoping she'd fall asleep. I try not to look at her.

"I guess," I say. "Just a shower though, please."

She steps into the water. I watch the drops of white light glisten where the water rolls off her shoulders. She keeps her promise; she showers then exits.

I stay in until my water runs out. I'm grateful for the towel she's left. I get mostly dry and go for my clothes. They're gone.

"Up here," Moon calls.

She's on the building's flat roof.

"Don't worry, it's an easy climb."

It *is* an easy climb and I hope Chase and Har don't pick this moment to come out of their tent and see me naked.

On the roof, Moon's laying on her back, naked on top of her clothes, staring at the stars. My clothes are laid out next to her. I follow suit and lay down on top of them.

There's something different about the sky. The stars are brighter than I remember. I can see them… glistening. I can see lines of white light coming from them and moving through the sky. Some of the lines reach the desert. And end where they reach pairs of animal eyes in the night. I become aware of the presence of dozens of coyotes near us. Moon has been talking…

"…when you run away you become someone else. Unless you're being chased, then you're running for your life, right? If you are running like that you are still you, you aren't who someone else says you are…"

Is that what I've been doing in California, running? What about Har? Are we brand new versions of us? Have we been chasing ourselves?

"…I don't normally tell people I want to kiss them, but you are going to be famous. A movie star. Maybe a film producer…"

"Did Chase tell you I'm in film?"

"No, I see it in the stars."

"What. How?"

"See that?"

She points to a star. When I nod that I see it, she directs my gaze to six others.

"That's Pleiades. The Seven Sisters."

I realize there are also stars in the black where I previously thought there were none. The faintest points of light. Along with dots all the colors of the spectrum.

"One for each world," she says.

"There are seven worlds? Which world are we in now?"

"I could tell you. It would take all night though. Would you believe me?"

"I don't know what you're going to say, how do I know if I'll believe you."

"I've seen it so many times before," she says. "People like to stay put. They don't believe even what they see with their own eyes and convince themselves all experiences fit into something safe and known. It's easier that way."

"Like that thunderhead?"

"Is that what you're telling yourself it was?"

"I guess so, I didn't think about it? What was it?"

"I don't know. That's the thing," she says.

I'm distracted by her flat stomach, the curve of her hip, and her pelvis bone. I do not like that I am losing my resolve, so I gather my clothes. Chase is singing in the shower below.

"I refuse to make believe and make up meanings," Moon says as I am getting dressed. "That's why the world is so hard for me to live in."

I climb down as Har is walking out of the showers. He's heading away from the campsite and into the desert. I call to him to wait up.

"You two stargazing up there?"

"Something like that," I say. "Did you know there are seven worlds?

"Of course," he says. "Wait you just said seven seas, right?"

"No, seven worlds."

"Who told you that?"

"Moon," I say.

"Ah, Moon. And you believe her?"

"She said she saw it in the stars, the Pleiades. Its astrology and stuff. It makes sense. I mean, it did a minute ago."

"Constellations aren't real," he says. "They're something we make up from what we want to see. The only connections out there are the ones we give and that's just not real. When tonight is over and by that I mean after we shake it off and sleep it off, we got our lives to get back to."

"Where are you going?"

"Right now, I'm high as can be and I'm going to enjoy it on a walk alone in the desert."

He walks a few paces. Then stops and back tracks to me.

"One thing. When the shoot is done and I'm back in LA will you take care of her, please?"

I try to remember him being close to anyone, any woman,

any of the girls who've circled him. I cannot. Once he rescued a kitten from a dumpster and even that didn't end well.

"Anything for you, man," I say.

I feel a long way from home as he walks into the night. This is what being grown up must be. Feeling alone and overwhelmed and hoping you've got enough to make it through.

I lay down next to the smoldering fire. The hard earth feels good on my back and I take in the wood smoke on the clean air. I hear Chase in the shower. I know Har is out there in the desert. And I haven't seen Moon come down from her star gazing perch. It dawns on me to build the fire up again. No matter what Har says I know the four of us form a shape. I know this is not a made-up thing because when I close my eyes, I feel us—four points in the night. Feeling it means it's real, I decide as I pass into the world of sleep.

The sun is coming up over the hills; the rock alive with color where the new light touches. A quail darts past, its spiral head feather bobbing. I decide I'm going to sweat last night off and go for a run.

Har, Chase, and Moon wake hours later, at the crack of noon. On the drive back to San Diego they remain burnt out. Beneath the energy I have mustered I feel the drag too. I dodged a bullet. Yesterday could have been a real mess. I'm gonna get them back safe then have myself a light dinner and hit the books.

Chase's place looks shabby and sad in daylight. A bunch of sketchy guys are standing around, eyeing my truck as I help everyone carry their stuff inside. I can tell whatever substance I want can be had from them in a heartbeat.

I write my number and address on Har's hand in marker and tell him to call me later. He doesn't.

The next morning I'm studying on my balcony hoping Har's going to call before he goes back to work and realize I should have taken Chase's number.

In the parking area, two stories below, I see a little sunburst-yellow Miata pull into a spot. Moon's behind the wheel. She does a line on her dashboard then gets out and heads to the stairs. Did Har tell her where I live?

A minute later, my doorbell rings. It takes me only a second to decide I'm not going to answer. She knocks on the door. Has she noticed my truck is here? Probably?

The old me would do just one line with her and not care what came next. I come inside and peer through the curtains as she returns to her car and drives away.

Twenty minutes later my phone rings. Its Har. He tells me to meet him and Chase for happy hour at a bar called Jerry's Ice House on the strip at PB.

"Oh, you're a local now?"

"Shut up," he says. "My last night out before going back to work. I'm bartending."

Showboating is more like it.

When I leave my place, outside my door is the disposable camera and a pile of manilla envelopes, from Moon. Full of scripts and stories and movie ideas.

As I drive, I try to wrap my mind around her. She also writes stories? No matter who she is or what her skills are, a girl with a habit is going to do me in. After tonight, keeping myself together is my full-time job again.

Pacific Beach's concrete boardwalk is a California dream. Cyclists, roller-bladers, girls without drug habits are everywhere. Someday, when I have my shit together, I'm going to find one, for me. The wide path runs south to Mission Beach. Does it reach Ocean Beach beyond where Nehru is shooting? I prefer its surfer vibes and sleepy pace to all this flash and color and thumping music. I think of the wood boardwalk back home at Jones Beach.

The big front windows to Jerry's Ice House have been removed and I can see inside to the far wall; dozens of mixed drink machines are lined up side by side, washing machine looking things displaying sugary iced alcohol in bright neon colors, spinning and turning and churning. Young women in tube tops and tight shorts roam the cavernous space with trays of shots in test tubes. I haven't even stepped inside and I hate it already. I tell myself I'm going to stay, for Har.

I find Chase sitting at a tall table a few feet from the bar where Har is stationed. I can hear Har making platitudes about his special cocktails. They don't even serve cocktails here, he's serving ices from those machines. I don't think I've ever had a real cocktail. Maybe a sip at a Chinese restaurant once. Har rambles on about Russian things. Russian drinks. How Nehru's film is somehow connected to something he finds tragically hip about Russia.

The first time I saw him showboating like this, I thought he was desperate for the adoration. It didn't take long for me to realize he was desperate just to be seen, from living in his basement like another discarded thing. It's clear as the sky on the ridge where we saw the cloud that Chase adores him not because of, but despite of all this.

"Having fun?" Chase asks me.

"I'm here for Har," I say. "What do you think? Can we convince him to give rolled tacos another try after this?"

As she answers my eye is drawn to a woman beelining towards Har at the bar. I can't be sure, but I think it is Moon's girlfriend. Har is laughing and produces a bottle of vodka and some shot glasses; it looks like they're having fun. Har's smile sours. The woman grabs the vodka bottle and belts him across the face with it. Har folds face-down onto the bar. She hits him over the head, breaking the bottle with a spray of blood and vodka. She runs. I scramble over to Har. Blood is pouring from his head. The left of his face is torn up. I don't see his eye, only the bloody socket.

I call Har's Mom from the bank of phones in hospital waiting area. No one cares. I sit in the booth reflecting on how I know the number by heart, the same number it was on all the calls I made growing up. I'm not ready to go back in to see him so I call my parents.

My mom goes on about the snow they've been having and then implores me to come home and take a job back home. Dad is stoic about it all and tells me if I'm set on staying out West then to try and do what I can for Harrison.

The doctors say Har has a long road ahead of him. I decide I am not going to speak of this as I return to his bedside.

"My eye," Har says. "How am I going to look through a camera and set shots with a concussion and one eye?"

"I'll take care of it," I say.

"How," Har says.

I don't know, but I know I am going to go to the set and try to do something.

Ocean Beach feels like a place that hasn't changed since the 1960s, or at least my idealized notions of it. Quiet. Plenty of surfers and long-haired's going about their business. Nehru's trailers are parked across the street from the Blue Breaker Hotel near the pier and it stands out as very out of place.

I recognize Nehru from photos and television. Tall and thin, dressed in black with his trademark shock of rockabilly black hair gone salt and pepper. He's at the center of a posse of Hollywood types sitting in folding chairs. I don't like that there is trash and cigarette butts on the ground. They're watching an open fire hydrant gush water into the street.

"Harrison, who?" Nehru replies to me when I tell him I'm here for Har.

"Smoothie Boy," one of his people says.

"Oh yes, Smoothie Boy," Nehru says. "Speaking of which, we need smoothies. I'm going to have—"

"I don't get smoothies," I say.

"Then why are you here? What could you possibly—"

I go to my truck and retrieve a pipe wrench. It takes me less than two minutes to close the hydrant.

"I guess your location is back the way you need it and you can resume shooting. No need to thank me, this one's free."

Nehru and his staff watch for a moment then the back to

work motions begin. No one thanks me. This was a failure. I turn back to my truck and find Nehru walking toward me.

"How long is your friend laid out for?"

"I don't know. A while."

"We wrap in two weeks. I need a script supervisor."

"Me? I have a job."

"Doing what?"

"A plumber."

"Of course. How much does that pay?"

I tell him.

"I'll give you that, per day. Here. Here's, one, two, three days in advance."

He takes hundred-dollar bills from a roll from his pocket and hands them to me.

"Get him the shooting scripts," he calls.

"What do I have to do?"

"What you did just there," he says. "Oh and keep me on track. I'm so easily distracted."

"This doesn't sound fun. At all."

"It isn't. Listen, I say make yourself some fast money. Give it to your friend Smoothie Boy, or whatever, I don't care. If it all works out maybe you can give him a job yourself once he's back on his feet."

———

On my balcony, I sort out the continuity of Nehru's film. I figure out a way he can finish the shoot in eight days not fourteen if he listens to me. I can't wait to tell Har when I visit him later.

The phone rings. I run inside and grab it. It's Chase. She's frantic. Through her cries she tells me Moon has overdosed.

I race to her place and find her waiting outside with a black plastic bag packed full of her stuff. Two cops are leaning against their cruiser writing a report.

"I'm outta here," Chase says. "Can I stay with you? I can't go back to this."

When I arrive at Har's room the nurse doesn't let me in; she tells me he doesn't want to see me. I pretend to leave and when she turns the corner on her rounds I bolt into the room.

"Get the fuck out of here," Har says. "I told them I don't want to see you."

"Har, what the hell is going on?"

"I asked you one thing." He hits the call button. "To take care of her. What do you do? You steal my girl. *And* you steal my fucking job."

"That is absolutely not what is going on—"

The nurse comes through the door and gets in between us.

"You have to leave, right now, sir."

I let her lead me out.

"I never want to see you again," Har calls after me. "Both of you. Ever again."

It's been months and Har has kept his promise. Six weeks ago, they moved him from the hospital to somewhere, I don't know where.

I wait for Chase to leave the apartment. She's off on a buy which means I've got three hours before she's back. Nehru's film wrapped early and underbudget. The wrap party was a blast and I met a ton of Hollywood types; not all of them were assholes. We haven't heard from Moon but Chase apparently took her habit with her in the plastic bag.

I've got a film shoot lined up in LA and an apartment waiting in Venice Beach.

I leave Chase a note explaining that I can't live like this. Along with a copy of the lease. The keys. And enough cash to cover next month's rent. She's gonna blow it on smack, but I did the right thing.

I make one last call. I get Har's answering machine. Just like every call for the last three months. As I pull away with everything I own in my truck I wonder what became of Moon. I'll never know. I'm pretty sure she told me her real name on the roof of the shower in the desert but for the life of me I cannot remember.

———

It is my first interview since being back in New York and I'm nervous about the call. I realize I haven't thought much of Chase and Moon and Har for years when the memory of them and the cloud rolling over us floods into me in response to the first question.

"You came out west for Rehab. Worked as a plumber. And were studying to go back to school all before your first film, is this true?"

"Mostly," I say. "Beneath the Dark Snow of Winter was my first job, it was a Nehru Casteltinni film."

"Nehru's film sets are notorious for the... indulgences. What was that like for you?"

"Well a magician doesn't give away all his tricks, I probably shouldn't say."

"You're not condoning drug use?"

"No, I'm not. Like everyone in LA I do admit I had a time when that was me. Unlike everyone in LA, I personally didn't like that kind of life, with all due respect. That's why New York is home again. It's different for me here."

"What's the first thing you did coming back to New York? Besides making the movie and now opening the new Production studio. Hit up your favorite pizza place?"

"Ha, I wish. Yes, I love the pizza. But no, first thing I did was get clean, really clean. Second thing was pay off my parent's mortgage. If the Company goes the way I plan, third thing on my list is to buy them a summer home."

In my mind's eye I see the bottle connecting with Har's face and I can answer no further questions.

New York City, 2007

It's been a rough year for film. I lost another production to a studio in New Zealand. A producer friend of mine told me how he went out with and slept with an actress we work with that I've held a candle for, for years. I have half a mind to take the rest of the year off.

I leave work early to grab a comic book on Bleeker street that I'm supposed to have read for a production. A woman walking down the stairs from the astrology shop above catches my eye.

"Chase? Is that you?"

Her hair is no longer that California blond, she's dyed it black and its cut short and modern but it is her.

"Wow, what are you doing here?"

"I was just going to ask the same of you," I say. "You're in New York?"

"Ten years now. I'm in banking. I work as a mortgage broker over in Union Square."

"Wait. My offices are in Union Square. Ten years and I've never seen you?"

"I work a lot," she says

"So do I."

"You clean? I'm clean."

"Yeah, me too," I say.

Bleeker Street is a flood of people. A thousand lives. A thousand stories passing by.

"I'm heading back up to 14th," she says. Want to walk?"

"Yeah sure."

She extends her arm the way Europeans do. I link mine in hers and it is nice.

"Hey. You ever hear from Harrison?"

"I used to," she says. "For a bit on and off. I got tired of his shit and stopped about ten years ago."

"How was he?"

"Last I heard he was a greeter at Walmart somewhere." She extends her lower lip and blows a strand of hair from her face. "Wow, this had to be over ten years ago."

A pang of guilt hits me over how attractive I find the unconscious little gesture.

"That's good? I guess…"

"He hated it. And so you don't have to ask, he still hated you.

Don't feel bad, to be fair he hated everyone, even me. Most of all himself."

The sun is going down. Being in her company makes me think of how long it has been since I've seen the stars.

"What was it, twenty years ago, we were out in the desert? I always think of you all Thanksgiving time."

"Twenty?" she says. "Try more like fifteen, I'm not *that* old."

"You look great."

"Thanks, every year counts."

"I wish I had photos. I never developed Moon's camera. Sometimes I wish I had."

"That whore. Holy hell, I haven't thought of her in forever."

"Yeah, me too."

That's a lie. I can see Moon posing in front of the glowing cloud as if the glossy thick paper were in my hands before me.

We arrive at the street across from the Christmas shopping village set up in the park surrounding the Union Square subway stop.

"You off for the day?" I ask. "I mean, you want to go for Mexican food, or something?"

"In New York? You know that's impossible."

"True—"

"Last night, I was thinking of my dad and my abuela and I made tamales."

"How's your dad?"

"In prison."

"I'm sorry."

"I'm not. I left him behind with California."

"Oh."

"And I swore to stop dating guys like him too."

"Tall, dark, and knowledgeable of all best drug plane routes? How's that going?"

"Don't ask," she says.

I wish she had laughed.

"Hey, you want to try the tamales I made? Not that you're qualified to know if they're any good."

"That would be perfect."

We find our way to the foot of the skyscraper that is hers. Her apartment is a couple of rooms high up. The living room and kitchen are a windowless rectangle. The door to her tiny box-sized bedroom is open; the space filled entirely by the bed. One wall is all window looking out into Manhattan's dusk.

I watch her put the tamales in the oven. Take out two fancy glasses and mix two drinks. There was a time when I'd never had Mexican food. Or a cocktail. Watching her is hypnotic. There's something on her mind she cannot mask. I remember how good she looked in the Photo-mat; tempered by the weight of things she's seen, her beauty is now much more profound.

"Which way to the restroom?" I ask.

"Other side of the apartment," she says.

I stand and shuffle through the dark. I stop at a doorway. There's a shape before me. My eyes, blurry from the dark, register that I'm looking in a mirror. But I'm in plumber's blue work clothes. I squint and for a second I think I'm seeing a younger visage of my dad. I move my hand to see if the image moves. Am I looking at myself?

I'm not looking at a mirror—five other man-sized apparitions appear in a row. I sense that they are all... me. I cannot see clear enough to discern faces or clues from what they are wearing. I just... sense them; presences as real and true as the certainty when I know it is going to rain a seconds before a cloudburst.

"Hey, not there, make a left," Chase calls.

I'm standing facing a wall. No mirror. No doorway.

I walk left. In the bathroom I feel throbbing aches in all the places I shot up long ago. My arms. My legs. Behind my knees. These pains are not real, I tell myself. Why now? Why do I want to use now? Why do I yearn for that oblivion? This call of the void is not real either, I tell myself. It has to be some kind of sadness. Some mournfulness for lives not lived.

"You were coming from that astrology place on Bleeker," I say as I take my place again on the couch. "How was it?"

"Oh, that?" she says and brings the drinks and sits next to me. "I was telling my friend not to worry, that I won't be coming round for a while. I don't believe in that shit anymore."

"Someone once told me the stars don't know or even care if you believe in them and their relationships or not."

"That's such bullshit," she says. "Please don't tell me you're into that."

"Do I look like I am?"

She answers by downing her drink. I follow suit. Its strong. I'm not used to alcohol and I can't not think of Har. Even after all these years I think of Chase as his girl and I have a pang of guilt for what we're about to do.

Seconds into our kiss I realize it is the best kiss of my life. Her lips are communicating something. This is reverse oblivion. My mind is full of a thousand things I want to tell her. My hands are in her hair. Then under her blouse and on her back. She's grasping at me as she leads me across the room. "I want you. Now." She whispers then bites my ear. She pushes me on to her bed with a force that startles us to a halt.

I gently pull her to me and for a few minutes we lay together, breathing heavy, watching the last of the day in the sky.

"You ever think of the cloud?" I say.

"That thunderhead?"

"Yeah. That day you told me I'd never look at the sky the same way again. You remember?"

"No. Sounds like something I'd say. Was I right?"

"So right," I say under my breath. "Wish I was there now. We should just leave here and go."

"What are you whispering? If I did say it, I was so fucking kidding or high out of my mind. I never want to go back to California again. It can fall off into the ocean with the big quake for all I care."

She leans to kiss me; gently pulling me closer.

I think to speak up and ask her out loud and for real if she'll go back to the desert with me. I close my eyes and can feel her. One point in the night. Is it because the distance between us is so minute? Once the shape that was us was three-sided. And then four. Is it possible to feel that ever again? It is hard to believe in things. It is easy to spiral on, head down. On lighted paths real for certain. Maybe Moon isn't dead and is out there somewhere. Maybe Har is going to speak with me again, someday.

I clear my throat to ask. The last light of the day is disappearing in the skyscraper crowded sky. Instead of speaking, I press my lips to the sweet curve between her shoulder and neck and let her take me.

DO NOT whistle and IT will NOT come to YOU, oh LAD

"**K**eep still and quiet, Lad. Real ghosts don't have a message for us like in the Signalman," Professor Vanessa says to Richie.

I think it's weird that she calls him "Lad." She's what, nine-teen? Only three years older than us. She calls me Lad too, so whatever. She can say anything she wants in that English accent of hers and I wouldn't mind though.

Richie ignores the slight to his favorite author.

When I recruited him he didn't contemplate being under the boardwalk on a school night, watching for real ghosts instead of discussing the Ghost of Christmas Future.

"It's okay, Lad, nothing's gonna happen to you. I've got my Specialist's Hat on."

I like the way spirals of her long, black hair hang from it, past the fringes of her jacket, a hippie-chic leather thing that reaches the middle of her black-tight-clad, long legs.

"You coming to Ghost Club tonight?" she said this afternoon.

None of us who cut class and hide out in the art room believe she's a real professor.

"What's that?"

"Me and you. At Long Beach. And some ghosts."

I got the sense this somehow would involve kissing. Richie knows I have hope Alana will fall for me, for real, despite her infatuation with Tommy and his band, so he agreed to come.

After hour two, I feel like Sally in the Great Pumpkin patch. The reek of wet fur and something… dirty hits me on the cold breeze that whips in from nowhere. Richie's fallen asleep.

There it is," Professor V whispers.

In a weak yellow light, that isn't the moon and isn't a ship I discern a figure that wasn't there a second before, loping towards an overturned wire trash can.

"That's not Jacob Marley. You ready?" she says.

A wheeze escapes Richie's gaping mouth. The figure goes still in response. Then disappears.

I should have taken Richie and just ran.

Next to him, where there was nothing before, the black shape from the shore appears and sits up, mimicking awakening. Up close it is hairy and bristly like an urchin. Professor V gasps. A sound of delight.

The shape has no face. Only bristles where features should be. It gropes the air as it stands. Professor V reaches for it and it slams into her. Before I black out, I think I am watching a lover's embrace only it stuffs itself in her mouth and disappears inside.

———————

I come to, and see Professor V walking into the ocean. Richie stands on the shore watching. Silently. A silence he's kept to this day.

———————

Professor V never returned to the art room. Richie never spoke to me again. Alana didn't fall for me. There is only the emptiness of where those relationships should have been.

———————

I know Christmas is coming when I wake up choking and think urchin spines are slipping into me. The smell of wet fur passes leaving only the void and the dead cold of winter.

The Exorcist's
Red-Haired Daughter

The French Quarter, New Orleans. 30 years ago.

She watches through the open door to the back room where she's sitting in the near dark. Long, straight, red hair. Bright primary no-question-at-all-it-is-dyed red. No color on anything in the entire Botanica even comes close.

Her mother, the witch who owns the place, rings up the stuff I've placed on the counter. Tiny souvenir juju bags I'll take home as gifts for my dorm mates. A book on Chinese Astrology. A glass bottle of spell powder.

The guide book entry for the shop said the owner has a short fuse and little patience for tourists, which piqued my curiosity.

"Open Roads, a fine choice," she says, with just a hint of a Southern drawl. "Be careful what you open the doors to though. Before I pack it up, would you like instruction on how to use it?"

"Oh, I've used spell powder before," I say. "I like to put it in the hot wax I seal envelopes with, you know for special letters or just wishes and things I write and put away for myself."

This apparently is the wrong answer because she looks offended. I sense a scolding is about to happen.

Through the doorway I notice her daughter watching with devilish delight.

The witch blows a strand of her jet-black bob of hair out of her face and points to a window propped open by a metal hammer.

"I was about to say something very different, then I saw my hammer," she says. "I bought it for putting in nails to hang herbs to dry on. It's meant to pound nails. It was created to build things. Yet, see how I'm using it? I'm not wrong. It's the perfect size and the only thing here strong enough to keep that old window from slamming down when the wind blows. Not every tool needs to be used as intended. Thank you for the unexpected lesson young man."

"You're welcome," I say with a nervous smile.

As she wraps the glass bottle of powder in brown paper the telephone in the back room rings.

"One minute, please," she says to me then disappears through the doorway. I hear her answer and speak.

"Which year are you?"

It's the witch's red-haired daughter. She's behind the counter across from me running her finger along the cover of the astrology book.

"Pardon," is all I'm able to say because she's so attractive.

I can't stop looking at her. She doesn't mind. She smiles. Tilts her head like she's posing.

"Your birth year," she says.

"I think I'm year of the dragon."

"Oh, we're not compatible," she says. "But I don't care."

She touches the top of my hand. Runs her finger up my fore-arm. It feels amazing.

Rick and Michael are out getting sloppy on Bourbon Street and here I am with this beautiful girl.

"Stay away from him," her mother commands as she stomps back to the counter.

She gathers my items in one swoop and stuffs them in a bag.

"Here, take your purchase. Time for you to leave my store, young man."

She escorts me to the door and locks it behind me.

I do not turn around until I'm halfway down the street. The red-haired girl is there gazing out a second-floor window above the shop.

I want to wave but don't want any trouble with her mom.

I stop at the grocer on Dauphine Street, purchase a half of Muffaletta sandwich and head back to my room.

My hotel's courtyard, an interior oasis framed by three story brick walls, has become a social scene. People are gathered around umbrella-covered tables happily drinking and smoking. The tiny rectangular pool is full to capacity with guests holding drinks in plastic cups above the water line. A man pushes through the glass doors of the pool house and goes into the adjacent changing room trying not to spill a bucket of ice fresh from the noisy old machine.

I rise above the sound of them celebrating the night as I climb the three flights of stairs to my room. The wooden floor is crooked and warped, anything on the floor will roll to one side. Exposed ancient wooden rafters run the length of the low ceiling.

It's what Rick and Michael call French Quarter charm. I don't see the appeal. Even on our last day of our week here I still don't see their fascination with everything New Orleans.

The phone rings. Speak of the devil, it's them at a pay phone on Bourbon Street drunkenly imploring me to come out and party. I tell them I'm in for the night and I'll join them for breakfast before our flight tomorrow.

I sit in the big bed, unwrap my sandwich, glad to be alone in the peace and quiet. I can't stop thinking of the red-haired girl. The way she ran her finger up my arm. It's been three years since Jackie went away to school and her parents made sure she broke up with me. One day on Spring Break when I was home at my parent's house, she came in through the bathroom window, like the Beatles song sort of, and was standing there waiting when I got out of the shower. I never saw her again after that and haven't been with anyone since.

The phone rings.

"I told you fools no," I say. "I'm not coming out."

"Come to the window," says a female voice.

I drop the receiver and go. I slide open the black out blinds revealing an alluring female form silhouetted by streetlight. Tall and thin, the hypnotic contour of a woman straight out of my dreams is there behind the diaphanous, sheer curtain.

I push the covering aside and open the window. The witch's red-haired daughter ducks to avoid hitting her head on the frame and climbs in.

I start to speak. I think I actually mumble a word or two about my ex and the bathroom window but she pushes me, then pushes me again sending me stumbling backwards onto the bed. She holds me down and kisses me forcefully.

"I lied," she says, allowing me some air. "I think we're very compatible. I was just trying to throw my mother off."

She kisses me again. A quick, playful kiss that ends with strong bite on my lip and her backing away.

She lifts her shirt, takes it off, and throws it.

"Can you imagine me with tattoos," she says.

The concave hollow of her belly is perfect alabaster white. The curve of her hip bone disappears under the top of her faded blue jeans.

She wriggles free of them and jumps back onto the bed. Back on top of me. She's so tall she can place her palms on the ceiling. She grips the rafters, presses herself onto me and grinds and writhes and moans.

At some point I realize the phone is ringing, then there is only the sound of her telling me how to feel, telling me what to do.

I do my best to comply then disappear into a haze of pleasure.

I wake and my first thought is, oh shit I've missed my flight.

My second thought is, oh no, she's not here.

I only see her clothes left strewn around the room.

I check the bathroom. Nothing. Then I notice a note stuck on the mirror above the sink.

I laugh. Such a cliché. Right out of every bad story and urban legend Rick and Michael ever told. At least its not in red lipstick.

Stay in touch, okay? Write to me. Come back and visit anytime.

I pack my bag. I gather her clothes and decide to put them in a drawer. I wait until the last minute to make sure she's not coming back then I go downstairs to check out and meet the guys for breakfast before our flight.

Breakfast is beignets and coffee with chicory in the French Market.

Rick and Michael are hung over as sin but it doesn't stop them from boasting about their so-called exploits last night. Except for the extreme amounts of alcohol and being on Bourbon Street, all are things I'm sure didn't happen.

They wouldn't believe me even if I wanted to tell them about the red-haired girl, so I do not.

Back to school in upstate New York is the same old fraternity parties, and other parties, and crowded, loud bars. All of them microcosms populated with those looking to fill the holes in themselves with hedonism, or at least with something. At times the debauchery reaches Bourbon Street levels of abandon. I sense a dishonesty in Rick and Michael in their thinking that this level of inebriation is fun. Maybe it is a tacit acknowledgement that life is something one needs to be numb to, to endure and they are getting a head start. Getting so drunk like that is just… drifting. Letting the current of nothingness take you, nowhere. They're not alone, most everyone in this "scene" will graduate and drift in different ways, and on different currents into thoughtless, unconscious lives.

I receive a letter from my dear high school pal, Leon who is working in a cannery in Alaska, instead of college. We should all get a job on a cruise ship, together, his letter says. You know, sail the seas. See the world. This is the fastest, cheapest way to do it while we're still young.

I write my reply and seal my letter with wax and spell powder from the Botanica in the French Quarter. I can't help but think of the witch's daughter running her finger along my arm. Of how I felt seeing her at the window. Of her white, perfect skin when she lifted her shirt.

Walking back from film class in the art building I decide to tell Rick about my encounter. His insight surprises me.

"Sex is real," he says. "We're young, maybe it's the only real thing we know about life right now."

I decide to write to her. I seal my letter with wax and spell powder.

When I return home to my parent's house for the summer a reply is waiting for me. From her mother.

"Stay away from her. Stay away from New Orleans," the letter reads. "In fact, never come back."

My disappointment is muted by the whirl of summer. Beach parties. Chasing pretty girls. Late night conversations with Rick and Michael about photography and film. I have an awareness that times like these are not forever and on the other side of this our transition to adulthood is waiting.

The last semesters of school and graduation and hopes and dreams and the mundane things life is built of eclipse my memories and fantasies of the red-haired girl.

My friendships drown in the rise and falls of love and loss and in the fascination and despair of trying to bring artistic visions to life in a world not built for such things.

Currents take us. Separate us. Scatter us to the winds and

corners of the world, even those friends who are just next door become strangers. This is not just *my* life; this is the way life sometimes goes for us all.

New Orleans, May 2023.

I return to the French Quarter after so many years for the occasion of the opening night of the Cure's Songs of a Lost World tour. A gift to myself, an indulgence to my thirst for travel and in-person experiences after Covid times.

Will it capture the sense of community lacking in my life? Probably not. Will it alter where I've found myself, alone at the end of a trajectory I always feared?

No. Of course not.

When I heard Robert Smith sing the lyric, "…it's all gone…" I felt it. I felt him. I believed despite the successes and luxuries in his life that he knew the same kind of loss as me. The same loneliness after relationships and breakups, after careers and dead ends.

Sometimes people self-destruct. Instead of facing down their problems and working out their issues, they implode. And all that is left for the people who were in their life, the people who trusted them, who gave all to them, is the empty space where a relationship had been. This is the story of my life. Its not unique and it is no longer tragic, it just… is.

The freedom to pick up and go on a trip like this is a small consolation. One I would trade for a life of picket fences and happily ever after without question.

I arrive at the hotel Rick and Michael and I stayed in decades ago a couple of days before the show, to give New Orleans another go; to try and find my connection with the city of art and music and spirit like so many artists before me.

The young clerk at the front desk is strange in all the wrong ways. His stand offish-ness and reserved demeanor is a rarity for New Orleans, and makes me feel uncomfortable.

I decide to take my bag to my room myself. I roll my luggage out of the blessed air-conditioned lobby into the courtyard. I'm greeted with the soft echo of gurgling water from two small fountains, new additions since I was here last. The brick wall of my building is covered with ivy. The pool house has been freshly painted white. There are vending machines, microwaves, and a sleek new ice machine. White venetian blinds, tilted open to let in light, hang in a new large glass window of the changing room.

Despite the facelift it hasn't changed much in the decades since the night the red-haired-girl came to me.

I was thinner. I had more stamina then. I moved through the world more on instinct than by thought. I remember life having spontaneity and passion to it that I yearn for now, a certain magic and unpredictability I wish I could have again, even if just long enough to capture a fleeting instance of it in a photograph.

I put my bag in my room, cool off with a shower and change then take myself out for a meal at a place on Jackson Square.

"Just one?" my waitress asks.

She's tall and thin and clad in all black. A tattoo of a snake on her lower leg wraps up and around and continues onto the part of her thigh beneath her skirt.

"Here for the show?" she asks.

"Oh, yeah. Saint Robert," I say. "I forgot I was wearing my shirt. You going to the concert?"

"No, not me. I gotta work."

There's something genuine and vulnerable about the way she says it. I notice the lines not covered by the make up around her eyes. How her hands are the kind that know hard work. At first, I thought she was half my age.

Is it possible she is *her?* All grown up now and we have met again, here in the Quarter?

"Do I know you," I say. "I mean have we met before? A long, long time ago."

"Where might that be," she says.

"I don't know, here," I say. "I mean I was once here when I was just a stupid kid."

"Oh, I just moved here. I don't think so," she says.

I fear I've made her uncomfortable and I regret it. She was just being professionally friendly and hoping for a decent tip like anyone would.

For a second I think I will compliment her tattoo but I decide the kindness I can give her is to not say anything.

"Ready to order?" she asks.

My meal of shrimp and grits is delicious and the rest of our interactions are with pleasant smiles and no more conversation.

I walk back to my room carrying a bag with beignets and a gift can of coffee and chicory from Café Dumond. As I climb the stairs, I realize I have no one to gift the coffee to.

I fall asleep with my clothes on and the bag next to me on the big bed.

I wake sometime in the quiet of night and glance through my window at the courtyard. It's so tranquil— the perfect place to enjoy my desert alone and in peace.

I plug my phone in to charge, grab one of the clove cigarettes I've brought for the concert, and go back down the stairs into the humid night and murmur of the fountains.

I park myself at one of the round picnic tables with the sun umbrella still up and I realize I'm not alone. Someone's in the pool.

A woman rises from the shallow end, water dripping from her naked form. She's tall and fit. A tattoo of a serpent is wrapped around her left leg. It winds up her torso, with its head on the bottom of her neck just where the line of her straight, black hair ends.

She's facing the pool house but I can swear she's my waitress from dinner.

She covers up in a towel and reaches for something at the edge of the pool. There's a solid, metallic clang as she picks up a thin sword, the kind one would use for fencing. The polished blade catches the blue glow emanating from the pool lights beneath the water line.

She carries it into the pool house then into the changing room without noticing me, or if she does without a care to my presence.

The blinds are partially open. I can see she's dropped her towel and has the blade in her hand. She's moving with it. Practicing moves. Practicing a routine for a show or a martial arts kata.

She tilts her head back and swallows the sword. The entire blade disappears into her mouth.

I know some sword swallowing is real and some is misdirection and showmanship. This has to be an illusion.

She pulls the sword from her throat and runs her finger along the edge of the blade. I recognize the same delight; the same way the witch's red-haired daughter touched the astrology book; the moment floods back to me.

Is this her? Is this her all these years later? All grown up like me?

I don't mean to intrude. She's not wearing any clothes. I make noise. I announce myself.

"Hello, hello," I say, as I walk past the pool and open the glass doors.

She's there before me, in the room with the ice machine, gracefully twirling the sword above her head in slow, sweeping arcs.

I could have sworn she was the waitress from earlier but it is not her, she's someone who looks a lot like her but it's someone totally different.

The woman turns in a circle and lowers the blade, spinning it dangerously close to her legs.

"I'm sorry," I say. "I was out there having a snack and I saw you and I thought you were, that you might have been—"

"Wouldn't I look better with tattoos," she says.

The very same words the witch's red-haired daughter spoke to me. How could I ever forget?

"What? What did you say? Why did you say that?"

She runs the tip of the blade along her foot. A line of crimson wells up.

I wince.

"Oh man that's sharp, please be careful."

She moves the tip of blade to her thigh and gives it a thrust. It goes right in. She pushes. It pushes straight through.

"Ahhhh, no. Why did you do that? What are you doing? You're hurting yourself."

There's no blood. It has to be a trick. Something like the sword swallowing illusion.

I try to reach her, try to get her attention. Her gaze is blank. It's like she's unconscious. I don't get any recognition of my presence. Is she in some sort of a trance?

She pulls the blade out. One smooth motion. Blood spurts from the gash.

She stabs herself again. And again. And again. Spraying blood hits the white walls.

"Stop it. You're hurting yourself."

A jet of blood splashes the ceiling. The room is wet and red and coated with what was inside her seconds ago.

She thrusts the blade into her foot. Then pierces her other thigh.

"Stop it, stop it, stop it!"

I run to her.

She's laughing. Covered in her own blood and laughing. Blood on the ceiling drips on me as I grab her arm.

I can't stop her; I can't take the blade. She's too strong.

"You're hurting yourself, stop, stop, stop!"

Her laughter continues as if I'm not there. I slip on the slick floor trying to wrest the blade away and crash down on my ass.

I slide around trying to get up as she keeps stabbing herself. I get to my feet and run for help.

The front desk guy is cool and composed and says nothing at the sight of me covered in blood.

"There's someone in the courtyard," I say. "She's hurting herself. She needs help, I mean she's hurt, call an ambulance."

"Yes, sir," he says. "Don't worry. We've got it under control."

"Under control? Call an ambulance, do something."

"I got this," he says.

"No, you don't. I need you to do something. This isn't a leaky toilet, call the police."

"You were told never to return here," he says.

"What? What did you say?"

"Sir, I said I got this," he says, in a flat monotone.

I dash back to the pool house. My bloody foot prints are all over the place. A line of blood has leaked through the bottom of the glass door and is seeping towards the pool.

The woman is motionless on the floor, the blade next to her. She's almost bled out. I've never seen so much blood.

———

I race up the stairs to my room to call the police.

I grab my cell, bobbling it with my bloody hands. I wipe my hands on the sheets and fumble the phone trying to dial.

There's no signal. I move around the room, dialing 911. I can't get signal. I go to the room phone. There's a tone. Will 911 work on it? I try.

It's ringing and ringing and ringing.

There's a knock on the window.

How can that be? I'm three stories up. Bars appear on my cell. I dial 911 again. No one picks up. There's only ringing and ringing and ringing.

There's another knock at the window, more insistent.

I see from across the room a woman is there. The witch's red-haired daughter, looking as she did decades ago, her red hair bright and distinct against the darkness of the night.

I go over and let her in.

"How'd you get up here," I say and I realize I'm asking the question to myself.

All those years ago when she came in through the window, I never even questioned it. I saw what I wanted to see. And in all the years since, I never gave it a second thought.

"Was that you? At the restaurant. Down in the pool house?"

I don't even know her name. I never asked her name. She never gave me her name. Never said it. I never used it. But I sent her letters, I must have wrote something.

Behind her through the window I see the courtyard is clean, no blood, no bloody footprints. The pool house is quiet and still. And empty. No exsanguinated woman. No blood. No blade.

"What year were you born," she asks.

The question is just… off. What kind of question is that after appearing like this in the middle of the night. It's a fucking weird replay of our first interaction from that day back in her Mother's Botanica.

It's all wrong and I'm afraid.

"Year?" I ask.

"Yeah, year, the astrology book," she says.

There's no astrology book here, only me panicking at the woman about to die in the courtyard. Yet I'm caught in the unnatural gravity of the dialog.

"Year of the… dragon," I say.

"We're not compatible," she says. "But I don't care."

She pushes me. Pushes me again and I stumble backwards onto the bed.

She pounces. Her hair catches on something. It's a wig. It

slides off center revealing a bald head beneath. It's scarred with lines— old incisions traversing patches of stubble.

Her back too is a patchwork of old cuts— a pink and white map of surgery incisions, a history in flesh.

A solitary scar thicker than all the rest runs up her belly and into a Y on her chest. She'd been opened up. Slit up the middle, like for an autopsy.

The moment I first saw her forces its way into my mind.

She's sitting in the dark of the Botanica's back room, then in an instant she just appears behind the counter. I never gave a second thought how that happened. What else have I disregarded, what else have I been unconscious to, in my life?

The epiphany is stifled with the pressure of her body pushing down on me.

She lifts her hands like she did that night, reaching for rafters that are not present, and grinds.

I can't get her off me, she's too strong.

She grinds, and writhes, and moans.

The door flies open. Someone bursts in. A woman. Her skirt, her hair a black swirl of motion.

"Get off of him," the woman shouts.

It's her mother, the witch from the Botanica.

She rushes to us, plants herself at the foot of the bed.

She has things in her hands. A bottle of orange powder. A bottle of murky liquid.

Everything is moving so fast. She's spraying us with the water. Shouting words I've never heard.

Her red-haired daughter continues moaning, writhing, grinding, not reacting to a single thing. Then in the blink of an eye she just stops moving, disappears, and is gone.

And I'm lying there in the bed with the witch from the Botanica standing over me.

She looks… exhausted.

"Thank you," I say, grateful for the stillness. "You saved me. What was…? I mean, how…Your daughter—"

"You stupid fuck. That's not my daughter. I don't have a daughter. I would never bring a child into this sick, fucked up world. You couldn't just go to Bourbon Street like the rest of the sheep, and stay where you're supposed to and do what you're supposed to, no. Don't you remember me? You must not remember me. I told you never to come back. I even sent you a letter."

"I'm sorry. I should have never come to your shop. I would have never met your daughter then. She's like a disease I caught or something, one of those things that stays with you."

"You're the disease. You're damn right you should have never come. You can see things. Things can see you. You don't get it. You don't understand. She's not my daughter. *You* brought her to *me*. She's something *you* manifested. You left your sick manic pixie fantasy in *my* shop."

"I did what?"

"She's the unwanted gift that keeps on giving. Just when I think I've done her in. Bam, she's back."

"I didn't do this. I didn't do anything—"

She takes a deep breath, opens the bottle of orange powder and throws it all on me.

"Be gone. Be gone from here," she says. "Get out of my city. Go. Go home, go anywhere you want. Anywhere but here. Get out and never come back."

I'm still speaking, asking her a barrage of questions as she turns her back and just walks away.

I take the longest shower of my life and then I shower again. I think about packing my stuff and leaving right now. I decide I will stay one more night, for the concert, as sleep takes me.

I wake before dawn. The red-haired girl is standing next to my bed watching me. She's pristine and unscarred. Her red wig is combed and in place.

"I'm sorry," I say.

"It's not your fault," she says. "Don't believe what my mother says. She's a monster. I had cancer and she couldn't wait for me to die."

"That's so awful," I say. "I didn't know."

"I'm the one who came to say *I'm sorry*," she says.

"I have to go," I say. "Your mother tried to banish me or something. I'm leaving after the concert. I guess that means I'm never going to see you again."

"That makes me sad," she says. "But I understand. People come and people go. Do you find that too?"

"I do," I say. "It's the way it's always been for me."

"If you must go there's one thing you can do for me before you do."

She rambles a list of instructions. Something to buy in a shop on Royal Street and where to take it. I'm so exhausted I fall in and out of sleep as she's speaking and I'm not convinced she is even real or here at all.

I sleep the day away and wake in the afternoon. The courtyard and pool house are all cleaned up. Or was there nothing even to clean at all?

I go down into the shady oasis and sit at the same table as last night and smoke that clove cigarette.

Was it all some sort of a waking dream? All of it. Long ago. Last night. Even in my room at dawn, was she a projection from my own mind? Could it be?

A couple of guests wearing Cure t-shirts stop and say hello to me and make a moment of small talk as they cross the courtyard. Music and bands and concerts can be quasi-religious like that. They can fill the holes in us left from a lack of ritual and bring a modicum of a sense of belonging to our detached, modern lives. The friendly chit chat is welcome.

I finish my smoke and head out to make my way to the Super Dome for the concert. As I pass the young man at the front desk, he looks up from what he is doing.

Our eyes meet and he gives me a nod. There's something good about it, none of the discomfort of our previous interactions present.

The concert is cathartic. I follow the flock of fellow concert goers back to the Quarter and find myself inspired. I keep walking.

The night air and moving does me good. I enjoy passing the storefronts and the open doors into all kinds of different spaces, all full of culinary and musical delights.

I follow a low rhythmic beat into a clean, narrow alley and found I've wandered into the entrance of an almost hidden bar all tucked away. I park myself on a stool at the polished wooden bar top and admire the glow of the place's tea light candles in the copper wrought, low ceiling.

I order a French 75. The bartender is elegant. All in dark clothes with long dark hair back in a tight pony tail. She pops the cork on a bottle of champagne and makes my drink. She's attentive and professionally friendly and courteous. I tell her my story about the witch's red-haired daughter, and she listens.

"You know, I think maybe I know who you're talking about," she says. "It's possible I went to high school with her daughter. She was the one who had cancer and her mother was all overprotective and didn't let her go out or do anything before she passed away."

She returns to my place at the bar after a few minutes and checks on me and my drink.

"There's a story that says she haunts the Quarter," she says. "One of those urban legend things. Like, she lures young men to their deaths, or something. I mean there are so many stories, so many ghost stories, it's hard to keep track.

Her mother though, yeah, she's for real and is a real piece of work. I know her store. I know exactly who you're talking about. It's a dice roll with her. She might tell you a wonderful fortune or might yell at you to get out of her store, I guess that's the New Orleans equivalent of get off my lawn.

Yours is a hell of a ghost story. If you ask me ghost stories aren't true. There's always something else behind them, especially around here. You know, they're all made up or embellished to sell things."

I tell her I'm ready to pay for my drink.

"You barely touched that. I'm sorry. Did I offend with my take on your story? I didn't mean to."

"No, it's just, I have somewhere to go. Something important to do."

"At this hour? I can make you another or something different if you didn't like the drink."

"Someone asked me for a favor," I say. "And I've decided that I'd like to go and do it before I go home."

The witch's Botanica looks that same as it did those years ago. I spy the array of powders, and jars, and talismans and shelves full of all sorts of books and esoteric things to shop for the through the front window.

The little window on the second story, where the red-haired daughter watched me from, is dark.

Her mother lived there then and lives there now. I know she's up there. Sleeping.

It's okay. I'm not here for spell powder.

I grip the knife in my hand. It's a finely made thing. An antique machete I purchased on Royal Street as the witch's red-haired daughter told me at dawn. It just needs a bit of a cleaning and some polish.

It's meant for cutting brush. It was created to clear vines and branches. To make paths through swamp.

Will it open roads for me? Or new paths? It may be time to cut a new path through life.

I try the door of the Botanica. It is locked.

I just need it to open *this* door. So I can complete the favor I promised.

Bring it to her mother, she said. And you'll know what comes next.

It's not a sword, but it will do. Not all tools are meant to be used as intended.

I try the lock with the tip of the blade. It doesn't give. It doesn't open.

I realize I've got a paper bag with handles in my other hand. I look inside. It's the can of coffee I bought as a gift. Did I come here to give the witch the coffee, and apologize before leaving town? Or to show her the blade like her daughter asked of me. I'll have to figure it out.

I sit down on the curb to think about it. I put the bag and knife down, light up a clove, and take a long drag.

How did life take me to this moment? With everything gone. How is it that I'm out here in the dark, wondering how I got so old.

the ghost with
my father's coin

We decided to finally get together, in the same place in the same time to celebrate the end of all the epic level shit we'd been through in the past few years. A black celebration, our four-day black celebration we decided to call it, to celebrate life, by immersing into all the good things of bustling, burgeoning, haunted New York City because like the song goes, we'd seen the end of a long, long string of grim, black days.

DAY 1.

There is a ghost in the airport terminal.

The ghost is me.

I'm the ghost almost everywhere. I certainly feel like one.

I've gone as far as they will let me and I'm waiting for her behind the barrier ropes. The guard is afraid of me. Even though I am speaking gently and courteously.

Hundreds of people. Thousands of stories. All together, in flux moving through the passenger arrival tunnel to luggage pick up. She appears among them. No ghosts are with her. As far as I can tell.

The most beautiful people in the world sometimes do not see themselves as beautiful because of what the world has thrown at them. The world is also adept at mistaking kindness for weakness and for making all sorts of mistakes of perception and false conclusions about even the little aspects of truth we mortals can grasp.

Turn back the clock five years and we are almost strangers talking excitedly about flying ointment. She calls me to ease the sting of helping a poor hurt fox shed this mortal coil. We talk all night analyzing the fragility and majesty of what it means to be alive. Now, thanks to the mundane magics of human hands and the fact that planes want to stay in the sky, here we are.

"How was your flight?" I ask, hoping it was pleasant. And uneventful. And free of unsavory people in close proximity.

"I tell you later," she says.

We waste no time and head to the good places of my past, the few of them that are still around and hanging on.

The Italian bakery smells like the 1970s, at least the sweet and innocent parts of it. We carefully select little cakes and receive them in a paper box tied with red and white striped string and take them to Jones Beach.

"This is the parking lot where a hippie told teenage me I should listen to Tangerine Dream."

"This is the boardwalk where the little lizards I once told you about live."

Mountains of quintessential, billowy white clouds float over the shore. The moon surprises us with its daytime presence.

The restaurant that was once a bath house is closed for the season. We are ghosts standing among the vacant tables on the terrace, gazing into the vast empty swimming pools. As a child I was taken here as part of summer camp. I remember the feeling of being an outsider as clear as the smell chlorinated water on one of those long gone humid, August days. We know what it is like to be different. To feel different.

On the train to Manhattan, we discuss the connection between Kate Bush's Hounds of Love and an M.R. James story that was made into a film.

New York's streets are made of stories. Stories in stone, stories in flesh; the past, present, and future here on this sidewalk all at once. She is pleased I am able to see this too.

The Empire State Building is lit in purple, especially for us we decide. We go right up, right to the spire to greet the night and perceive the psychogeography from the top of the city. I think I can feel the building's metal skeleton sway and my vertigo takes hold.

We retreat down to the observation deck.

The square terrace is ringed by tall metal bars turned in, making it almost impossible to fall, so the fear in my brain quiets. The wind is alive in the October chill; I think it wants to have its way with us, all of us present for daring to whimsically venture to a place so high.

"You okay? Now it's your turn to look a little white," I say.

"It's like on the plane," she says.

"We can't fall," I say. "No way we can with these things."

"It's not that," she says. "When we got up there, to the highest altitude. It's hard to explain…"

"Try me. I want to know," I say.

Next to us, a young Asian couple maneuver against the metal bars, trying to get themselves and the sprawling, lit-up, city centered in their selfie.

"It wasn't a fear of falling," she says. "I could hear the blackness. I could hear the space between the stars calling out. I was afraid of going up and up and not being able to stop. Being up there and free of gravity. Free of the bonds… of earth. I could see myself going and going. Becoming invisible. Becoming… nothing."

The wind gusts. Flexing its elemental might. I make sure she is okay and we return inside.

"Me afraid of falling down, you afraid of falling up," I say.

"It's not fear," she says. "The call, it's just…louder up high. I don't always want to hear it."

I remember there used to be a photo booth near the elevator. On my sixteenth birthday my friends "kidnapped" me from my room and anti-social tendencies and took me here. I lost touch and lost track of them long ago. I still have the rectangular photo strip though. Is it all that is left of *that* me? Of those times and those dreams?

Friends are witnesses of each other. Briefly sharing existences before, as all things do, they slip into the void, as is the natural way. It is the natural way to disappear.

This monument, its shape forcing on us a mandatory way to see the night sky, looks same as ever from the outside, while inside is all changed. This is the opposite of the way *we* grow old.

Penn Station is full of strangers. My blank, solo train rides out of the city have become so familiar, the emptiness has been inverted into feeling like home.

Tonight, I am not here alone. We traverse the liminal space together.

DAY 2

Gothic and grand, Cathedral of St John the Divine's stone carved facades grow more enchanting as dusk falls. We are here for a concert in the crypt to celebrate the Autumn season.

Candles placed in strategic clusters around the cavernous space create pockets of light where guests are gathering. In one of the lit-up areas are tables with spreads of food laid out for us. Shrines to all things and religions, testimonial displays to the spirit of mankind line the walls.

I have not been here since the fire and rebuild; I remember there was once a shrine with a large meteorite. As I look for it, she points to a ghost rising from the wooden pews. It floats up to the ceiling's stone arches high above and passes through the ceiling. We watch for more as if we are watching for shooting stars. After a moment, another phantom emerges. A man with a white curly wig of the kind I associate with George Washington. He turns his head and contemplates us watching him.

"We all disappear into the black," he says. "That is how everything ends."

Then he floats up, disappearing into the dark.

"What if the black is how everything *begins*," I say.

She shrugs, opens her mouth and releases a singular, pristine note. The tone resonates with sonorous echo.

She sings a run of notes, a phrase of a familiar, operatic song. A man, a real non-ghostly man, veers away from the food table to us. "Bravo," he says with his hands clapping softly.

"So utterly gorgeous, right?" I say.

Our host appears in the midst of the guests and taps a glass with a fork.

"It is time," he says.

We follow him. Out a side door. Along an outside Cathedral wall. Down a winding flight of non-descript steps lit by candles.

Descending thought the basement levels feels like passing back in time. The exposed pipes and storage boxes are a glimpse of the guts holding the structure together. One last set of stairs takes us into the crypt.

Three stone sarcophagi dimly lit from above are the focal point of the space. Three rows of folding chairs are arranged in a half circle before them. Ancient, thick wooden beams running the entire length of the low ceiling are scarred with burn marks.

The musicians file in from various positions and entrance points and incorporate the darkness and areas of light in their performance. My mind is still in the chamber above, with her vocals echoing in stone.

We celebrate the close of another day alive by quietly saluting the night with piping hot Moroccan peppermint tea in a nearby place still open after the concert.

She gets up to use the washroom and in the space she just vacated is a ghost. It is the man with the white George Washington style hair from the Cathedral sitting there non-chalantly with his wig removed. He has two golden Sacagawea golden coins over his eyes. A cloak of inky black crow feathers is draped on his shoulders.

He dips his incorporeal fingers in my empty tea cup and touches the remnants, as if seeking a fortune.

I stifle my trepidation and speak.

"Reading my tea leaves?"

"They say nothing," he says. "I am here to teach you. How to go up. Past the sky. Into the black"

He returns his wig to his head and then disappears.

DAY 3

The lonely Illuminated Manuscripts area on the first floor of the Metropolitan Museum used to be my secret refuge, my favorite place in New York. Since one of the Met's remodels, it is a place that exists no more. I used to take myself there on my birthday to spend time in its dim, labyrinthine maze of displays. Then I'd find my way to the café in the corner, a small area no one else seemed to know about or frequent, its windows allowing just a modicum sunlight into the glorious eternal gloom.

We are here for the Temple of Dendur, the tiny Egyptian shrine rescued from the waters of Lake Nasser and brought to its modern, spacious new home looking out on Central Park through a wall of glass. Nestled in the center of a huge, ultra-high-ceilinged space built especially for it replete with shallow pools of water with a stone crocodile, the shrine itself is structurally basic and otherwise unremarkable. Its enduring appeal is an implication, a subliminal affirmation perhaps, that if things such as this little temple are worthy of great undertakings to be rescued that there is hope for refuge from the floods that threaten to swamp us.

We wind through the Egyptian wing passing countless items, numbered and on display behind glass.

A small mummy resting in an open, wooden coffin along with some urns catches her attention.

"Do you see it?" she asks.

She doesn't wait for my answer and walks in a square, a few steps up and over and back again; zeroing in, on something.

People pass us with only a mild curiosity.

"I didn't think this would be an active place," she said. "I feel something. Something's here."

The ghost from the tea house last night emerges from the low ceiling; arms folded over its chest.

Its feathered cloak stays perfectly in place as it descends. He sinks through the floor without acknowledging me.

She walks off at a fast clip, not stopping at any of the exhibits.

I catch up with her in front of a large, black stone sarcophagus, almost buddha-like in its proportions. It is flanked by two cat-headed statues also made of black stone.

"It's magnetic," she says. "Do you feel it?"

I'm not sure I feel anything, maybe a slight a tingle in my back.

"I think it was once part of a portal or something," she says. "Now it's just a pretty piece of something broken."

I pace around it with my hand extended. As I round the final turn there's a pull on my shoulders. I feel myself lifting.

"Help," I say softly.

"What," she says.

"Something's pulling me up," I say. "I'm levitating."

She looks at me, looks down at my feet, then puts her hand on my shoulder.

"No, you're not," she says.

"My stomach feels like I'm racing up in an elevator."

Dozens of Museum-goers file past. Some briefly stop at the sarcophagus before moving on.

"Nothing's happening," she says. "And you're okay. I got you."

After a moment we pass through the door that opens into the Temple of Dendur's sunlit home.

It's graffitied stones have seen several iterations of me and now they have seen one more.

———

Night falls and we take a taxi to the centerpiece of our celebration, an event in Greenwood Cemetery. The cabbie thinks we are odd and asks us why we are going to a cemetery for a date but takes us anyway. On her phone she plays recordings made by a departed person most dear to her. Those stories are not mine to tell so I won't repeat them.

The cemetery is alive and full of revelry, not a phantasmagoric spirit to be found.

We pass into a dark stretch of the path, an area shielded from starlight by trees.

"About your vertigo," she asks. "Why are you afraid of heights?"

The wind can't reach us here. No one is near enough to hear.

"Twenty years ago, my friends and I went to Four Corners and camped out in the desert," I say. "As part of the trip each of us asked our fathers for a task, for a funny little thing for all of us to do. One of those things was we each had to bury a coin out there.

So, we were climbing around on one of those beautiful mesas and I decided that's where I was going to leave my coin. The climbing was pretty easy going, nothing serious but there was one part where we had to go over a small but deep fissure. It was only about a foot or two wide but it went straight down. You could easily just grab hold of the rocks and pull yourself up and over it. It would actually take a bit of maneuvering to fall in, but if you did it would be bad.

I was the last guy to pass and something in me said 'no' and shut me down.

My friends came back to help. Help consisted of sitting there under the sun and writing poems together. I remember thinking what I wrote was the best I'd ever done. Vultures circled overhead curious as to why we were not moving as we sat and wrote and read to each other. Then we burned them, one by one, offerings to the mesa.

I remember the ashes floating away. With the last of our writings committed to smoke I was able to go on. I went right over the fissure one, two, three.

I left my coin up there, on that mesa, in a shallow hole under a big rock. I also left a part of me. Words and thoughts I've forgotten now. Though I know they contained something real about me. Something time has eroded, hopefully not erased. Something harder to find in myself now."

I know I said I wouldn't talk about the story she told me in the cab but it was a story about losing a piece of yourself too. When we lose someone, to time, to death, or the labyrinths we find ourselves wandering in, something about *us* is also forever changed.

There are days when I'd give anything to be on top of the Empire State Building with my long-lost old friends. Or on that mesa with my poetry-writing brothers, who while nearby are long gone, long changed from the selves I used to know.

"Okay," she says. "I think I get it now."

"You do," I say, playfully. "Tell me."

She looks both ways making a show of that fact that no one is watching and dashes off the paved path onto the expanse of tree-covered graves.

"Okay, I will," she says. "Just follow me."

We run off into the beckoning darkness.

In our hotel room all feels right in the world as I am about to fade into sleep. I try to picture the words of the poems we burned all those years ago, or capture even an inkling of what they were about.

An image of a horse skeleton and the husk of an old truck buried in sand under the desert's vast, starry sky enters my mind.

We've got the lights just right, just the right amount of the city's flashing, shifting colors coming in through the crack we've left in the black out blinds.

A flash of red light glistens on something in the corner. The ghost from the tea shop is there, the city's scintillations reflecting in his coin eyes. He's watching me.

I am too tired and too content to care.

DAY 4.

The airport guard is still afraid and watches me suspiciously as I watch *her* disappear into the bustling flux of living stories coming and going.

The coin-eyed ghost is here. Watching me, watching her.

"Okay ghost," I say. If you're going to haunt me you need to make yourself useful. Why don't you act like an old-fashioned ghost and foretell or warn me about something."

"I will tell you three things," the ghost says, blankly.

"That's good," I say. "Three things is very classic-ghost behavior. I'm listening."

"First," he says. "Your cat's end time is near."

"She's twenty-one. That's a given. Tell me something I don't know."

"Second. You will come upon a river of spirits during a lightning storm in New Orleans. They will all speak to you at once. In the miasma you will hear the words of your grandfather."

"Cryptic, but a good one. Sounds fun. What's the third one?"

"Third," he says. "You will hold your father's coin that you buried on the mesa again."

"Okay," I say. "That was unexpected. I doubt it."

"I can show you where the coin is. I can even give it to you. And your burnt up words. I can help you remember them."

"You… say so much and know all these things," I say. "How? Who are you?"

He removes the coins from his eyes. His eyes are my eyes. I recognize them. He is me. He is the part of me that died up on the mesa. All grown up and just like me, only different.

"Thanks, for now," I say. "Maybe I'll go find that coin myself. And I'm gonna try to remember those poems too. If I wind up changing my mind, I'll get back to you."

He disappears. Two coins drop from the air and land on the floor with a clink. I leave them be.

I look into the crowd for a glimpse of her.

She's gone.

Her presence was a light shining on me and my chest hurts with her absence.

There is a ghost in this terminal.

The ghost is me.

I'm alone in the airport, talking to myself.

———

My cat greets me by opening her eyes for a moment before resuming sleep.

I close the door and see I've left the box of Italian pastries from the other day on my kitchen table.

They've been out there too long, I know I should throw them away. Instead, I sit and take a bite of one.

Loves we seek again

The flower is said to bloom once every three thousand years. It grows only on the shores of the River of the Dead so it doesn't live in this world, it only appears from time to time.

Some believe it can bring the deceased back to life.

It's come to this.

In a suit again, after decades and decades. Tight around the collar. My hair pulled back. Stomach full of distaste from being around these men and women I want nothing to do with, all done up like me, too. All here, wherever here is, with their extravagant offerings for our unknown host. All seeking the flower.

It's quite the setting for a party. A huge dock made of the finest woods surrounded by shallow, calm ocean for as far as I can see. Out in the middle of nowhere, the Maldives or some-where in the Indian Ocean, my best guess. In the clear sky above, a vast stream of stars and multi-colored celestial objects glow in breathtaking, cosmic glory. Submerged lights illuminate slow moving dark shapes and smaller blurs of color I take to be fish.

A few dozen of us seekers orbit each other and the table in the center; it is piled high with offerings. Most of them briefcases. Full of ungodly amounts of cash and other riches, I'm sure. There are some creative deviations among the selections. Framed works of art. An alabaster statue. A large cage containing what I think is an exotic, brightly colored bird.

Waitstaff appear out of the dark when needed, their elegant uniforms shifting from black to shades of purples and dark blues, like the deep sea, like the night. Masks of impeccable silver cover their faces. I don't trust my perceptions and I wonder if it was possible that I was drugged as part of the secrecy involved in getting here.

I awoke this afternoon in a luxurious, sparsely-furnished, spacious room over tropical blue waters, my personal staff nowhere to be found. I figured I arrived by sea-plane but I do not remember. After a shower and some rest, I dressed, grabbed my offering, and walked the long wooden walkway connecting my room, one of many, to this gathering place.

A pair of men snatch martini glasses from a tray a silver-masked staffer is holding. The taller of the two gives his glass a swirl. A tiny vortex of metallic golden orange flecks appears in the liquid before it returns to crystal clear. He's old, but not as old as me. Despite all the work, and medical miracles and advances buoying us into the future with a semblance of youth, you can still tell, you just can.

They gravitate toward me.

"Love we seek again," the stocky one says with a gruff voice as if it is an introduction.

He's in his fifties and like me, isn't made for suits and formal dress; he isn't comfortable here. I can read loss all over him. Its fresh.

He repeats his sentence twice in small talk tones as if he's making perfect sense, as if I should understand whatever he means by it.

"I beg your pardon," I say.

"The name," he says audaciously. "The name of this so-called flower."

Before I speak, the tall one interjects.

"Love-s, we seek again, with an s, is the name of this gathering," he says, correcting his friend. "The flower is called—"

He speaks a word in a language I've never heard before.

"Best of luck to you," I say as a preamble to extricating myself from their presence.

"I'll drink to that," the gruff-voiced one says. "For the amount of money I just left on that table, you better believe I want the best of luck to *me*."

"Your sweet Shannon is worth it," his friend says.

"She better be," he says.

I smile and back away before they can talk *at* me with more tedious details of dead wives, sexual conquests, tales of the ones that got away. They believe the flower can bring their dead loves back to them. They want to be the one our host selects to see it.

I remember when I was fifty like him. My last hopes of any chance of romantic love in this lifetime dissipating with my last feelings... for anything at all. All the illusions of the world were falling away from my eyes left and right and I found I could see the path to everything the world could offer and make it happen if I wished. I could manifest *anything* except for what I really wanted.

I'm not special. I know these two dolts can do it too, so can everyone here. Hopefully I'm different, or just different enough.

As I step back and turn away, I bump into someone. There's the sound of chimes and I'm face to face with one of the staff; starlight moving across her silver mask in a glistening stream. In my mind's eye I see fireflies and bats and swirls of water color paint.

"Do you seek the flower?" she says.

"I do."

Her voice is one I know. One I once knew.

She's like the rest of the staff, an enamel pin of a white flower on her lapel the only difference I discern. A flash of memory hits. She's the Maître D' who escorted me off the sea plane… I think…

"Tell me of the love you seek again. Was she a woman of uncommon grace and beauty like your friends here—"

"Oh, nothing like that. And they're not my friends."

Her face is behind the expressionless mask, yet I can tell I've sparked her interest.

"Your offering," she says gesturing to the table.

I've brought a painting my friend made for me one night during our high school days. We were waiting outside all night, on a line to buy tickets to a concert.

I hold the wrapped three-foot piece of board out to her.

"It's a piece of art. Hardly original," I say. "It is the most valuable thing I own, though."

"Oh, Mister Rumab, from a man of your wealth and stature I'm sure it must be a priceless treasure," she says.

I can't tell if she's mocking me.

"I'm not sure it's worth anything," I say. "But it can't be bought. And my friend who made it is long, long gone."

She takes my gift and places it on the table with the rest.

"I never thought I could feel out of my depth again," I say. "I never thought I could feel *anything* again, so congratulations."

She extends her hand outward in a small, efficient gesture, with her fingers moving. I think she is reaching for me, to shake my hand, maybe.

In her upturned palm is a tiny folded thing of pristine, white paper. A miniscule origami flower.

"Go back to your room," she whispers, the words so soft I am not sure she is even speaking out loud.

"Or stay here if you wish. When the party is over, I will bring you to the flower."

On the walkway I think I see a human form among the shapes in the water. I move to the edge of the planks and glance down.

A school of thousands of tiny oval shaped, light green fish explode in a myriad of directions as I lean over, then reform into a cloud in a graceful underwater murmuration.

No one's there.

I push through the door into my room happy for the blessed quiet and stillness, flop onto the bed, undo my tie and un-button my damn top button.

I drink bottled water and take my medications.

Cheers to another day alive, I say to myself. My eighty-first birthday is soon. My niece and nephew and their families will come out of the woodwork and get in touch to acknowledge me. Maybe an old friend or two will as well.

When you are fifty, like the gruff-voiced man back in the party, you think there is an off chance that you will have romantic love again. Maybe it will be fate. Maybe it will be luck. Maybe, for any number of reasons, you may even encounter someone you loved that you want to see again, or someone who once loved you might seek you out. You'll see the reasons why you split more acutely, should this happen. You'll see what you thought was love, was different kinds of desire. You'll see the crashes and coincidences of youth and the things you thought were fate and destiny and love for what they were.

Leon, my dear old friend Leon, wise beyond his years, knew these things, even back when we were teens, a time when I was so, so clueless about most everything. These were the days when all we did was spend our time painting, and hanging out and seeking fun; seeking connection. We were in the throws and pains of the rise and falls of our first loves. Well, mostly me. He always seemed okay; he always seemed to have it together despite the extreme chaos that was his life.

Like the great rockstars who died too young and became legends, Leon became more than a dearly departed friend. He always was the living breathing embodiment of the spirit of art to me and he left this earth too soon to become or stand for anything else.

He was the spirit of yes. He was the spirit of not accepting no, he inherently did not and could not, and in that way, he was not meant for this earth. He was the spirit of believing that anything could be done. And it should be done now. When he died, when that fireball of a highway wreck claimed him, it took something more than my friend from me…

... what do you mean you don't know how to surf, Leon says.

"I mean. I suck. I have absolutely zero balance."

"Have you ever tried?"

"Kind of."

"Kind of? That's a no. Let's go."

"Okay, we will."

"No, I mean now."

"Now, right now?"

"Yeah, right now. We're grabbing my board and going right now."

We left a thriving party, an unheard-of sin at the time, full of our friends and girls and the music of the Cure and the Smiths and the Lion and the Cobra album playing loudly and went to Long Beach where he proceeded to try to teach me how to surf. Turned out, it was true, I could not surf. But that was not the point. Following the passion and the immediacy and the singularity of purpose of the notion was a rarity and there was power in obeying what it directed.

I came to know such things are not the way of the world and it was one of the many things about him this world did not oblige.

Such as how he took it upon himself to supply me and our little circle of art student wanna-bes with tubes of paint that he deftly shoplifted from our circuit of art stores, despite our many protests. I'd call him a Robinhood of sorts, only he wanted zero glory. In fact, after he promised to stop, he quietly and surreptitiously planted choice tubes we coveted and could not afford in all of our art boxes. It was his way. He could not exist any other way.

His way put him at odds with the law more than once. One incident, that I barely believed, ended with a car chase going the wrong way into the Mid Town tunnel. That had him locked up for a while. I can't drive through the tunnel without thinking about him.

There were many more quiet moments than explosions. Most of our time was spent in the liminal spaces of the basements of our parents' houses. Sometimes just he and I, sometimes groups of us would gather and paint quietly, sometimes with music on softly, way into the small hours of night.

We'd paint everywhere. One summer, upstate, the night was alive with so many bats and so many fireflies, the air itself was magic, and we could not resist painting out among the trees in the moonlit dark. While they did not quite understand, the adults in our world recognized we had something special. We were doing something they could not, holding off the ravages of time and creating pockets of infinity. Plus knowing where we were and that we were painting was something wholesome and safe, so it was encouraged.

My offering. I remember the winter night he painted it. We decided we would "sleep out" on the line outside the ticket window to buy tickets for the Cure's Disintegration tour. It was dreadfully cold. We painted on scraps of cut board and shivered and listened to the album on tape. I awoke at some point and the darkness was gone and I was warm. I opened my eyes and there was only white light. Dawn was breaking. We had fallen asleep and it had snowed over us, coating us in an inches-deep cocoon of gentle, insulating snow.

That summer, at the concert with friends in Giant's Stadium, the opening chimes of the album played as the sun was going down. The crowd surged so fiercely everyone in our group were torn away from each other and weren't able to reunite until hours later in the parking lot.

That's how I remember him most of the time. His presence next to me as I'm gently buried in snow. And being carried away from him on a wave of human enthusiasm, like that at the concert only with a mortal finality.

With time and distance and the first steps of adulthood sweeping us into the currents of our adult lives people can become more than just who they were. Not something different or diminishing to their actual selves that we know, this is more of gaining an additional, almost archetypal status. Leon took on this status to me as our young lives took us into our separate futures.

Where others succumbed and surrendered their dreams, surrendered the things they cherished surrendered their passions, Leon lived in the way he always did.

Until he lived no more.

No matter what happened, no matter where I was, I always had that painting with me. It was a one of a kind and made just for me.

In the polished surface of the ceiling to floor window, I see a reflection of the Maître D. Her black dress is slit up the side revealing one of her legs. It gleams with a metallic, silver sheen same as her mask. Outside in the water behind her, the submerged lights are dimming.

Was she in here all along?

She's holding my offering, Leon's painting. It's unwrapped.

"Why this," she says.

The four images, each a tree in a different season, in bright neon paint on the rectangular board seem so simple, so rudimentary almost among the elegant lines and understated luxury of this place.

"Cash and treasures seem… an almost meaningless gesture from people with wealth," I say. "Surely our host is looking for some sort of sacrifice, something true, something pure to judge us on."

"I am the host," she says.

And I realize who she is.

Teresa. Leon and my high school classmate. She was at the party we left to try surfing. She was his first love. She was his "one that got away."

After high school I heard she left town and traveled around the country. Then from time to time I'd hear from Leon that she was somewhere parts distant around the world. Eventually she settled down and opened shop as a silver smith. A terrible accident with molten silver maimed her legs and brought her within inches of her life.

I heard she was the last of us, the last of Leon's friends to speak to him before his death.

"You," I say. "It's been so long. I knew I recognized your voice."

"You," she says. "You didn't go to our fiftieth class reunion."

"I should have. I always wanted to talk to you about Leon, what he meant to you, maybe learn about some piece of him that only you knew and stuff like that, but I never did."

"Is this why you seek the flower?"

"Yeah... I admit it. I want to bring him back, if such a thing can be true. It can't be though, can it? Maybe I can speak with him. Can I? I would very much would like to speak with him again."

Her silver mask, a form fitting, second skin of metal covering her entire face disappears as I speak, revealing the visage of the girl I remember. Blue eyes, small nose, high cheeks, lips with an alluring curve to them. The only sign of her age is her once blond curly hair has gone a rich shade of almost silver-gray.

"What I really want," I say. "When you get right down to it, what I really want is to feel again… anything, to feel just something, yes. What I really want is to feel. Feel like the that way we used to, the way he and I used to. You knew him. You loved him. Maybe you knew him better than me so you know what I mean. This feeling. This purity of thought, my thoughts of him are all wrapped up in it, they're almost one and the same."

"Ah, *this* is why you seek the flower."

"It is."

"Come outside, I will take you."

She pushes gently on the window and it pivots opening into an outdoor garden of potted flowers. Fragrant, night blooming jasmine colors the still night air.

In round pots next to the jasmine vines are three-foot stalks topped by spidery red blooms as big as my hand their filament thin petals outstretched like deep sea creatures awaiting prey.

"This is a beautiful spot," I say. "Leon would have appreciated it. He'd probably get us to set up out here and paint and take it all in."

I reach to touch one of the delicate, red tendrils.

"Careful. Poisonous," Teresa says.

"Is the flower here? Was it so near me all along?"

Teresa shakes her head no.

And looks to the ocean.

Something's out there, moving in the dark. Something large. A whale or a shark, up from the depths?

No, it's a boat. Slowly moving towards us. A wide canoe of

rich teak wood. There are no paddles or oars. No motor. No one is helming it.

The boat bumps against the dock and comes to a halt. Teresa and I get in and the boat slowly spins until we are facing out to the open water.

We coast into the night.

There are shapes in the water. I try to see but only make out human forms. One nears the surface and I see its face, aquamarine blue and speckled with green, before it submerges.

We're moving left and right, taken by a current, a river in the ocean, the lights of the complex dim in the distance. After a few minutes we are out of sight of them, out of sight of land or anything. There is only the quiet night and the river of starry sky above.

The boat slows and we glide onto the shore of a tiny island, no more than an acre or two. It is all sand a wooden platform in its center. Atop the platform is a life size statue, a buddha-like bronze figure.

We get out of the boat. Silently. There's no reason to speak. This is where she's taking me.

As we approach the shrine, I see the figure's hand is outstretched in the gesture Teresa made to me when she gave me the origami flower.

A wave a fear washes over me that I've lost it.

In the figure's hand is a tiny flower. A tiny white thing; a miniscule bell made of petals no larger than a finger nail.

No stem. No roots. It is just a bloom.

"It roots in another here. Another now," Teresa says.

"Can this be true?" I say. "Is this other here and now the River of the Dead?"

"What do you think?"

"There's part of me. A real big part of me that hoped the flower could let me talk to Leon. I admit, I was even holding on to the possibility that it could bring him back."

Teresa looks at me and her contemplation is utterly inhuman. She strikes me as a curious thing, a non-human thing, playing with an insect and the insect is me.

"You're not her," I say.

"I am her," she says. "Also, I am not her. I can be. For today, for now, let's just say I am."

"If you're not her, why pretend?

"Shall we say it makes this easier... perhaps less frightening to you?"

"Should I be afraid? What do I have to be afraid of?"

"The unknown? Tell me, I want to know."

"I don't care about the unknown," I say.

"What do you care about?"

"I'm not sure I know anymore. Nothing hurts me. Does this mean I don't care about anything? I want to feel again. I want to feel, like I used to."

She says something but it comes out all wrong. Her neck has come apart into tendrils of flesh and silver cords, squirming and wriggling around each other that reform into her solid neck after a second. The sound of her words is like a that of a fish that somehow learned to speak like a parrot.

"I'm scared now," I say.

"I'm sorry. I didn't mean to. Don't be afraid. You can smell the flower; you can even touch it if you are gentle."

I move my face closer.

The smell is rich and complex. A bouquet of sweet florals that I know all mixed in with sweet aromas I am certain I have never encountered before. I sense a note of something I am not sure I am perceiving with my nose. Is this the smell of darkness? The aroma of sunlight and salt on skin is there with that darkness too. There's a hint of soil and loam. And something that makes me aware of the celestial river of stars glistening above me. A stray thought jumps into my mind— does the River of the Dead absorb light and sensation instead of radiating it?

I take the tiny bundle of petals between my fingers, lift it from the figure's hand, pop it in my mouth and swallow.

"That's new," the Teresa-thing says. "I chose correctly. You *are* the most interesting."

There is a hint of something sweet. A hint of something bitter. The texture is smooth and dry very much the taste and texture of earthly flower petals, nothing magical at all. Then there is the taste of nothing.

"Did you not contemplate that there might be seeds?" she says.

"No," I say. "What will happen? What's going to happen now?"

"I don't know," she says.

A gust of warm wind blows off the dark shallows. I sense movement in the water. Unseen shapes are there just below the surface. Presences. With their attention on us, their attention on me.

"You'll probably forget me," Teresa says. "And most of this."

"Most?"

"A little bit may linger. Myth and rumor. That's how they start. Fragments of truth out of context that grow."

She gestures with her hand, the same movement as when she presented me with the white paper origami. A swirl of silver orange flecks appears in the air, a little vortex of stars, same as in the cocktail at the party, flies free of her hand. I cannot look away. It captures my attention, consumes my thoughts and all goes majestic, gleaming metallic orange, then black.

I'm outside my room. My packed bag in hand. It is dawn.

I was right about sea planes; several are floating aside the dock as guests embark. Others are putting away to open lanes in the water. One plane gains speed and takes to the air.

Silver masked staffers are hauling bags and escorting guests two by two to the planes. One is slacking off with their mask removed sitting with his legs hanging over the side of the dock, having a smoke in sight of everyone.

The atmosphere, any semblance of the party's magic has dissipated with the growing daylight.

The gruff-voiced man staggers into my view, still apparently drunk, his arm around two women.

"Where did all the loot go," he rambles. "A submarine? I told you it was some sort of a scam."

"Only two to a plane, sir," one of the staffers admonishes him.

He chooses one of the women to board a plane with him. I watch it put out to open water.

The unchosen woman sees me watching and walks to me.

"Do you think it's a scam, too?" she asks.

"Could be," I say.

"I have a thing for years and numbers," she says. "Three thousand years, wow, if such a thing was real, I mean, whatever the reality of it is maybe years don't correspond to our sense of time."

"Like a koan," I say. "As in, when is a flower not a flower?"

"Yeah, like that," she says.

"Heading home?" I ask.

She shrugs.

"I thought he'd pick me, now he's off to wherever with my friend, well whoever she is."

"A question," I say. "Before you decide what's next. I want to ask you. Can you surf?"

"As on a surfboard? Why do you ask?"

"Yes, as on a surfboard. And it is a very important question to me. You know, waves and water and sand and blue sky."

"That's all pretty important," she says.

"To me, for sure."

"It is," she says.

"So, can you?"

"Well," she says. "Actually, I never thought about it. So, I don't know."

"You don't know? We must find out."

"Now?"

"Yes, now, of course now. Or as soon as we can we must…"

"Okay, then, yes," she says. "Let's go."

Together we head over to the queue to board the sea planes.

"So, what do you do?" she asks.

"What do you mean? Like, what do I do when I'm not looking for three-thousand-year-old flowers?"

"Yeah, okay. Start with that."

"I do this," I say, reaching into my pocket for the origami flower. "I have something for you, a token of good luck before we fly."

And the day unfolded. Another path became clear. Not the one that I was anticipating. Not the one I'd hoped for.

I'd like to say that this was where we kissed. That a wave of bliss washed over us and we flew out into the sunrise. I'd like to say that this was the point where everything became clear and it was a happily ever after, but that's not true. It *was* the point where a couple of good stories began, though. And some of them, if I'm lucky I'll live long enough to tell you another day.

PUBLICATION HISTORY

"Scarecrow and the Imposter" — *Original to this collection*

"Above the Buried City" — *Shivers VII* (2019)

"Twenty-Nine Palms in Reverse" — *Vastarien: A Literary Journal* (2022) — *Nominated for a Pushcart Prize*

"A Loch Ness Monster Under the Light of the Southern Cross" — *A Darkness Visible* (2023)

"Ghosts of the Pantal" — *Nightscript, Vol. 8* (2022)

"Tiki Bar at the Edge of Forever" — *American Cannibal* (2023)

"Where the Jaguar King Lives in the Dark Heart of the Wood" — *Nightmare Abbey #6* (2024)

"The Fourth Bell" — *The Beauty of Death 2: Death by Water* (2017)

"The Hand of Fire" — *The Jewish Book of Horror* (2021)

"Phantom Constellations" — *Creatures of Liminal Space* (2025)

"Do Not Whistle and It Will Not Come to You, Oh Lad" — *Weird Fiction Quarterly: Ghosts* (Winter 2024/2025)

"The Exorcist's Red-Haired Daughter" — *Original to this collection*

"The Ghost With My Father's Coin" — *Original to this collection*

"Loves We Seek Again" — *Original to this collection*

about the author

Daniel Braum writes short stories that explore the tension between the psychological and the supernatural. He intentionally adopts the term "strange tales" for his "Twilight Zone-like" stories in homage to author Robert Aickman and the intentional ambiguities of his work.

His debut short story collection *The Night Marchers and Other Strange Tales (2016)* was re-released in 2023 in a new edition from *Cemetery Dance Publications.*

His short fiction can be found in his collections including *Underworld Dreams (2020)* from Lethe Press, the illustrated chapbook *Yeti Tiger Dragon* (2016) from Dim Shores Press, and *The Wish Mechanics: Stories of the Strange and Fantastic (2017)* from Independent Legions.

His novella, *The Serpent's Shadow* was released as a Cemetery Dance eBook in 2019 and as a trade paperback in 2023.

An illustrated volume of his work titled *Creatures of Liminal Space* was released by Jackanapes Press in Spring of 2025.

His stories have also appeared in many magazines and anthologies including the *The Best Horror of the Year Volume 12* edited by Ellen Datlow and *Shivers 8* edited by Richard Chizmar.

Braum is an American writer who lives and writes in New York.

Find him at: https://bloodandstardust.wordpress.com

www.ingramcontent.com/pod-product-compliance
Lightning Source LLC
Chambersburg PA
CBHW030637020726
47493CB00006B/1758